FIVE, SIX ... GRAB YOUR CRUCIFIX

REBEKKA FRANCK, BOOK 3

WILLOW ROSE

Cover design by Juan Villar Padron,
https://juanjjpadron.wixsite.com/juanpadron

Special thanks to my editor Jean Pacillo
http://www.ebookeditingpro.com

Follow Willow Rose on BookBub:
https://www.bookbub.com/authors/willow-rose

Connect with Willow Rose:
willow-rose.net

PROLOGUE

T HE MAIN DOOR to the dining hall was ajar when the Priest approached it. A small knot of women and men stood watching, their backs turned to him as he walked closer. They were humming, chanting. The light from the candles was flickering, the spectators casting long shadows on the bare walls. Someone was screaming. Not ordinary screams. These were screams of evil from a possessed soul, screams from the pit of Hell. In the middle the Priest spotted a figure. A young naked girl was on her knees. Crying out, screaming. Her face was deformed and almost hairless. A big lump grew out of her forehead, making her face lopsided. She was torn with pain and strained. Her eyes glowed green when they stared at the Priest. She threw herself at the floor, screaming in agony and pain, her knees bleeding from hours and hours of kneeling.

She stared at the Priest who thought he saw the girl's skin turning green and fuming. Then he looked at her hands. They were covered in blood. The girl lifted them and pointed at the Priest. Blood dripped from her fingers and ran down her arm.

"YOU!" the girl screamed.

The word hit the Priest like a clenched fist in his face and he felt himself stumble backwards. The voice was so forceful, nothing like the girl's normal voice that the Priest knew so well.

The Priest lifted his hand holding a crucifix. "In the name of Jesus," he stuttered, still overwhelmed by the force of this demon that possessed the girl. "In the name of Our Lord and Savior Jesus Christ I command you to leave this girl." But his voice was too weak; he knew that all too well. Evil spirits didn't listen to weak voices, they needed strong forceful commandments, and they needed to be driven out of the body.

"Filthy man. Shut up!" the naked girl screamed.

"In the name of Jesus, I command you ..."

A loud scream followed. The girl kept staring at the Priest. Then she laughed. Not the sweet laughter of a normal twelve-year old girl. No it was the laughter of death. The Priest felt her cold breath hit him in the face. It gave him chills. The naked girl threw herself on the ground, then got up and screamed again just before she bent over and ran as fast as she could towards the wall, banging her face into it, tumbling to the floor, bleeding from her mouth and lip. She looked at the Priest with a grin, licking the blood from her lip.

"She wants this," she said as if the demon was talking through her to the Priest. "She invited me in; she wants to come with me. I'm taking her."

The Priest walked closer then lifted his hand with the silver crucifix in a chain high in the air. "NO!" he yelled. "I command you to leave this body! I command you to leave her now!"

The girl stared at him. Then down at her body. Her skin

was moving, almost bubbling, boiling underneath. The glowing green eyes were lifted and locked with the Priest's. He fought hard to tamp down his growing fear but felt himself stagger backwards. These eyes were not of this world. The pupils were dilated and looked like black holes leading to eternity, an eternity of pain and agony.

Like they were a gateway to Hell.

The priest lifted the cross, trying to cover himself with its holiness, protecting his eyes, shielding them from the evil staring at him, trying to drag him to Hell with them.

"Who are you?" he asked.

"I'm the one who was within Cain," the girl stated with a devilish voice. "I am stronger than death. No one is stronger than me."

Then all sounds were drowned out by a sudden outburst of flaming timbers falling. Windows were popping, glass shattering everywhere, flames creeping up the walls making them black with soot. The Priest stared at the girl. Her face was plastered with a mixture of grinning and agony. Soon long lashing flames were licking the girl's legs and body. Through the hissing crackling sounds of fire the Priest could hear the girl laughing.

The Priest woke up in his bed screaming the words:

"She's coming. She's coming!"

The priest inhaled deeply a few times trying to catch his breath, slowly realizing it had all been nothing but a bad dream. He squinted at the alarm clock in the corner. Almost midnight. There was still time to get more sleep. He considered going to the bathroom to pee, but the soft pillow held a stronger appeal. With a relieved sigh he put his head back on the pillow and went back to sleep.

The sound of the wooden floor creaking followed by footsteps outside of his room roused him only a few seconds later. In the still darkness he reached to his nightstand and grabbed his crucifix.

1

"THE WHEELS ON the bus go round and round, round and round ..."

We were all singing along in the car. Even Sune who had once told me he would never sing for anyone in public again after a girl once laughed at him when he had sung a serenade written for her in his teenage years. I looked at him while repeating the verse for the fifteenth time since we left Karrebaeksminde. He was smiling as widely as I was. We had been looking forward to this vacation for weeks now. Since Christmas. I turned my head and looked at the kids in the backseat. My dad was sitting between them with an arm around each of them. He had grown as fond of Sune's son Tobias as he was of his own granddaughter, Julie.

"It's right up there, you have to take this exit," I said and pointed at the sign saying Arnakke.

Sune took the exit and soon we were lead through a thick pine forest with nothing but trees reaching into the sky surrounding us. I rolled down the window and took in a deep breath of fresh forest air. I looked forward to leaving the city behind and getting away from everything.

Even if Karrebaeksminde was very small for its size it was still a town with people and cars and work. Once Sune and I decided that we wanted to go on vacation together with the kids and Dad, we agreed that it had to be somewhere away from everybody and especially from work. Arnakke was still on the island of Zeeland, but it was further north and far away from the area that Sune and I normally covered for the paper.

This was going to be very relaxing, I thought to myself as Sune drove further into the deep forest.

Arnakke was a small town with only three hundred and ninety-four inhabitants. The area around Arnakke had been inhabited since the Stone Age. The name meant "eagle's neck" since there used to be a lot of eagles fishing in the fjord that was called Isefjorden. You could still spot them occasionally, I was told, but it was rare now. I looked up at the sky between the trees but saw only crows. The road was slippery from the wet snow. The trees covered in the white powder. We had packed the car with sledges and winter clothing. I looked forward to tumbling in the snow with Julie and building a huge snowman or a snow cabin. I inhaled the icy air deeply into my lungs. The kids complained that it was getting cold in the car so I rolled up the window. I looked at Sune. This was going to be great, I thought. Just me and the people I loved in a small cabin far from everything, taking long walks, sledging down the hills.

Just what the doctor had ordered.

He actually had ordered me to relax, to get away from everything. The emotional stress I had put myself through the last couple of years, had begun to wear on me. On top of it I had almost been killed six months before and I had had a hard time sleeping ever since. I kept waking up at night screaming and crying, scaring Julie who thought she had to constantly take care of me. That was not how it was supposed to be. I was supposed to hold her hand when she had bad dreams, not the other way around.

I sighed and looked at her. She was playing a game with Tobias; they were laughing and teasing Dad who laughed happily. Julie had been so tough, so strong through all of this. I had no idea how she managed to be like that. I knew I had almost reached my limit. At least that was what the doctor had told me.

"No one is supernatural and can do everything. You have to face that you have limits as well. You have to know these limits and learn to respect them. Otherwise you might burn out."

His words had scared me like crazy. I had seen numerous colleagues break down from the pressure of the job and never come back. Being a journalist wasn't for the weak, but even the strong had limits, I had learned. I was stressed all the time and felt like I was never good enough.

Probably hadn't helped that I had to fight for my reputation ever since I helped overthrow the government six months ago by writing a story about the Prime Minister who allowed lobotomies performed into the Nineties on criminal teenagers that no one knew where to place or to do with since they were too young to go to prison, but kept getting themselves in trouble.

It all occurred before she was elected Prime Minister, yes, but she had been Minister of the Health Department and that was enough for the opposition to claim that she should step down. Now a new election was on its way and I had faced everything from threats of a lawsuit filed against me to attacks on me as a person in the media exhibiting me as a bad mother leaving my sick husband when he needed me most and having an affair with my photographer who was also a criminal.

Luckily they had left my daughter alone so far, but I was terrified that they would approach her again like they had when they tried to force me to not run the story. She had been the one persuading me to run it. I would never have done it if she hadn't wanted me to. But she was so right. If you don't stand up to a bully, they will bully someone else. I had no idea exactly who was behind all of these media attacks but I knew that it wore on my strength having to disavow all those rumors they kept writing about me. I wasn't going to let them discredit me but I was just about to say that I'd had enough by now. It was so childish and wouldn't change a thing in the end.

I didn't understand why they kept doing this, since the Prime Minister had already stepped down. There was no more to save. It was over. So it had to be all about getting revenge or something, I thought while Sune put his hand on my leg with a smile. I put my hand on top of his. He had been my rock in this. We had been together for almost six months now and every day seemed to get better and better. I guess I was falling for him really seriously. And it scared me like nothing else in this world. Last time I had let myself fall hopelessly in love it had ended so wrong, so bad. I never wanted to go down that road again. Would it be different this time? Sure. But it could still go terribly wrong. There was always the risk. Then everything would be destroyed. Our kids loved each other almost as much as we did. They would be devastated if we were to split up. And since Sune and I worked closely together, it would make it impossible for us to work together again. I was afraid to risk that since he was the best photographer I knew. I had realized that he was as much a part of the stories as I was. I couldn't be this good without him. He made me good.

Sune grabbed my hand and squeezed it lightly. "No thinking about work," he said. "That was the deal here. We are on vacation."

I smiled and exhaled deeply. "I know," I said and closed my eyes for a second. "I'm going to enjoy every second of it."

"Good."

Sune took a turn and we went even deeper into the pine forest. We passed a sign in front of a closed gate.

"Keep out!" it said. "Private property."

I remembered having seen the gate before in the news on TV. This was where the oft-discussed religious sect "The Way" had their headquarters in some old abandoned camp area where there used to be a children's school camp. I remembered pictures of the old wooden log cabins taken by a news photographer for a paper, someone who had crossed the heavy gates and fences somehow in an attempt to take pictures of what was going on in there. Rumors had circulated about exorcism rituals and other stuff that no one knew if it was true.

They were widely known to recruit confused young people by drawing on their weaknesses. Their leader who called himself "The Priest" had appeared in the media a few times some years ago before they clammed up and refused to talk to anyone anymore. He was quite charismatic as far as I remembered. Called himself the reincarnation of Isaiah. But other than being severely delusional he seemed quite harmless.

The sect was big in the Nineties but I couldn't remember having heard about it in the last fifteen years, maybe even longer. I wondered if they were in there as we drove by and turned left onto a dirt road where piles of snow made it hard to drive. Sune cursed and hit the gas pedal. The car moved again slowly, going straight up the hill. Soon a few houses, mostly small cabins appeared between the trees. I could spot the fjord in the distance. The view was spectacular. The white snowy landscape was so calm in the cold. Sune stopped the car in front of a small wooden cabin. I got out and inhaled the fresh air. The kids tumbled out on top of each other and threw themselves in the snow.

"Put on your winter jackets first," I said.

But it was too late. They were soaking wet, throwing snow in the air and letting it fall on their faces, making snow angels in their sweaters and jeans. I threw their jackets at them and they got up dusted off the snow from their shoulders and hair, laughing. Then they put on their jackets and ran into the yard of the cabin while we unpacked the car.

I looked at the wooden cabin just before I went through the red painted door. Yes this was going to be a relaxing vacation. Then I pulled out my phone and turned it off.

2

M AYBE HE WAS just being jumpy, the Priest thought to himself as the silence again lingered over the cabin. He listened for more sounds coming from the hallway, but it was quiet now. It was nothing but a bad dream, he kept telling himself. A very bad dream, but nothing to worry about. It had been years since the Priest had last thought about the girl. Not that he had forgotten about her that simply wasn't possible. Who could ever forget someone like that?

The Priest sat up in the bed and pulled the curtain slightly. It was full moon outside. That was probably why he felt so strange inside. He always slept badly when it was full moon.

"Nothing to worry about," he mumbled to himself.

But he couldn't escape the feeling that someone was walking around outside his door. Could it be some of the other church members? Maybe someone was lost. They had just recruited a group of four young people. They always a hard time sleeping the first couple of days. The guilt towards their parents or friends that they had left to follow the Priest into that warm embracing hands of their God, the fear of something new. It was always hard to overcome in the beginning. But they would eventually. The Priest and his disciples would make them strong enough to resist their parent's approach, strong enough to face them once they tried to get in contact with them and try to get them to come back. Some would cave in, and the Priest would help them fight it, get over it and persuade them that their family was here now, that those parents never did them any good.

Most of the young people that they recruited had run away from home several months ago. His disciples found them in the streets or maybe outside a shelter nearby where they spent the night but always went outside to smoke. Then his disciples would approach them with promises of a better life. Most would run or laugh in their faces, but every now and then someone would ask to know more and then his disciples would take good care of them. Tell them they were loved. Tell them they didn't need their parents anymore or anyone else for that matter.

Yes, that had to be the answer. If there was someone out there it had to be one of the young ones who were lost, maybe got out of bed to get a drink of water or maybe looking for someone to talk to. It happened every now and then that they sought comfort in the middle of the night, when the nightmares and bad dreams became too overwhelming. These kids had often been through a lot, too much for such a young person. That was the mission for the Priest and The Way. To help these young people get rid of all these evil thought patterns and bad behavior. And the Priest knew exactly how to do that. First they had to accept that they had evil inside of them. That it wasn't their fault, but evil was holding them down, destroying them with wrong thoughts, telling them to do things, evil things. Once the demon was detected in the person it had to be commanded to leave, it had to be driven out. Evil had such a stronghold upon our youngsters today. Well it always had, he thought to himself as he found a bathrobe and put it on. It wasn't like being possessed with evil demons was anything new. People on the outside just didn't understand. They didn't see things the way the Priest did. He could spot an evil demon in any person at any time just by looking at the person. And he had the power to make it leave. God had granted him that power.

He had come to him in his bedroom more than thirty years ago. He had shown himself in a strong light and told the Priest that he should leave his Catholic church and start a new one. He showed him faces of people who had been possessed by demons and had died without the demon being exorcised. The hell of pain and agony they lived in now had made the Priest fall to his knees and cry before the Mighty God. He had screamed: "Please let me help those people, please teach me to help them."

So He had done. The next day the Priest quit as a pastor at his church and started reading about demons and exorcism. God had guided him on a trip where he visited churches all over the world that used exorcism to treat people from all sorts of deviltry that possessed them and caused them to live a life in pain. He had brought back his new knowledge to Denmark where he started his church and written a book about it. A book the church members were told to memorize and always keep close to them. This was their Bible now. Soon people came to him from all over the country wanting to be set free and he had helped them. He had helped thousands of people so far. That made him happy, so very happy. The agony of the faces burning in that awful way he had seen the night when God had spoken to him wouldn't leave his mind and he was driven by the desire to prevent more people from ending up like them. That was his goal, at any cost.

There had only been one he couldn't help. One soul whose demon had been too strong. From his readings the Priest knew that once you've lost to a demon it was going to run loose. It would eventually try and take over. Death was its only weapon. Nothing could settle a dispute like death. Nothing could display who was more powerful in this world like death's sting. He particularly remembered a story from a book about a demon that a priest hadn't managed to cast out in Vietnam many years ago. Afterwards the entire town had been killed, children, women, burned alive or cut to pieces. Like some special viciousness had been let loose.

In the years after the Priest had given up on the girl he had expected the demon in her to come back somehow. He expected the demon to come back after him and his disciples, eventually turning the lands into a slaughterhouse. But nothing had happened. Not yet.

The Priest walked towards the door leading to the hallway with all the rooms where the other members of the church slept heavily. If anyone was out there, lost or looking for a shoulder to cry on, then he would be there to help him. As long as they worshipped him - and believed what he believed - he would help them.

Just as the Priest reached for the handle it turned on its own.

3

T HE FIRE IN the fireplace was slowly growing and soon crackling in front of us. We had played all afternoon in the snow outside. Our cheeks were red and I ached all over but in a wonderful way. In the way that you knew that you had used your body and been outside. Now my cheeks were burning from the heat in the fireplace. I had put on warm, dry clothes while Sune prepared dinner with Dad. They were both whistling and humming along while they cut vegetables and prepared a nice roast beef for us. I looked forward to a good meal now. Being outside for hours always made me build up an appetite.

I was poking the fire and trying to make it burn more. Then I threw in some more wood. I dusted off my fingers while Sune called the kids to the table.

"Time for dinner!"

The kids were giggling as they walked down the stairs. Sune smiled at me when he placed the meat in the middle of the table. It smelled heavenly.

"Did you wash up?" I asked the children.

They looked at each other. Then they nodded. I stared at

them in disbelief. "Try again," I said and pointed at the down-stairs bathroom.

They raced towards it. Julie won. Then they laughed. I sat at the table next to Sune. Dad carved the meat.

"So what about a game of Scrabble once we're done?" Sune asked.

That had become our favorite game ever since we started hanging out a lot more during the weekends with our kids. I looked at him and took a piece of meat.

"Sure. But don't weep when I beat you," I said with a grin.

"Ha!" Sune exclaimed.

I laughed and looked at him. He looked great. I loved the Mohawk. It looked nice on him. Even if I knew he probably wouldn't keep it like that once he passed thirty-five, I still hoped that he would. It made him so different from anyone else I had ever been with. Different was good.

The food was - as expected - just as heavenly as it smelled. I ate till I was about to burst. So did the rest of us. The cold fresh air had made us famished. After dinner I cleaned up while Sune and Dad chatted in the living room by the fire. I enjoyed watching them from a distance. They seemed to really hit it off. Even if Sune wasn't quite the kind of type my dad had ever pictured me with, he wasn't one to judge a person by his or hers looks. He liked Sune. He liked him even before we became an item. But I did have a hard time telling him about us. He had liked my ex-husband Peter as well. He had liked him a lot. I could tell it was hard for him to accept that I wasn't going to go back to him even if he hadn't treated me very well in the end.

"He was sick, Rebekka," Dad would say whenever his name was somehow brought up in our conversation. "One of these days he will be back for you, feeling much better and then what?"

"He won't be back," I kept saying. "He's too embarrassed. Plus I'm pretty sure he has moved on with his life by now. It's been two and a half years. And so have I."

Sune laughed loudly while the kids found Scrabble in a suitcase and put it on the table. I prepared coffee and found the box of chocolate I had brought. I kept it in a safe place since I was trying hard to watch Dad's diet. He had a stroke a couple of years ago and after the last doctor's visit he was told to try and lose some weight and lay off the salt. His blood pressure was too high.

"Yeah! Chocolate," Julie exclaimed when she saw me bring it in.

"Wait for everybody to sit at the table," I said and put it in the middle so everybody could reach.

I won the game as usual. Sune was grumbling while we packed up. He really couldn't stand to lose. Dad brought the kids upstairs and put them to bed. Then he told us he would turn in as well. I looked at Sune and smiled. He smiled back. We had learned to cherish the few moments we had to ourselves.

We walked into the kitchen and found a bottle of red wine. Sune opened it and I found two glasses in the cupboard. Sune poured the wine.

"Let's go outside," I whispered while showing him a packet of cigarettes I had smuggled with me in my suitcase so neither Julie nor my dad would see it. Sune nodded and went to get our jackets. He liked to smoke now and then just like I did. It had become sort of our thing, like kids in school sneaking off somewhere to have a cigarette.

Sune brought me my jacket and had already put on his own. The wind was freezing as we walked onto the porch. We found a bench and wiped off the snow before we sat down. I sipped my wine while Sune lit a cigarette. It was a beautiful night. So incredibly peaceful. The sky was clear and being away from the city and all its lights we could now see all the stars. It seemed like they continued for eternity, making me feel so small and insignificant. The full moon was right above our heads shining down on us making the snow glitter. Sune handed me the cigarette and I took it. I smoked and drank some more wine which made me feel warm inside even if the cold felt like needles on the skin outside.

"This is really nice," I said exhaling. "I feel really relaxed."

Sune looked at me. "That's good," he said. "That's really good."

The forest surrounding us was as quiet as death. Not a single branch moved. It was like everything was frozen.

While enjoying the silence I killed the cigarette in an ashtray. Then I drank some more wine. Neither of us wanted to speak. We enjoyed this calmness, this complicity. All day with kids yelling, screaming, fighting, laughing does that to you. Once it was gone you just had to keep quiet and enjoy the silence. Sune put down his glass on a table and leaned over me. Then he grabbed my glass and put it next to his. His breath smelled good as he approached my face. I felt a chill of excitement. My heart was beating faster. It was always like that with Sune. We never had much time to be intimate so it was always like the first time with him; it was always new, exciting. His lips were warm as they covered mine. He held my head between his hands while he kissed me intensely, demanding. Soon his hands were all over me. While he was kissing my neck and nibbling my ear I felt his hand on my thigh climbing up along the jeans, stopping at the top, finding the button and opening them. Soon his hand slid down and he started touching me. I felt an arousing excitement like shock waves through my body. Sune was moaning. His sex was hard against my leg.

"I want you so bad," he said under his breath.

He found the zipper in my winter jacket and opened it, and then his hands found their way to my breasts underneath my sweater. I closed my eyes and enjoyed his touches. It was a strange situation but it felt good.

"Do you want to go inside?" he asked.

"We can't," I moaned. "Someone might wake up and hear us. The cabin is small and not very soundproof."

Sune kissed me again. His hands were touching me. Then he fumbled with my pants and managed to pull them down to my knees. I opened his. I touched him gently and led him to me. He entered me with a small shriek of pleasure. I closed my eyes and let him ride me.

We were both almost at our climax when suddenly the silence in the forest was broken by a terrible scream. It felt like glass shattering inside of me. The sound of it caused me to shiver. It was ghastly and gruesome at the same time. Birds took off from treetops, dogs started barking. Sune froze and stared at me. We both went completely stiff. Never in my life had I heard this kind of screaming. Sune pulled out and put on his pants. The screaming continued. It was horrifying and I felt waves of chills all over my body.

"Where is that coming from?" Sune asked.

I got up and walked into the yard. I looked around and tried to detect where the sound could come from, but seemed to echo off all the trees in the forest and sounded like it came from more than one direction.

"I don't know," I said and looked at him. His eyes were filled with as much terror as I imagined mine to be. "Do you think we should do something?"

Sune sighed. "How? We don't even know where it is coming from?"

"Maybe someone needs our help?" I asked.

Sune nodded. I looked at the cabin and thought I saw something move inside the living room. The curtain was pulled and Julie was looking out at us.

"It woke up the kids," I said and started running back.

I opened the door and hugged Julie. "What is the awful noise, Mommy?" she asked while holding her ears. Her hair was messed and her eyes hardly open.

"We don't know sweetie. It'll probably stop soon. We need to get you back to bed," I said.

"But I can't sleep with this noise!" she exclaimed angrily. "It's so loud. It hurts my ears."

"I know," I said. "I have an idea. I brought some earplugs in case Sune was snoring too badly. You can have them."

I went to my purse and found the earplugs. Julie looked at me with her big blue eyes as I returned. She was shaking. I felt her arm. It was freezing cold.

"I'm scared Mommy," she said. "Who is screaming like that?"

I stroke her gently on her cheek. "I don't know sweetie. But I'm sure it'll stop soon."

"Can you come sleep with me?" she asked.

I sighed deeply, since I really wanted to spend the evening with Sune. But her eyes convinced me otherwise and the screaming had kind of destroyed the moment along with my mood.

"Okay. I will. Here," I said and pressed in the first earplug, then the second in the other ear.

Then I grabbed her around her shoulders and looked in her eyes. "Better?"

She looked at me like she didn't understand. I knew then

that they were working as intended. She could see that I was talking but not hear me. They weren't ordinary earplugs, these I had gotten from the army when I was in Iraq. Julie wasn't going to hear a thing all night.

"I'm going to sleep with Julie," I said to Sune.

He looked disappointed at me. I shrugged. "It's too eerie to be in the mood for anything anyway," I said and pointed at the outside from where the screaming hadn't stopped, only increased in intensity and depth.

He nodded. Then he stroked me gently across my cheek. "I know. It's just so rare we get to ... you know."

"I do know. A rain check?"

He smiled then kissed my forehead. I scowled in Julie's direction. We hadn't yet kissed in front of the kids. They knew we were seeing each other, we had told them that much, but somehow I think they had the idea that we were just good friends. We were never affectionate physically in front of them. Maybe that was a mistake but I feared Julie's reaction. I had no idea how much she knew or how she would react. So I guess I kind of postponed it, which annoyed Sune greatly. He wanted to be able to kiss me whenever he felt like it and he was certain that Tobias didn't care at all. Maybe I was just being overly protective; I thought as I climbed into Julie's bed and held her tight while Sune called the police.

Outside of the windows I could still hear the screams shattering the night. I realized now that this kind of scream wasn't normal, this kind of screaming was filled with suffering and anguish to a point where it was almost inhuman.

These were the screams of someone dying.

4

T HE PRIEST WAS screaming from the top of his lungs. The pain, the agony inside of him was unbearable. His screams attracted his church members, some of them his closest friends through many years. Now they were looking at him with despair and helplessness. He was lying on the floor his body curled up, shaking in pain. He was throbbing, sobbing trying hard to speak to them but no words left his mouth, only screams and vomit every now and then. His skin felt like it was boiling underneath. His blood was raging through his veins.

Oh the pain. This excruciating pain was eating him from the inside. Were they just going to stand there and look at him? He heard them talk amongst themselves, discuss what to do, but no one dared to touch him. No one wanted to come too close. Another wave of pain rushed over his body and caused him to throw up. As he did, a clump of hair fell off and landed on the wooden planks. He sat up on his knees and touched his head. Then he pulled another clump of hair out without even feeling it. Then he pulled even more out and to his astonishment threw it on the floor. He was drooling when another wave of pain rolled in over him and he screamed in anguish. His skin was bubbling, sizzling and when he touched it, lumps of skin just fell right off. He threw up again and felt how he was urinating at the same time and realized that he was lying in his own excrement.

A woman, Isabella, the one he had trusted as his right hand, his apprentice, the one who was supposed to take over for him once the good Lord had taken him home, kneeled in front of him. Her eyes were terrified. In her hand she was holding his book and she was reading phrases from it, phrases he had written and told them to repeat again and again. The people surrounding her hummed and chanted while she mumbled the words in Latin.

The Priest screamed his suffering out as another wave of pain rolled over him. It felt like something was eating him up from the inside, devouring his internal organs one by one. It was burning, so badly burning.

"The ..." he managed to stutter just before another pain forced him to fall to the floor again. He was trembling like he was having a seizure. Then more vomit. Now his head started to hurt. He held it in agony. Was it going to explode? It felt like something was pressing from the inside, trying to get out. The Priest screamed while holding on to it and tossing his body around while strange voices filled his mind and drowned his thoughts.

The people watching started yelling. "Go demon! Leave this body immediately! Leave the Priest now. I command thee in the name of the Lord and savior Jesus Christ. Leave this body and this place."

The Priest crumbled up while moaning and groaning. Then another pain from his stomach hit him like had he been shot by an arrow or punched by someone. He screamed again this time louder than ever, causing Isabella to stagger backwards in fear. He roared out in pain and screamed at her. She threw herself backwards. Others grabbed her and pulled her away from the Priest.

Then he went quiet for just a second. He gasped for breath, got up on all fours and lifted his head. He stared at the people surrounding him. When they saw his face they jumped and drew backwards holding on to each other as if they were staring directly at the devil. A gasp, someone cried, others cursed the devil and tried to cast him out of the Priest. Then he opened his mouth.

"The ... The ... girl," he stuttered half choked. Drool ran down his chin and neck, blood was coming out of his nose and eyes, running down his face. Then he threw up again. This time only blood came up. His body was shaking, trembling, and his arms and legs could no longer hold him up. He fell with his face flat in his own bloody vomit and excrement.

"The ... girl," he whispered as life slowly oozed out of him.

But no one heard the last words the Priest spoke. They were drowned in Latin phrases and commandments telling the devil to leave this body now.

The last thing the Priest saw was his own crucifix lying on the floor in front of him, smeared in blood.

Then the good Lord finally had mercy on him and took him home.

5

WHEN THE SCREAMING finally stopped I found it hard to fall asleep. The eerie feeling inside wouldn't go away. As the morning approached hours later I finally managed to get a couple of hours of sleep before Julie woke me up. Her eyes looked tired. I helped her pull out the earplugs. She smiled then kissed me.

"The screaming stopped," she exclaimed.

I nodded, and then put my head back on the pillow. "I'll just take half an hour more," I grumbled.

Julie shook me. "No Mommy, we have to get up. I'm hungry. Tobias is awake too," she said and pointed at Tobias lying in the bed next to ours.

His eyes were open and he looked at Julie with a huge smile. "Let's go downstairs," Julie said and jumped out of the bed.

I put the cover over my head. "I'll be down later," I growled.

I heard them leave the room then walk downstairs. My dad was awake; I could hear him say a singing "Good morning" to the kids. Apparently he hadn't been awake like I had.

I turned onto my side and tried to fall asleep again. It was after all vacation so I was allowed to treat myself. But much to my surprise I couldn't fall asleep even if I felt like I needed it so badly. The screams had somehow burned themselves into my brain and wouldn't leave again. I kept hearing them over and over again and it gave me the chills.

The door to the bedroom opened and I felt someone crawl into my bed. I opened my eyes and stared into those of Sune. He was smiling. His Mohawk was messed up and lay flat on top of his head. I touched his face gently.

Sune crept under the covers to me and held me tight.

"I can't stop thinking about those screams," I said.

He kissed my neck. "Me either," he said. "I keep wondering what it was. What could make a person scream like that?"

"Pain," I said. "Excruciating pain. Unbearable pain."

Sune lifted his head and stared at me. "What are you thinking?"

I shook my head. "I have no idea what it might have been. All I know is that it was something serious. Something awful."

I turned and grabbed his face between my hands. Then I pulled him closer and kissed him for a long time. Feeling him, drinking from his lips.

"Well a good morning to you too," he said with a huge white smile when I let go of him.

"Do you want to get some breakfast?" I asked.

"I'm starving," he exclaimed and patted his stomach. He hadn't put on a shirt yet. I loved to look at him. He was very tall and well-built. He leaned over and kissed me once again. Then he got up from the bed. "Are you coming?" he asked.

"I'll take a shower first."

Once I came down after my shower I couldn't find any of them in the kitchen. They were all sitting in the living room by the TV watching something. It was the News, the 24-hour news channel. They had breaking news to report. I crept up behind Sune and hugged him from behind.

"What's going on?" I asked.

Dad looked at me. "The screaming last night ..."

"So you did hear it," I said. "I thought you slept through it all."

"No it kept me up all night. Haven't closed an eye since it started. Once it was over I thought I might as well get up. Couldn't fall asleep again."

"It was Anders Granlund, better known as the Priest," Sune said. "You know, the leader of that sect."

"The Way?" I asked.

"Yes. You know their camp is located pretty close to here," Dad said.

"Yes. We drove past the entrance yesterday on our way here," I said. "Was it him? What happened?"

Sune shook his head. "He died last night. They believe it might be some sort of strange disease. He fell ill during the night. Then he had sort of a seizure. Could have been an allergic reaction or something. He was throwing up and had diarrhea for hours apparently before he died."

"A disease?" Julie asked with frightened eyes. "What if we get it?"

"They don't know if it is a disease yet. You heard what Sune said. It might have been an allergic reaction," I said to calm her down.

"But when will we know?"

I saw anxiousness in her eyes. I walked to her and hugged her gently. "They'll find out soon and then they'll tell us we don't need to be afraid." I looked at Sune. "Has anyone else fallen ill in the camp?" I asked.

"Not to their knowledge," Sune said.

"There you go," I said. "It's nothing to be afraid of. They keep to themselves up there and don't have much contact with people around them so even if they do have some virus up there - which I don't think they do - it's highly unlikely it will spread."

Julie looked at me with a smile. "Now turn that thing off," I said to Dad who held the remote. "You're scaring the kids. Plus we need to get something to eat."

Dad prepared a huge meal for breakfast. But none of us ate that much. I kept thinking about the Priest and what could have possibly made him scream like this. I found my purse and retrieved my phone. I sighed and held it for a while in my hand almost like I was feeling its weight. Then I turned it on. I knew I never should have. Twenty-five voice-mail messages. All from my editor Jens-Ole. I knew what they were about but listened to one anyway.

"I know you must have heard about the death of the sect leader by now. You're in the area. Call me."

I looked at my family sitting around the breakfast table. Then I sighed and called him back.

"Where the hell have you been?!" he exclaimed.

"On vacation. Where do you think?"

"I know. But you're the only one right now who is close to the scene. Could you look into the story about the Priest?"

"I'm here with my family. I'm supposed to relax, doctor's orders remember?" I said.

"If I say please?"

I sighed again. Sune looked at me. Our eyes locked. He knew what was going on. I knew he had brought his camera as well. Just in case. This was that kind of case. I was intrigued enough to look into this story.

"Just one article about the Priest, his death and the place up there and then I'll let you off the hook," Jens-Ole pleaded.

"You know they'll never let us in," I said.

"I know. Take some pictures from the outside and then talk to the locals about them. Could you do that? Please?"

I exhaled. "Okay. But just the one article."

"I promise. Cross my heart and all that," Jens-Ole said. "I'll leave you alone the rest of your vacation."

"Yeah right," I said with a smile. Then I hung up.

Sune approached me. "Let me guess. Jens-Ole?" He whispered.

I nodded. "Just one story," I said.

Sune sighed deeply and shook his head. "I thought we were here so you could relax."

"I know. But aren't you intrigued? Just a little bit?"

"Of course I am. But we are just doing a portrait thing right?" he asked.

"Yes," I assured him. "Just the story about the Priest seen from the eyes of the locals and then pictures from the place, probably just be the fence and the 'keep away' signs."

Sune looked at the children. They had found a video-game and plugged it into the TV. They would hardly notice we weren't there once that thing had started.

"Okay," he said. "I'll grab my camera."

6

AS EXPECTED THE place outside the camp was swamped with people when we arrived. TV cameras, journalists, photographers swarmed around the fence, peeking in, waiting for the sect members to show themselves and maybe give a comment. Just a picture of someone walking behind the fence would make the front page.

I greeted the few that I knew from earlier in my career, then joined them waiting. Sune started taking pictures of the fence, the signs telling people to stay away and that this was a private property. He had a way of making himself almost invisible, able to sneak around unseen and take the best photos. He would never just stand in a crowd to get the same picture as everyone else. I studied him as he slowly moved further and further away from the crowd and into the forest while following the fence. I knew he was trying to get closer somehow and maybe be able to zoom in close on the camp through the trees. Maybe he would catch a glimpse of someone in there, maybe one of the young persons that the sect was suspected of brainwashing. While Sune disappeared I wondered what it was like to live like that, in a camp with people telling you what to think and what to do. I could vividly imagine how it would be appealing to young people with many problems. Kids were so fragile at that age, so easy to manipulate. That they exploited their weaknesses made me sick to my stomach.

Before we left the house I researched a bit on what had been written over the years about the sect. And I didn't like what I had seen one bit. On more than one occasion they had been investigated by the police, but never charged with anything. The media reported that their leader the Priest was simply too smart to get caught doing anything illegal. One person who had managed to get out after five years in the camp had in the one and only interview he had ever made ten years ago, told that the Priest deliberately targeted young people who had run away from home or were living in the streets. He lured them to the camp with promises of a better life. Then he used them for labor, cultivating the fields on the estate, caring for the sheep and cooking and cleaning. They weren't to have any contact with the world outside and were told to never contact their families again. They told them that they didn't know what was good for them; they would never understand or accept their new way of living. The other sect members were their family now. The Priest would tell them how to think, what to think and what not to think. That was the difficult part for me. The brainwashing part. They were so impressionable at that young age.

The man who had escaped said that once they arrived at the camp the first thing they would do to them was to have a "cleansing ceremony" which was just another word for an exorcism during which the Priest and his followers would clean the newcomer of all the bad things and evil demons that possessed them. If a person got the bad thought patterns back they would do another ceremony. When he was asked about how the ceremonies were performed he started crying and ended the interview.

That was the closest anyone had ever come to learning what was going on behind that tall fence I was staring at right now. Where the sect had all its money from there were many guesses. Some said that they had a huge billion-dollar donation back in the nineties, others that they had inherited the money from an old member of the sect who had died a few years ago. Others speculated that people had to donate all of their money to the sect once they joined it and more than one millionaire had joined them over the years. Most famous was one of this country's biggest movie-actresses Isabella Dubois who was known to have given up her entire career and donated all of her money to the sect. She had never commented upon the matter to the press.

Suddenly I noticed Sune; he was walking fast along the fence towards us. A few seconds later he was running. When he approached me he leaned over and whispered:

"Someone is coming out now, I got a picture of someone getting into a car and driving towards the exit. Better get ready when the gate opens."

I nodded and placed myself strategically right in front of the gate so when the car approached and the gates opened I had the best spot. The other journalists didn't suspect anything was going on until they saw the black car and then they started swarming it. The gate opened slowly and the car tried to press its way through the crowd, but they were too many and the driver had to slow down in order not to hit anyone. I knocked on the window in the backseat. Nothing happened. The many photographers blocked the car while shooting pictures, trying to capture whoever was behind the black windows. I knocked on the window again and suddenly it moved. Through a small opening a set of eyes stared at me. I recognized them immediately as those belonging to Isabella Dubois.

"Care to comment on the tragic death of your leader?" I asked.

Isabella's eyes were moist when much to my surprise she spoke: "It is a very great loss not only to our Church but also to the rest of the world."

I felt the other journalists push up behind me forcing me closer to the car. I tried to stand still but it was hard. Sune stood right next to me, shooting picture after picture.

"Do you know who will be the next leader of your Church?" someone yelled behind me.

"Who will take over?" another asked.

"Who's in charge now?" a third person yelled.

"Will you release the members to their families?" I asked.

Isabella Dubois shook her head slowly like she couldn't believe us. Then she rolled down her window further. A great wave of silence washed over all the journalists. It may have been her beauty or her astonishing authenticity that had once spellbound so many from the movie screens all over the country for years. Isabella sighed deeply before she spoke:

"Anyone who comes to our camp comes here by his or her own free will. And they are the lucky ones. What happened last night marks the beginning of the end. Evil will rise all over this land and you will all end up burning in hell."

The journalists stared at her, speechless. I could tell by the look in her eyes that she truly believed what she had just told us.

"Are you saying that the death of the Priest wasn't an ordinary death?" I asked.

"You all think I'm crazy. I know that perfectly well," she said. "But we have known this was coming for years. We have been waiting and preparing for this. Don't say you weren't warned."

"You didn't answer my question," I said.

Isabella looked at me with her icy blue eyes. "No it wasn't an ordinary death. And neither will yours be."

"Was that why you didn't call for an ambulance?" I asked. "The call didn't come from your camp, did it? It came from one of the neighbors."

"You're focusing on the wrong thing," Isabella said.

"Then what is the right thing we should focus on in your opinion?" I asked.

"That this land is damned. We should all be preparing for the end. If that demon can take the Priest it can take anybody."

On that word Isabella rolled her window up and the car started moving down the road. Photographers followed it some of the way taking more pictures. Then it was gone. A journalist approached me. He was an older guy, kind of old school with a green vest, beard and a very laid back attitude.

"Can you believe that story?" he asked. Then he looked at me. "Great questions by the way."

"Thanks."

"Well no use in staying here," the journalist said. "There is a story to be written and they have shrimp and fish filet in the cafeteria at the paper today. Wouldn't miss that, huh?"

I smiled. Knowing his type, he would have a couple of snaps with that as well.

Sune returned just as the journalist left. He handed me his camera. I flicked through the pictures on the display. They were great. He had even captured Isabella in the camp just before she got inside the car. She was talking to a couple of other church members looking serious.

"Perfect," I said and smiled.

7

N EXT STOP WAS the local people. Arnakke was a very small town of mostly a lot of houses and summer residents. We chose the closest neighbor to the sect's camp and knocked on the door. An elderly woman opened. She introduced herself as Esther, smiled widely and invited us in for coffee. We sat on the couch in her living room that reminded me so much of my grandmother's. Heavy curtains, carpeted floors, old naturalistic paintings on the walls and the windowsills packed with trinkets, birds and small rabbits made in porcelain. The old lady was still smiling when she brought the coffee. She poured some in our cups and offered us Danish butter cookies to go with it.

"I guess you've heard about what happened last night at the camp?" I asked and sipped the coffee. It even tasted like my grandmother's used to. I took in a deep breath and remembered her for a second.

"Oh, yes. Wasn't it awful? Horrible. If I didn't know better I would think he was being tortured."

I nodded and ate my cookie. "Actually we heard it too," Sune said.

"We are here on vacation with our kids and have rented a house on the other side of the big road," I said.

Esther nodded. "Well it wasn't the first time that kind of thing happened, but it was definitely the most horrific one of them."

"What do you mean it wasn't the first time?" I asked and sipped some more coffee. After standing outside for hours in the snow it felt good to get warmed up again.

"Well, we do hear occasional screaming from up there. I don't know what they do to each other. But it doesn't sound nice, that's for sure."

"So you're saying that you've heard it before?" I asked and noted it on my notepad.

"Well not quite the same. Last night was worse than any night I have ever heard, but yes I hear screaming from up there every now and then."

"Do you have any idea what causes it?" Sune asked.

Esther shook her head. "No. But I have called the police more than once. But once they arrive at the camp to check it out they never can find anything, they tell me. Screaming is one thing, but if nobody is hurt or hospitalized then they can't do anything. The Church members tell the police that the screaming is part of a therapy they offer the young kids in order to get rid of their rage." Esther stopped and looked at the window. It was snowing again. "But the screams I hear aren't screams of rage," she said with a small still voice. Then she looked at me. "It's of pain and deep suffering."

Esther picked up her cup and finished her coffee. Then she lifted the pot with a smile. "More coffee anyone?"

I took a refill and flicked through my notes. Esther took my hand. I lifted my head and stared into her eyes. "There are rumors, you know," she said.

"What kind of rumors?"

"There was one kid that disappeared. Many years ago. She was a local kid that they took in because no one else wanted her. Her mother had died from cancer, leukemia and her dad died even before they came here. They were from Ukraine. Back when it was still part of the Soviet Union. They got out of there once the Union fell and they were able to travel. They moved here. Just the mother and the child. But there was something seriously wrong with the kid. Her mother and father had both worked on the Chernobyl plant when the accident happened and all the radiation was spilled. She was pregnant, the mother. The father died a few weeks after, but the mother survived miraculously. She gave birth to Edwina. But she wasn't well. She looked strange. A few months after her birth she had a lump growing out of her head almost as big as her entire head. It made her face crooked. Even her eyes were scary to look at. They glowed greenish, the story goes that it was from the radiation inside of her that she had been exposed to while still in her mother's womb. She looked like a freak and people couldn't stand being near her. So the mother and child moved away for a new beginning. They ended up in our small town where the mother worked at the local grocery store. She kept the girl at home so she wouldn't scare anyone, but rumors started about the mysterious woman and her child that she didn't want the world to see. The young girl would stare from the window at the other kids playing outside in the street, longing to be a part of their play, but once they spotted her they ran away screaming. The mother home schooled her, and she hardly ever left the house."

"Poor kid," Sune said.

"Oh no," Esther exclaimed shaking her head heavily. "See, we all thought the woman kept the child away for her sake, so she wouldn't be bullied, but it was really for our sake. The kid was evil. I don't normally believe in things like this, but she was definitely possessed with something evil. If it was a demon or what I won't go into, but that kid wasn't human. As I said something was terribly wrong inside of her."

"How do you know?" I asked thinking this conversation had taken a strange turn.

Esther sighed. "Once the mother died from the cancer that was eating her for many years, the girl had to be placed in foster care. They found a nice family in Vipperoed, a city close to here. Soon after the family was struck by one accident after another. Not even months later they lost their younger daughter because she fell from a treetop and broke her neck. The parents found her in the yard when they ran to see what had happened. When they looked up into the tree they saw Edwina standing on a branch staring down at the dead girl. They later swore in the police testimony that she was laughing. The kid was that twisted. The family could no longer have her in their home so they gave her back to the authorities. A few months later they were both diagnosed with cancer, leukemia. Just like the girl's mother. Whoever took the girl in after that was struck by deathly accidents or cancer. They all died. In the end the social workers didn't know what to do about Edwina. She was getting more and more strange and would pull out her own hair and pee on the floor. Soon she began to suffer from convulsions. Unable to speak, scream or call for help she would later explain that she felt as if a huge body of weight was sitting on her, on her chest, holding her down. Like a supernatural force. She claimed she heard voices, which told her she was damned and that she was going to 'stew in hell.' Doctors grew concerned when she explained that the voices were giving her orders, they were whispering to her. Her behavior was out of control. They tried to put her in a psychiatric hospital for months, but it didn't improve her behavior. The doctors had to give up. Even strong medicine didn't help. I know all this because my daughter used to work as a social worker. She heard all the stories that were told about 'the Chernobyl-kid.' That's what they called her. It's said that all her victims dream about her in the moments before they die."

I stared at the old woman in disbelief. Never had I heard such a strange story. "So the church took her in?" I asked trying to stay to the facts.

"Yes. No one else would take her so the county accepted it just to get rid of her even if she did fall in the hands of a sect. Barely a teenager the Priest granted mercy on her and like so many before him he believed that he could help her. I guess he didn't succeed. The last thing I heard she had disappeared. No one has seen her in many years. Luckily, I guess. I was afraid she was going to kill them all."

It was with a strange feeling that I said goodbye to Esther. I promised her that her picture would be in the morning paper. I knew it wasn't going to be much of what she had told me that I was going to actually put in the article.

Back in the car Sune exhaled deeply before he turned the key and started the engine. "Are they all completely insane up here?" he asked.

I laughed. "I'm afraid so."

"Let's get back to some normal people," he said and put the car in gear.

I was already looking forward to spending time with the kids and drinking hot chocolate as soon as the article was done.

8

THEY HELD A meeting. The third one today, Hans Christian thought to himself as he sat down on one of the chair in the meeting room at the camp. People's faces were strained with fear, including his own. The death of their dear leader last night had planted an anxiety among all the church members and especially those who lived at the camp for a long time, like Hans Christian who had been there for twenty-five years.

He had met the Priest back when he was just Anders, a young pastor with ideas that Hans Christian could relate to. Anders had convinced Hans Christian to join him and his cause. Hans Christian had taken cash advances on his dad's credit cards and given Anders all of the money. Hans Christian came from a very wealthy family so with the money they were able to rent the property that they had lived on ever since.

It was an old abandoned school camp where school classes used to come back in the eighties. With his dad's money they rebuilt the place and soon moved in. Hans Christian had helped recruit new members to build the congregation and raise more money for their cause. Anders had some wonderful ideas and Hans Christian had no problem standing behind them and eventually made them his own. His dad had tried to get the money back and filed a lawsuit against both of them, but eventually he dropped the charges, probably because Hans Christian's mother had convinced him to do so. She was a smart woman and knew perfectly well that if they should ever have a hope of seeing their son again, then filing lawsuits probably wasn't the way to do it. Besides too much evil had been between them over the years.

Hans Christian didn't feel bad for taking the money at all. No he thought he had deserved it after all that his dad had put him through. Keeping his mouth shut about the sexual abuse of his older sister that he had discovered by coincidence when he walked in on them in the wine cellar. Hans was only thirteen looking for a bottle of wine to bring to a party. His dad was bent over his sister with his sex in her mouth. Then he had taken a bottle and handed it to him. From that day on they had an agreement. He wouldn't tell about Hans Christian's drinking and stealing expensive wines from his cellar and Hans Christian kept quiet about what he had seen him do to his sister. Hans Christian had never been too fond of his sister anyway so he figured it was a good deal.

Later in sessions with Anders he had spoken about this for the first time and repented his actions for hours kneeling in front of the Priest, till his knees were bleeding. Now Hans Christian was a free man, free from the sin and guilt. He still had scars on his back from the beating Anders had provided him in order to drive out all the evil from his soul, but it had been worth it, every striped scar from the stick. Now he was free.

Hans Christian looked at his friends around the table. It

was the first time he had seen their faces like this. It wasn't just the sorrow of having lost their leader and guru Anders the Priest, it wasn't only the insecure future of their church that caused them to suffer and look strained. It wasn't even the mob of journalists waiting outside the fences, waiting for them to make a mistake so they could write their lies in their papers.

No Hans Christian knew why they were grabbed by this sudden angst. It was the thought that this might be the Priest's prophesy that finally came true. Nobody dared to speak about it but they all thought the same.

The Priest had spoken about it for years. Ever since that night in 1998 when the full moon had shone above Isefjorden just like it did last night. That night when the Chernobyl-kid had looked at him with those green glowing eyes and...

"So what do you think, Hans Christian?" Isabella suddenly asked him.

Isabella Dubois. How he hated that name and those icy eyes. Hans Christian had been the Priest's favorite until she came along and ruined everything. Suddenly the Priest had declared that she was going to be his predecessor that she would take over once he was gone. Hans Christian had loathed her from the beginning. She was a conniving snake. Suddenly Hans Christian was frozen out by the Priest. He was no longer invited to the important meetings where the important decisions were made. He was shoved into the cold and the Priest hardly looked at him anymore. Just because of her. And now since the Priest was gone she suddenly wanted his opinion? Was Hans Christian a part of the leader group again all of a sudden? Did he want to be?

"Well I guess I think it is important that we keep on as usual in order to keep the youngsters calm. They're scared to death. We need to get back to normal at any cost."

Isabella nodded to his surprise. "I couldn't agree more," she said.

Hans Christian was surprised that she had even asked for his advice and he had never thought she would agree with him.

"The worst thing we can do is let panic get the best of us. So let's get back to doing what we normally do and proceed with the ceremonies that we had planned for this week. Anders might not be here anymore, but he still lives on in us. In this place we have built for his cause, for our cause."

Hans Christian scoffed at her last words. Like she had ever built anything. She was still a teenager when they had started this place and now she acted like she owned everything. Sure she was beautiful and he got why everybody adored her and listened to her every word. She was like the ice queen in Narnia he would say, but not many would probably agree with him on that. He saw her evil though even the Priest hadn't managed to do so. She had driven this church too far, he thought. She had made them do things Hans Christian didn't like. That was when the Priest had started to freeze him out. After the night, with the kid, with those green eyes, oh how he could still see them. He remembered them staring at him. It sent chills up his back just thinking about them. After that night, Hans Christian had declared that if this was the way things were going, then he wasn't in anymore. To his surprise the Priest had just accepted that and then kept him out of everything. Hans Christian hated him for that. But even more he hated her for turning the Priest against him. The man he had loved for many years. A love that was higher than any other love he had ever encountered. It was deeper, more profound. And now he was gone. Hans Christian didn't even get to say a proper goodbye.

Last night had been horrendous. Hans Christian had

been the first to run for the Priest's room once he heard the initial scream. He wanted desperately to call for an ambulance, but Isabella had refused. "No ambulance can help him out of this," she had exclaimed. "We need to do it ourselves."

So they had tried to drive the demon out of the Priest's body, but with no luck. Terrified they had watched him die a slow and agonizing death. Reduced to nothing but a squealing, drooling monster bathing in his own excrement.

Just before he took his final breath Hans Christian could have sworn he saw a reflection of the Chernobyl-kid in the Priests' eye. She was looking directly at Hans Christian and pointing in his direction.

9

THE ARTICLE ALMOST wrote itself, I thought when I re-read it to make sure I had gotten it all in. It was quite good. I had left out all Esther had told about the Chernobyl-kid and instead just written that one girl once disappeared from the camp and was never seen again, but that it was a rumor and that there were many rumors engulfing the sect. The portrait of the Priest was pretty standard, written based on what I could find about him in early interviews and other articles written over the years. I called Sara at the newspaper in Karrebaeksminde and had her collect everything she could find about him for me. It was an okay article but probably not much better than what all the other papers had.

Sune's pictures of the camp turned out to be excellent and as soon as I had gathered everything there was only one thing left for me to do. I called the local police to hear if there would be an investigation of the death of the Priest and if they had the autopsy ready. I spoke to the head of the police department in Vipperoed. He was nice, but couldn't tell me much.

"So far we consider the death to be natural," he said. "There is no indication that it should be otherwise."

"What about the autopsy, what does that conclude?"

The officer cleared his throat and spoke in a strange high-pitched voice. "We haven't received that yet," he said.

"Will there be any charges against the church members for not calling for an ambulance?" I asked. That was one of the things I mentioned in my article as slightly suspicious.

"I don't know yet," he said. His voice was shaking strangely. He was about to hang up when I stopped him with another question:

"Why didn't they call for help?" I asked. "What was their explanation?"

"I really have to go now," the officer said. Then he hung up. I lifted my head and looked at Sune and the kids playing the video game. It all seemed a little fishy, I thought while tapping my pen on the table. What could their excuse possibly be to not call for help right away once the Priest had fallen sick? Were they that afraid of the world outside? Were they that self-sufficient that they thought they didn't need the world surrounding them?

Sune beat Julie in a game and they all screamed, waking up Dad who had been snoring from the couch with the paper across his chest for hours. I laughed when I saw Julie's dissatisfied look. It was good for her to lose every now and then. She was good at almost anything and she needed to learn to lose without throwing a fit. She crossed her arms in front of her chest, and then sat on the couch with an angry sound. I looked at my laptop, and then wrote in the last statements from the police about not pressing charges, for letting the man die without calling for help. Then I pressed 'send' and closed the lid. I smiled and walked over to Julie. I sat next to her.

"Wanna try to beat me?" I said.

She growled then looked at me. "Okay," she said and got up.

At least five games and two hours later I finally gave up. Even as hard as I tried I couldn't beat Julie. She was way too good. It gave a boost to her self-esteem and soon Tobias took over trying to beat her.

I threw myself on the couch with a sigh. Dad had begun preparing dinner, Sune helping him. I went to the kitchen and joined them in some grown-up playing. I enjoyed watching the two men I loved chopping vegetables, discussing recipes and exchanging cooking tricks and ideas. This was really an area they had in common and where I was left completely out. Instead I grabbed the paper and started reading it. Sune brought me a glass of red wine that I enjoyed while they cooked. Every now and then I lifted my head and stared at the two of them feeling like the luckiest woman on the face of this planet.

Sune grabbed a glass of wine of his own and when he was done chopping onions he approached me. He sat on the chair in front of me.

"So are you thinking what I'm thinking?" he asked while sipping his wine.

My eyes left the paper and locked with his. "My dad is right there!?" I whispered surprised.

Sune shook his head. "No, that wasn't what I meant." He paused to laugh. "I meant the autopsy. Aren't you curious as to what killed him?"

"The Priest?"

"You know anyone else that died within the last twenty-four hours?" he asked grinning.

I paused and stared at him ignoring his remark. "Is the internet connection good enough for that up here?"

"I should think so," he said. "Otherwise I have ways to make it better."

"The police said they hadn't received it yet. But I would love to read the statements made by the other church members. I would like to read their explanation to why they didn't call for help."

"That's easy to find," Sune said and sipped some wine. "I bet they don't protect their systems very well out here in the country. Don't think they get many cyber-attacks."

"Then by all means go ahead," I said.

10

————

H ANS CHRISTIAN WAS tired of meetings and discussions.
All day long they had been talking about how they
should proceed without the Priest. Even when Isabella left
the camp for three hours to go whoever knows where, they
continued the meetings, discussing how they could keep it all
up. In his honor, they kept saying. They treated him like had
he been the messiah himself.

Hans Christian had at one point believed that he was
Jesus who had come back to get all of them. Maybe the Priest
had even believed it himself. But then he started telling
people that he was the reincarnation of the prophet Isaiah.
Hans Christian had never cared what he thought he was; to
him he was a god. He was the most beautiful human being to
have set his foot on this forsaken earth. Back when it had
only been Hans Christian and him, Hans Christian had
adored everything about him. Every word he spoke, every
gesture, everything he did could only come straight
from God.

Hans Christian had worshipped the Priest. He had kissed
his hand, he had let him drive out demons by beating him,

he had let him tell him how he was supposed to live right, to be righteous. The Priest had explained to Hans Christian that he was and always would be a sinner and that he deserved to be punished for that. He had told him that he was evil, that within all humans lived evil demons that made us sin towards God. He had also explained to him how they needed to be driven, commanded out before anyone could be truly set free. Even if it was painful to the flesh, even if it meant suffering for hours on the cold stone floor while repenting for your sin, bleeding from the wounds the whip left on your back. Jesus had bled for us; it was only fair that we bled for him.

All that Hans Christian had accepted but when it came to the youngsters in the camp he disagreed with the Priest on many things. He didn't think they were evil, when Hans Christian looked into their eyes he saw no malice like the Priest did. He saw young people barely out of childhood who had been hurt, some of them gruesomely. Some of them had been misled, they had done stuff they never should have done, but they were not evil in Hans Christian's eyes. They needed guidance and direction and they needed all the love the disciples could give them. They needed someone who understood them for once in their lives. These were troubled kids with many problems; they didn't need to be told that they had evil living inside of them. On that subject Hans Christian had disagreed with the Priest and he had protested when he thought the Priest went too far with them. He had told him straight up that it was not right to punish them like that. But the Priest didn't want to listen. He had a new apprentice now, Isabella, and she had new ideas, that the Priest wanted to try out. She was the one who had led the cleansing ceremony that night in 1998 when ... Well after that it was like everything went in the wrong direction.

Hans Christian sighed and sat heavily on his bed. It had gotten dark outside of his room. He wanted desperately to sleep but he felt bad inside. He felt bad because his best friend and great love had died the night before and he had watched it happen without doing anything. He felt a huge load of guilt. What if they had called for that ambulance? What if they, for once, had asked for help from the world outside? Could he have been saved?

Hans Christian sighed again and put his head on the pillow. He closed his eyes gently and soon pictures of the Priest flickered before him. So many wonderful years they had had together building this church. Hans Christian had thought about leaving many times throughout the years and now he was thinking about it again. But where would he go? This was his home and had been for almost thirty years. He had helped built this camp, it was his and the thought of leaving it all in the hands of that woman was appalling to him. But without the Priest then what was the point? Leaving the church wasn't an easy thing to do. Hans Christian would lose everything. His only friends and family, he wouldn't have a job anymore and he would certainly miss the youngsters with whom he had worked for many, many years. A lot of the grown-ups in the camp making the decisions today were someone that he had recruited and taken care of when they were just young teenagers in trouble. Now they were like his family.

No one ever left "The Way" once they came here. Neither would he. It was his family and he had to take the good with the bad. Just like a regular family. Plus he was an old man by now. There wasn't anything for him out there in the world. He would only be miserable.

Hans Christian exhaled deeply thinking how he would try and improve the conditions for the youngsters from now on. He would fight Isabella who obviously didn't care much about them. They were scared to death now the Priest was gone. They knew how Isabella looked upon them.

Hans Christian looked at the starry sky outside his window one last time before he finally dozed off.

11

A FTER DINNER SUNE started working on the computer while I helped the kids get to bed. When I returned downstairs Dad was slowly dozing off on the couch in front of the TV. Sune had poured the rest of the red wine into our glasses and his magical fingers were working on the keyboard.

I grabbed a chair next to his and took my glass from the table. He was concentrating and I had worked with him long enough to know that I had to keep quiet. He would speak once he was ready.

"Ha!" he exclaimed not long after.

"That was fast," I said and leaned forward. I looked at the screen and had to admit that I understood absolutely nothing of all the letters and numbers in front of me.

Sune grabbed his wine and sipped it. "It was almost too easy," he said. After putting the glass down his fingers danced yet again across the keyboard and soon after he turned the screen for me to look at.

I grabbed the laptop and pulled it closer. He had found the police report made this morning with all the statements taken from the church members present when the Priest died. I scrolled while skimming them. All stated they had been asleep when the screaming woke them up. I stopped at Isabella Dubois' statement.

"If you click here you can hear the recorded audio from the interview," Sune said and moved the mouse over an icon. Then he pushed the button and a voice filled the room. The voice of an officer telling us the date, case number and who he was interviewing. First he asked her a couple of questions about her name and status and so on. Then he asked her to describe what happened.

"I was petrified. I remember the screams penetrating my dreams and waking me up with a start. My heart was pounding. At first I thought it had been nothing but a dream, but soon I realized that the screams were still there and now they were even worse. They were coming from the building across from mine. I put on a bathrobe and ran across the courtyard thinking that it might have been one of the youngsters who had hurt himself somehow or maybe he was having a bad dream. But I knew deep inside that this kind of screaming don't come from just an ordinary nightmare."

"How do you know that?" the officer questioning her asked.

"You just know. These were screams of deep pain. These weren't screams of this earth."

"What do you mean by that?" the officer asked.

"I have heard my share of people whose souls were screaming from beyond the grave."

"Like dead people?"

"No. Yes. People who are possessed. These were screams like that. Coming from a devil trying to take over a poor soul," Isabella said.

"So what you're telling me is you thought Anders Granlund might have been possessed by a devil, is that it?"

"Not might have been. He was. I have seen it so many times before and this was the strongest one I have yet met. That was why we couldn't drive it out of him. We weren't powerful enough. It took him with it to the pit of hell. And you know what happens when you can't expel a demon?"

"No, I don't," the officer said.

"It comes back to get you. If you let it win it will come back after you. It happened to the Priest once before in '98. There was a demon he couldn't drive out and it came back to get him. Bigger and stronger than ever. The Priest knew it would. He has told us for years that this was bound to happen. We all thought we would be able to drive it out once that happened though. But I guess we aren't as strong as we thought."

"So let me just get this straight. You're telling me, that you thought Anders Granlund was possessed by some demon that had come back to get revenge?" the officer said.

Isabella Dubois sighed annoyed. "Why am I even trying?" she exclaimed. "No one ever cares to listen anyway. You simply don't want to understand, you don't want to see the evil that has taken a stronghold of this land, of this area. It will take over and kill everybody if you don't stop it. Don't you understand the importance of spreading the word about this?"

The officer was silent. I imagined that he was shaking his head or maybe just staring at Isabella Dubois in disbelief. I knew I would have.

She exhaled annoyed. "Let's just get this over with," she said in a harsh irritated voice. "I can't help people who don't want to be helped. But don't say I didn't warn you."

"Please explain to me what you saw once you entered the

building where the screaming came from," the officer said. His voice sounded heavily burdened and slightly resigned.

Isabella Dubois sighed. "I saw people standing in the room."

"Who did you see and where were they at the time you entered?"

"It's hard to remember. I don't think I remember everybody who was there. I wasn't exactly looking at them; the screaming was going right through my bones. My focus was on the person it was coming from.

"Try anyway," the officer said.

Isabella sighed again. "Alright. I guess I saw Mette Grithfeldt, she was standing on the left next to Soren Sejr, Hans Christian Bille and Mogens Wammen."

I found my notepad and started scribbling the names down. Sune was drinking his wine. Isabella Dubois continued:

"In the center of the room I saw Peter Hansen standing with Camilla Morsoe." Isabella paused. "Yes I guess that's about it. Others came running to the room after I had arrived but I can't remember who they were. I was focused on helping Anders."

"Okay," the officer said. "What were they doing in the room?"

"Well they were paralyzed. They were all staring at Anders who was lying on the floor, curled up in a strange position. He was screaming and throwing up; blood was coming out of his eyes and ears. His hair ... he tore it off in huge clumps. It was horrible to watch and there was nothing we could do to help him. Excrement came out of him everywhere and it smelled nasty in the room. The worst part was the pain I sensed he was feeling. It was like something was eating him from the inside. Like the demon was killing him slowly from the inside, shutting down one organ at a time. In his hand he was clutching his crucifix. It was covered in blood coming from his mouth."

"So what did you do?" the officer asked.

I felt sick to my stomach. Sune stared at me. Our eyes locked and I sensed he felt the same way. What could possible kill a person in that gruesome manner? That fast? A disease? An allergic reaction? It didn't sound plausible to me.

"I had brought my bible and held it high in the air," Isabella said. "Then we decided to drive out the demon that had taken possession of the Priest's body. We all agreed there was no other way."

"And how do you do that?" the officer asked while exhaling. He didn't even try to hide that he thought about her and the sect. I guessed he was thinking just what I was. This group was insane, religious fanatics at their worst.

"We command it to leave. We rebuke it. We quote scriptures, chant and sing and praise the Lord till the devil can't stand it anymore. We tell the Lord to come and be in our midst and help us drive the devil out of this person."

"And how long does that ceremony usually take?" the officer asked.

Isabella chuckled. "It depends on the demon. It's size and strength of course."

"But it would take more than an hour?" the officer asked.

"We keep going until the demon has left the body and the place. It can take hours, sometimes days," Isabella said. "Sometimes they come back and then we have to do it again with a few months in between. This is powerful stuff it's not something that will leave you alone just because you tell it to. This takes hours and hours of pain and suffering and listening to the word of God cleansing your body. It's the only way to be set truly free. If you don't believe me then read your bible. Jesus and the disciples drove out demons all the time."

The officer paused. I could almost feel how he was shaking his head in disbelief. As was I. Then finally the question came, the one I had been waiting for:

"The alarm call came from a neighbor at twelve-thirty in the morning but what you describe for me we know from the other statements happened around midnight. Why didn't you call for help while your priest was in pain and obviously needed professional help?"

Isabella Dubois went quiet for a few seconds before she continued. "He was getting professional help. There is no one mightier than the Lord, the creator of the entire universe."

The officer sighed. "I meant an ambulance. Why didn't you call for an ambulance?"

"Because he didn't need it," she said.

"You don't think he could have gotten the help he needed in a hospital?" the officer said.

"No. You're focusing on the wrong thing here. This is a very strong demon and it had taken possession of his body, killing him from the inside. No doctor, no science could ever cure that."

I stopped the audio file and looked at Sune. "She really believes that," I said. "Completely brainwashed. It's insane."

He nodded. "I can't believe how anyone can think like that. Let a man die on the floor without getting help. It's way beyond cruel."

"I know," I said leaning back in my chair. I sipped my wine while scrolling through the rest of the statement. In the end Isabella kept repeating that we should all consider ourselves warned. This was just the beginning of our downfall. This demon would take possession of this entire land, this town and kill all of us. I scoffed and continued reading. The officer ended the interview by letting her know that she and others who were present in the room when the Priest died should be prepared for possibly being prosecuted for not having helped the deceased in his dying moments. This was an offense that was punishable by prison. Isabella Dubois apparently didn't care much about it since she ended the interview by telling the officer that they wouldn't have the time to prosecute her.

"This is the beginning of the end for all of us," she said.

I scoffed again and read it out loud to Sune. He shook his head slowly. "I have heard about religious fanatics but this woman is just plain crazy."

I laughed and finished my glass of wine.

"More?" Sune asked.

I looked at the clock. It was only eleven. It was after all vacation. "Just one glass," I said.

Sune got up and went to the kitchen to get more wine for both of us. He found some dark assorted chocolates that he brought back to the table. I swallowed one in a hurry like I thought it wouldn't make me fat if I hurried up and swallowed it. Sune filled our glasses again while I opened a new statement. This time the officer was talking to a man named Hans Christian Bille.

12

I T DIDN'T FEEL like a dream, Hans Christian thought to himself as he walked closer to the weird green substance in front of him. Somehow he knew it was anyway, maybe because the green stuff was pulsating as if it were somehow alive. It reminded him of the Jell-O that his maid used to serve him when he was a child. Green, wobbly Jell-O when all he wanted was a hug from his mother and her presence.

Hans Christian had been lonely as a child and the solitude was a feeling he hadn't been able to escape even as an adult, even when he met Anders and started the church. It lingered with him and he would never get rid of it. It was a part of him. Now standing in front of this weird mass he felt the lonesomeness stronger than he had in years. It felt almost like it was sucking all hope and happiness out of him. It grew steadily in front of him while he slowly shrank. It sucked life out of him. He was left with nothing but despair and the old familiar feeling of loneliness, the sense of never having been properly loved. The feeling was so overwhelming it forced Hans Christian to bend over in agony like had he been punched. He gasped for air as the green mass grew bigger and bigger in front of him. He reached out his hand towards it still feeling suffocated. As his hand touched it he spotted his own reflection in the green mass. He didn't recognize himself at first but the eyes were familiar. It was a boy, himself as just a young boy.

"Why do you look so sad?" Hans Christian said to the boy.

But the boy never answered. He started to cry. Not like children normally cry, but in a quiet way. He stared at Hans Christian while tears rolled down his cheeks.

"Don't cry," Hans Christian said and reached out his hand and touched the green mass. It felt sticky. He put his palm on it and pressed through into the wobbly mass. It felt cold and clammy and the shock made him pull his hand back. But he couldn't. The mass had closed around his arm and it felt like it was trying to suck him inside of it. Slowly he watched as his arm became smaller. Then he panicked. But it was like quick-sand. The more he pulled the deeper in the arm went. The green mass was still growing bigger and made smacking sounds like someone eating soup. Hans Christian moaned and tried to pull his arm back again but he couldn't. Soon his entire arm was sucked into the mass and his shoulder as well. Then he screamed. He screamed from the top of his lungs.

"Stop! Stop! Please don't hurt me. Help!"

But he was alone. Just like he had been as a child whenever he heard those footsteps in the hallway of the mansion he grew up in. The footsteps of his father coming to his room in the middle of the night. The smacking sound from the green mass made Hans Christian want to throw up. It was the same sound his father used to make when he put Hans Christian's sex into his mouth and began doing things to him he never could forgive himself for. It was the same sound his father made at the dinner table while they ate in silence. The same sound haunted Hans Christian for years making him feel uncomfortable eating with other people who smacked their lips, causing his anger to rise. Anger that could kill if he didn't restrain it. Hans Christian restrained it all he could. Over the years he had learned how to. Whenever anyone was smacking his or her lips at the dinner table in the dining hall at the camp, Hans Christian would leave immediately, go to his room and take out a whip from the closet. He would take off his shirt and whip his own back for hours until the pain was completely gone and he could hear the sound of the smacking lips no more.

Frantically Hans Christian was now pulling his arm trying to get it out of this weird green growing mass in front of him, crying in despair. Pictures of his father touching him, making him feel things he didn't want to, the forbidden feeling of pleasure, pleasure from being with his father who never looked at him or even talked to him, who always seemed to be disappointed in him, except at night when he climbed under his covers. Hans Christian was screaming and crying while fighting the green mass in the way he knew he should have fought his father but never had the guts to do. Because he wanted it. Didn't he? He wanted it to happen. He wanted to be close to his father, he wanted to feel his presence, the love, the affection. Even if it was in that way, a way he knew was wrong. At least it was something. It was the closest Hans Christian had ever come to being loved.

While Hans Christian was screaming out years and years of pain and repressed feelings he suddenly saw something in the green mass. His reflection was changing; it was no longer the young boy he had tried so hard to forget staring back at him from inside the green mass. Slowly the eyes changed, and soon the face changed. Out grew something much much worse than facing his long concealed pain. It was a girl, the girl. She was staring back at Hans Christian with her green glowing eyes in her crooked face.

Hans Christian gasped for air and froze. Then the girl laughed.

Hans Christian woke up screaming. Realizing it was just a dream calmed him down immediately, but the sense of inner peace didn't last for long. Barely had he put his head back on the pillow and closed his eyes, hearing nothing but his own rapid heartbeat, when suddenly another sound caused him to open his eyes again.

The sound of smacking lips.

13

HANS CHRISTIAN BILLE'S statement didn't add much new to the story except he clearly told the officer that he wanted to call for the ambulance right away but Isabella Dubois had told him not to. He was the only one of the people present who clearly had conscience enough to want to do something according to the statements that - except for Hans Christian's - were scarily alike. The officer kept asking him why he didn't just do it anyway, why he - and the others in the room - hadn't refused to obey the orders coming from Isabella Dubois? Hans Christian hadn't been able to provide a satisfying answer for that.

"That is just the way it is," he answered.

I noted that statement on my notepad, thinking that it was probably a very fitting answer. These were people who were used to being led by a strong leader and used to being told what to do, what to think and what not to. They obeyed orders or they risked losing everything. I had once written a story about a similar sect in Jutland a couple of years ago. A young woman had managed to break free and told me in an interview how it worked. It was appalling. Especially how they exploited her weaknesses, her fear of being alone. They told her she would lose everything if she left the sect, if she turned her back on them. No one would take care of her, and she was weak as a person, they told her, and not able to take care of herself. She needed them and she believed them.

For several years she let them exploit her. She had to work for them, cook, clean and be available sexually for the leader as should the rest of the women in the sect. Her mistake was to fall in love with the leader and follow him into this as just a very young woman. He had brainwashed her and over a couple of months changed her way of thinking. I was appalled by the way he had filled her with guilt and basically told her she couldn't do anything on her own, that she was evil by nature and a sinner and without him she would fall back to her old sinful lifestyle. Her parents had tried to contact her and help her get out, she later learned but she was kept away from them and everybody else. She was told her family and old friends weren't good for her. She was told to turn her back at them, on her old ways, and so she did. Ten years later she finally managed to escape but she found it hard to live a normal life, she was constantly afraid and suffered from severe anxiety attacks. All of her friends were gone and her mother had died.

Now she lived with her father who was all she had left. Members of the sect still came to her house several times a week to talk to her and tell her to come back. First they would tell her that they loved her and knew she loved them. Then they would tell her she was living wrong, filling her again with guilt and condemnation, telling her she couldn't do it on her own. That she was living sinfully. It was hard for her to resist them, since there really wasn't much left for her on the outside anymore. She had never had a good relationship with her father and it hadn't improved.

As I sat in the living room of the vacation rental and stared at all the statements made by the members of "The Way" I felt a chill run down my back. I thought about the young woman and where she was now, if she had managed to get her life back or if she had gone back to what she knew, what had become familiar to her? I remembered asking her if she ever considered going back. I will never forget that look she gave me. It scared me. She didn't have to answer and she never did. I could tell by simply looking into her eyes, that she thought about it constantly.

Sune leaned over in the couch and kissed me. "Where did you go?" he asked.

I smiled and touched his cheek gently. "Nowhere. Was just thinking about a story I once did."

"Ah. More work."

"I want to write this story," I said scrolling on the laptop.

Sune sighed and looked at me. "Can't say I blame you," he said. "It is a great story. I can't believe they wouldn't call for an ambulance."

I nodded pensively. "It's an important story."

"I think so too."

I picked up my cell phone. It wasn't too late to call my editor Jens-Ole. I found him under recent calls.

"I have another story for you," I said. "A spin-off from the death of the Priest."

Jens-Ole laughed. "I knew it. I knew you couldn't stay away."

Jens-Ole was shocked after I had told him the details of the story. He told me I could get the front cover. Then he hung up. I took the laptop to the dinner table and started writing. Sune turned on the TV and watched the late news. The story of the Priest was still there, but it had moved to the bottom of the run down and was just a small story stating he had died from what was believed to be food poisoning. So far people shouldn't be alarmed since none of the other church members seemed to have been made ill and they all shared the same food.

I got up from my chair and went to the kitchen to make myself some coffee. When I returned Sune had fallen asleep on the couch. I found a blanket and put it over him, then I turned the volume down on the TV and went back to the computer to write my story.

14

THE SMACKING SOUND just wouldn't go away. At first Hans Christian thought it was all in his head. It was a leftover from his dream. So he decided to ignore it. Forget it, think about something else. Happy thoughts. He thought about Anders and the first years they spent together building up the church and the camp. Those had been the best years of Hans Christian's life. They had talked for hours and hours, even sometimes staying up all night discussing their beliefs and why God had put them on this earth. They had a mission they both agreed. Anders had been amazing. So beautiful, so powerful and so anointed. There was no doubt in Hans Christian's mind that Anders was created for greatness. And he worshipped him for it. God had chosen Anders to be the leader, to be the Priest. He had shown him things in visions and when Anders spoke about it, it was like he was on fire. His passion was big and soon Hans Christian's was just as big. They wanted to save people from the evil lurking inside of them, that was their mission. They were going to cleanse them and free them from what possessed them and made them do evil things. It was an honorable mission and just like Peter was to Jesus in the Bible, Hans Christian had been Anders' faithful servant and disciple. He had followed him in everything, worshipped his every movement and word he spoke.

Until that night in 1998, he thought while the emotions flushed in over him. How many nights he had regretted what had happened. But mostly he regretted not having done anything until afterwards when it was all too late. Not until the day after had he told Anders how he felt about what they were doing, what they had done. Not until then had he told him that he didn't want to be a part of it anymore.

That was when he lost everything. That was when he lost Anders for good and became just another one in the crowd to him.

Happy thoughts, Hans Christian thought to himself as he thought the smacking of the lips became louder in his head. Get back to the happy thoughts. Thoughts about the good days, before … Hans Christian sighed and opened his eyes. What use was it to try and sleep now? He was an old man now and sleeping had become increasingly difficult over the years.

Hans Christian sat up in the bed. There it was again, the smacking sound. He sighed and got up. He walked to the window and pulled away the curtain. It was still a full moon. How he hated the full moon. Always reminded him of that girl. Hans Christian shivered at the thought. He never liked to think about her. Why was he suddenly dreaming about her? Well it wasn't that strange after all, Hans Christian thought. Not after what had happened the night before with the Priest. It was a wonder that he had been able to sleep at all after that event. It was a wonder that anyone was able to sleep this night. Hans Christian shivered again. He could still hear those screams in his head and now the smacking of the lips. Why was he tormenting himself so much?

The smacking sound seemed to come closer, he thought and turned around to face the door. Was he imagining things or was there someone out there? Maybe someone was in the kitchen? Hans Christian's room was next to the kitchen. Maybe one of the youngsters had sneaked in to get a late night snack? The building was after all a place where you could hear everything going on in every room. It wouldn't be the first time he was awakened by someone grabbing something to eat.

Hans Christian grabbed a cardigan and put it on. Then he walked towards the door, grabbed the handle and opened it. The smacking sound was louder out there. It couldn't be just in his head.

He loved this place, he thought to himself while walking and thinking about that time when they built it. He and Anders had built it together with love and passion for their mission. Hans Christian sighed deeply as he approached the door to the kitchen. He was going to miss Anders, even if he had turned his back on him, even if they hadn't spoken much the last few years.

The sound was much louder now and Hans Christian prepared himself to do a little scolding before he reached out for the handle. No one was allowed to eat outside of hours. He opened the door and stepped in with a small gasp.

With a trembling hand he reached into his pocket of the cardigan and pulled out his crucifix.

15

I WROTE FOR two hours and then the story was done. My editor had given me until midnight to finish it and a few minutes before the clock on the wall showed midnight I pressed 'send' on the computer. Satisfied I leaned back in my chair with a small sigh. This was a story no one else had, I was certain of that. The story about the religious sect who thought their leader was possessed by a demon and therefore didn't call for an ambulance when he was in fact dying of what they now believe is food poisoning. That was bound to be the talk of the town by tomorrow.

I yawned and got up from my chair. My back was killing me. The chair I had been sitting on was horrible. Good thing I wasn't going to work anymore on this vacation, I thought and went to wake up Sune and get him upstairs with me. I exhaled and looked at him. He was such a sweet guy. Was I in love with him? I believed I was. But I still felt he was so young, at least sometimes. There was so much he didn't know. Yet - being a father and all - he was really mature for his age and I loved spending time with him and Tobias. We had fun. Sune was a lot of fun to be with.

He opened his eyes and looked at me. "I guess I fell asleep," he mumbled.

"I guess you did," I said smiling. I leaned over and kissed his lips. They were so soft, so gentle, so sweet. So different from kissing Peter who had always been rough and demanding.

"I was dreaming," he said. "A great dream."

I put my head on his chest and enjoyed the resounding sound of his voice through it. "That sounds nice," I mumbled.

"It was about you," he said and chuckled.

"I like the sound of that. Keep going," I closed my eyes and enjoyed a rare moment of closeness.

Sune chuckled again. "We had a baby, you and I."

I opened my eyes and lifted my head. "We did what?"

Sune smiled gently. "We had a baby. You had it, but I was the father. You and I made a baby together. Isn't that wonderful?"

I froze completely while staring at him. I exhaled. "I think it is time for bed now," I said and got up from the couch.

Sune stared at me. "It was just a dream," he said. "What's going on? Why are you freaking out?"

"I'm not freaking out," I said sensing my voice becoming slightly shrill. I forced it to calm down.

"You're acting weird, then. Why are you acting weird?" Sune sat up on the couch and looked at me.

"I'm not acting weird. You're the one being weird about this. You were sleeping. I get it. People have dreams. Nothing to it. I dream all the time about stuff that doesn't matter, right? I mean, it doesn't have to mean anything."

"You're still being weird," Sune said and got up from the couch.

"No I'm not," I exclaimed a little too loud.

"Then explain to me what is going on, because I don't think I understand. Either you're mad at me for something or ..." Sune exhaled.

"Or what, Sune? What?"

He exhaled again. "I don't know," he said. "Maybe you have PMS or something. Maybe we just need some sleep."

I froze. "PMS or something? What kind of statement is that supposed to be?"

"I don't know. I don't understand women," he said.

"Try anyway. I don't like to be called mad when I'm not mad. I thought we were having a nice time here."

"Well I thought so too, but suddenly it was like you were mad at me for having that dream or something."

"Why should I be mad about that?" I asked defensively.

"I don't know, okay! Could we please just leave it?"

I gesticulated resignedly. "Alright. Whatever."

Sune sighed again. "I'm going to bed."

"For your information I don't suffer from PMS," I said as I watched him walk up the stairs.

"Okay," he said. "Whatever you tell yourself."

I snorted in anger in his direction. What the hell just happened there? I thought to myself as Sune disappeared up the stairs. How was I supposed to react? I was confused. I couldn't go up there now, he would only think he had won, so I had to stay at least a couple of minutes to make a statement. At the same time I was so tired I could sleep standing up so I really didn't want to wait. My pride kept me in the living room for another five minutes before I finally caved and started walking up the stairs.

I only went a few steps before I froze by the sound of another wave of horrifying deathly screams.

Sune came out on the stairs and walked towards me. The

screams went through my bones. "Should we call for help?" I asked.

"I'm on it," Sune said and walked downstairs to get his phone.

16

T HE PAIN WAS excruciating. Nothing like anything Hans Christian had ever experienced. Not even when he succumbed himself to the mercy and strict hand and whip of Anders the Priest. Not even when Anders beat out the demons from his body and made him free again. Not even that pain was anything compared to what he was experiencing right now. It was like needles, no more like knives trying to penetrate through his skin from the inside. It was as if his blood was boiling, his internal organs on fire.

People gathered around him after they had heard him scream. He lay on the kitchen floor crouched, crumpled up, vomiting blood and trying desperately to talk, but only being able to utter a few incoherent words. It was like his body was giving up, one organ, one cell at a time. Even his mind seemed to be tricking him. He thought he saw visions, people from his past in the room with him, along with all the church members staring helplessly at him while he was tossing his body on the floor, screaming while blood ran from his eyes, ears and nose. It seemed his body was slowly dissolving from the inside, as if something was trying to get out. In his hand he still held his crucifix and every now and then he tried to lift it and command this pain to go away in the name of Jesus Christ, but the words came out spluttering with blood and nothing made sense to him anymore. He knew who had done this to him, he had stared into the face of his killer, but then he remembered no more. Next thing he found himself on the floor of the kitchen in a pain so tormenting he wished he could just die right away. He wasn't afraid any longer. He wanted to go home. Home to be with Anders. His only problem was he wasn't sure he was going to be with the good Lord anymore. Not after having stared the devil right into the eyes.

"Help ..." he stuttered half choked by the blood in his throat. "Help me ..."

Isabella entered the room and kneeled in front of him. Hans Christian managed to lift his head and look into her icy eyes. He had expected to be met with cold or even maybe compassion, but he saw neither. Instead he saw disgust. Isabella had loathed him from the beginning and now he was more appalling to her than ever.

"We need to clean him," she said. "We might not be able to save his life, but we can rebuke the devil from him, so it won't take his soul. We can still save his soul."

They started chanting, singing and talking in tongues. Hans Christian moaned and groaned while more blood oozed out of him and onto the white tiles that he himself had installed many years ago. In all of the spectator's eyes he saw fear. They were scared of him, of what was happening to him. When he moaned and screamed in pain they drew back. Isabella lifted her crucifix in the air and yelled Latin phrases, commanded the devil to leave his body. Another wave of pain flushed through him and caused him to vomit more blood. He felt something in his mouth and spat it out only to realize it was a tooth. One by one he spat them all out on the tiles. He touched his hair and pulled it out in big lumps. Just like Anders had done.

In the seconds before he died.

"It's just like the Priest," he heard someone whisper.

Hans Christian lifted his head and locked eyes with one of the spectators, the one who had spoken. Mette Grithfeldt. He saw her draw back, fear and anxiety radiating from her eyes. Isabella was still chanting, singing, commanding, yelling at the devil. Hans Christian stared at Mette Grithfeldt trying so hard to speak to her, to all of them, to tell them to get out of here while they could, to escape, tell them that they weren't safe here anymore, but as he opened his mouth, torn by pain, only blood came sputtering out. Blood and one single word:

"...you ... you ..." Hans Christian heard himself say. He wanted badly to say more than that. He wanted to tell her to get away. Tell her to run now as fast as she could and never return to this forsaken place.

"Don't listen to him," Isabella yelled. "He is possessed. It's the devil trying to manipulate you. Don't listen to it, don't let him get his words inside of you. They'll poison you and eat you up. Don't let him get to you."

Mette Grithfeldt drew further backwards. Her eyes stared at him with horror. She didn't understand that he cared about her. Mette Grithfeldt had been Hans Christian's only friend when Anders had turned his back at him. That was why Hans Christian was approaching her now. He knew she would listen; she would understand if he could get the words across his lips and press them out through the terrifying pain. If he could find the strength to utter them, he would be able to warn her, tell her to leave. He cared about her. It was too late for him, but she could save herself.

But all he managed to do was to lift his hand and point at her before the pain became so unbearable he could no longer feel it or sense anyone around him. Everything drowned, their faces, their voices and suddenly it all went so quiet.

As life slowly oozed out of Hans Christian and reality became nothing but a blur he was certain he heard one last sound clearly and distinctly.

That of his father smacking his lips.

17

S UNE HUNG UP. He looked at me and then put his arm around me. Then he kissed my forehead.

"They're on their way. I told them I thought it sounded like the screams we heard last night but I had no idea where they came from. They said I wasn't the first calling about it and they were on their way to check on it now but it could take up to half an hour for them to get all the way out here. Guess we are just far from everything, huh?"

I held him close to me. My body was shivering. If it was the cold or fear I couldn't tell. The screaming was horrifying, piercing. "Do you think it is coming from the camp again?" I asked.

Sune shrugged. "It might as well be coming from somewhere else."

I exhaled. I was getting scared. Afraid that it might be some disease killing people or maybe something in some food we had all bought in the local supermarket or maybe it was in the water? I was thinking, speculating insanely. Could any of us have gotten this somehow as well? I looked up at Sune. He seemed calm, but concerned.

I glanced towards the door behind where the children were asleep. What if any of them caught it? What if Dad did? He had a weak heart. He would never survive it.

The door to the children's bedroom opened. Julie stuck her head out. I smiled and pulled away from Sune. Then I walked towards her.

"Could I borrow those earplugs again, Mom?" she asked.

"Of course you can. I put them in the top drawer in your room just in case. Let's go get them." I turned and looked at Sune just before I went into the bedroom following Julie. He smiled back. Tomorrow night, I thought. Tomorrow night we will be able to sleep together again.

This time the screaming didn't last as long as the first night. About twenty minutes later it was suddenly gone and I fell asleep next to Julie. My sleep was uneasy though mostly because Julie kept taking over my pillow and kicking me in my stomach, but also because I couldn't escape this eerie feeling inside that something was really wrong in this place. The screams scared me. It was one thing that a person died from something they didn't know what originated from, but a second death? Would I wake up to find another person had died from this around here?

I kept waking with a start, then fell asleep again dreaming creepy dreams about people dying while screaming and then waking up again. Every time I woke up I tried to calm my thoughts and looked at Julie while she was sleeping heavily. The full moon outside my window lit up the entire room and made me able to see every little feature of her beautiful face. I was so blessed to have her in my life, I kept reminding myself again and again. She was my pride and I would do anything to protect her. If this was some disease we were going to leave first thing in the morning. But what if it turned out to be already too late? What if we had been infected somehow?

I pushed the thought out of my mind again. I had to calm down. I was worth nothing without my sleep. I had to keep calm for her sake, for Julie.

Julie woke me up at seven o'clock by shaking me.

"Get up Mom. You promised to build a snowman with me and Tobias, remember?"

I opened my eyes. Both Julie and Tobias were staring at me with big expectant eyes. They were both smiling. "Please?" Julie said.

I sighed. Then I smiled. "Okay, okay. Just give me a few minutes to wake up."

The door to the bedroom opened. Sune stuck in his head. He looked as sleepy as I felt. "Kids, stop bothering Rebekka. Breakfast is ready downstairs. We'll meet you there," he growled.

"Yay!" Julie exclaimed and jumped towards the door. Tobias followed her in another great leap.

"Where do they get the energy?" I groaned.

Sune crawled under my covers and we spooned for a couple of minutes.

"Mmm," he mumbled while kissing my neck.

"That Tobias sure sleeps heavily," I said. "He didn't wake up at all even with all the screaming. Has he always been like that?"

Sune kissed my ear and buried his face in my hair. "He has always been a heavy sleeper just like me. I guess I'm just lucky."

"You sure are. Julie always wakes up. It has gotten a lot better with age, but earlier she used to wake from just the sound of the TV. It was quite hard on us when she was younger. She would hear a sound downstairs or outside the house and then crawl into our bed almost every night. To get proper sleep Peter always spent the rest of the night in the guest bedroom. It tore apart my marriage with him that we never slept in the same bed."

Sune went quiet. "Hm," he said.

"What?" I asked.

"Well, we never sleep together either," he said.

I exhaled. "I know. It will improve. I promise you it will. I'm determined to not make the same mistakes again."

Sune kissed my neck again and held me tight. "I know you're trying. And I know it is hard from time to time. But I need to be your priority as well. I need intimacy and I need to feel important to you."

I sighed. "I know you do. You are my priority. It's just hard sometimes, when you know what your child is going through. Missing her dad and all. It's been a couple of tough years on her."

"She's fine," Sune whispered in my ear. "She's a happy kid. You're worrying too much."

I turned my head and kissed his lips. Those soft gentle lips that made me feel so happy. "I'm sorry," I said.

He looked at me surprised. "Sorry? For what?"

"For acting weird last night. I guess I was just tired."

He kissed me again. Our eyes locked as he let go of my lips again. "I'm sorry too. I said stupid things. It was just a misunderstanding. I became scared that you freaked out because I had that dream."

"The one about the baby. Well, yeah, that was kind of silly, huh?" I looked down and tried to avoid his eyes.

"Sure was."

"Just a dream. Nothing more to it," I said and looked at him again, looked for confirmation that I was right, that there was nothing more to that dream. But I didn't find it. Sune went quiet. He was biting his lip.

"There is more to it?" I asked. "Don't tell me there is more to it!"

Sune gesticulated resigned. "So what if there is? Would it be so bad?"

I pulled backwards out of his arms. I sat up.

"What?" he asked. "Why are you reacting like this?"

I inhaled deeply and looked at him. "Listen to me, Sune. I'm thirty-eight years old. I barely have my life together as it is. I have an ex-husband who has gone crazy and a child who needs extra attention because she has seen things and experienced her own father fall apart in front of her eyes. I have absolutely no interest what so ever in having another child. Not now. Not ever. I made my decision a long time ago to never have any more kids so it is not something I'm willing to even discuss."

I looked at Sune. He looked like I had punched him. He was staring at me with moist eyes.

I sighed. "Did you really think I wanted more kids?"

He shrugged. "I guess I assumed that you might consider having a child with me. We're in love and I have to admit I have been wondering what our baby would look like. If it would have your eyes and my nose or the other way around?" Sune smiled when he said it.

I was paralyzed. I had no idea he felt that way. I guess a small part of me had feared that this was how he felt. "You never spoke of this," I said slightly stuttering. I was shocked to put it mildly.

"Well, I guess I was afraid of getting this reaction." Sune sighed and got up from the bed.

"Sune don't leave. We need to talk about this."

Julie and Tobias were calling our names from down the stairs.

Sune looked at me and bit his lip. "What's there to talk about? You've clearly made your decision for the both of us."

Then he turned around and left.

18

I ATE WAY too much for breakfast. That was what conflicts often did to me. It was the same when my mother and father fought when I was a child or if I got into a fight with one of them I would always end up comfort eating in the middle of the night or bring food to my room. Food was my weakness and I knew it. And now I was doing it again. I was eating breakfast rolls with butter and cheese while the ambiance at the table was tense to put it mildly. Dad was grumpy because his leg was acting up. It often did that when it was really cold like now. It had kept him awake for hours at night and today he still had a pain in it.

"I'll do the cooking the rest of the day," I said. "You just sit on the couch and rest, okay?"

He didn't like it much but finally agreed. Still he was groaning and mumbling at the table, complaining about the pain. Sune was acting grouchy as well. He hardly looked at me or even spoke to me. The air between us was tense and it made me eat more than I needed.

"So when are we going to build that snowman?" Julie whined. "You guys are taking forever to eat."

"In a minute, honey," I said and grabbed some pastry and poured another cup of coffee. I couldn't say I was looking forward to hours in the freezing cold. I was tired and cranky and really wanted to just lie on the sofa with the newspaper and a box of chocolates. The wind was pulling the trees outside the windows, the sky had grown grey and the clouds were heavy with snow.

"I guess we better hurry up," Sune said. "It is going to snow in less than an hour. It looks like it could last all day."

I swallowed my pastry and flushed it down with coffee. Julie and Tobias started putting on boots and winter suits.

"Come on, Mom. Jeez. You heard Sune. I really want to build this snowman today. You promised."

I swallowed hard then drank some more coffee. "I'm coming, I'm coming," I said and got up from my chair. I looked at Dad. His face was torn in restraint. "Promise me you'll leave all this on the table. I'll clean it up later, okay?"

He nodded with his eyes closed. I sighed and found some pills to kill the pain in a cupboard and handed them to him with a glass of water. "They'll make you feel better for a little while," I said. I kissed his forehead. "Try and get some sleep."

He nodded slowly and kissed me back.

Sune opened the door and the kids ran out with high-pitched screams. The wind hitting me from the open door felt like needles on my skin. I shivered and ran to get my winter jacket.

"I'll be outside with the kids," Sune said. His eyes were still hurt and distanced. He was barely looking at me.

"Sune ... I," I said and stepped forward with my jacket in my hand.

He shook his head. "Save it. I can't deal with this right now." Then he followed the kids outside. I heard then whine and laugh as they threw snowballs at Sune and he grabbed

Julie and rolled her in the snow. I sighed as I watched them make snow-angels. This was supposed to be a happy day, a joyful time and vacation. But as usual I had destroyed everything. What was wrong with me? Why did I keep doing this? If things didn't work out with Sune and me it would kill Julie. She loved him and she loved Tobias even more. But the thought that I couldn't give Sune what he really wanted and dreamt about killed me. I just really couldn't see it in my future. I couldn't picture myself having another baby. I really didn't want to. I wasn't prepared to do it just to make him happy, either. That was unfair to the baby.

After all having a baby was a huge thing in your life. I remembered having Julie and being surprised how hard it really was, how much it changed everything. Not that I ever regretted having her, I never did, but looking back at my life it had been a rough journey. I wasn't prepared to go down that road again. Not at my age.

Julie spotted me watching them through the window. She signaled that I should join them.

"Come on, Mom," I heard her yell from the other side.

I exhaled and nodded. "I'm coming!" Then I put on the jacket, my scarf and a pair of gloves. I looked at Sune when I opened the door. He threw a snowball in my direction and I managed to duck just as it was supposed to hit me in my face. I laughed. He laughed back. Then I grabbed some snow and shaped a ball and threw it at him. It hit him right in the middle of his face. Tobias and Julie squealed with delight. So did I, and soon Sune accompanied us.

We built the largest snowman anyone ever had built. At least that's what I told the kids. It had to be the world's largest snowman. No doubt about it. We managed to make it inside just as the snow began to fall again. We laughed and took off all our big winter clothes and threw them all in a pile on the floor. Then Sune started the fire while I went to the kitchen to prepare hot chocolate. My fingers and cheeks were hurting from the cold and soon they started to burn. I smiled while I watched Sune in action trying to get the fire in the fireplace started. I really liked him, I thought. I really didn't want to blow this. I went towards him and put my hand on his back. He looked up. His eyes seemed milder now. He chuckled, then he leaned over and kissed me on my lips. I blushed when I realized the children were watching us.

"Ew! Gross," Julie exclaimed causing me to blush even more. I felt like I had been caught in doing something wrong.

"Grown-ups are so disgusting," Tobias said.

I looked at Sune. Then we burst into laughter.

"Who is up for hot chocolate?" I said.

"I am. I am!" they both yelled one louder than the other. I looked at Dad afraid that they would wake him up. He was still sleeping on the couch. He didn't move.

"Okay," I whispered. "Let's go get some in the kitchen."

"Yay!" they yelled again and ran towards the kitchen.

Afraid they had woken him up I turned to look at my father again, but he still didn't move. I felt a pinch in my stomach. Usually he woke by the slightest sound. He was a light sleeper just like Julie and I. I stared at him from a distance, examining him. He suddenly looked very pale to me. Almost grey. Was his chest moving at all? Was he breathing?

Fearful I stepped towards him and placed a hand on his chest. I still couldn't feel it move. My heart was racing in my chest. Then I placed two fingers on his neck to check his pulse. It took a couple of terrifying seconds before I found it. It was there. A feeling of great relief came over me and calmed me a little. But the pulse seemed weak. Too weak even for someone sleeping. Another wave of fear rushed in over me and I started shaking him.

"Dad, wake up."

Sune stopped what he was doing and walked towards him. "Is there something wrong?" he asked.

"I can't wake him up. I think something is wrong. His pulse is weak and he is all pale."

Sune stepped in front of me and felt the pulse. Then he sighed. "It does seem a little weak," he said. "I think we need to call for an ambulance."

A panic started to grow inside of me. Not now, I thought while tears were piling up behind my eyes. I can't bear to lose him yet. Julie came up behind me and grabbed my hand. "Is something wrong with Grandpa?" she asked. I detected fear in her small voice. I pulled her closer while Sune found his phone and called for an ambulance.

"He'll be fine," I said. "I'm sure he'll be just fine. Don't worry."

I knew my words weren't convincing.

19

JULIE AND I got to ride in the ambulance with Dad. The paramedics had him hooked up to all kinds of things but he was still not conscious when we arrived at the hospital. Fear was growing in my stomach making me feel sick and nauseous. I remembered losing my mother a little too well and I wasn't ready to go through this again.

"Please don't take Dad, God," I mumbled again and again while we waited for any news.

Sune and Tobias joined us soon after. They brought a bag filled with books and toys and Tobias managed to make Julie forget for a while why she was there. I wondered why we didn't all just remain children for the rest of our lives. They knew it didn't help anything to worry. Why did we as adults insist on torturing ourselves like this over all kinds of things, most of the times silly stuff? Life was so short. Still I couldn't escape the anxiety. It was in all of my body, in every cell now and made me feel sick. Sune brought me water, coffee, sodas and chocolate bars that I swallowed like I was in a hurry. He held my hand.

"I'm sorry," he said. "I didn't mean to put all this on you. I really didn't."

"It's not your fault. You can't help it if you feel the way you do," I said and stroke his cheek gently. "You're so young. Of course you want more children."

He bit his lip and nodded. "I just never considered the fact that maybe you didn't," he said. "It was selfish of me."

"I'm the one who has been selfish," I said.

Sune lifted my hand and kissed it. "Let's never fight again," he said. "I really don't like it."

I chuckled. "Me either. But I'm afraid it's very often a part of grown-up life and relationships."

Sune looked at me with a grin. "Then let's not be grown-ups. Let's never ever grow up."

"Like Peter Pan?" I asked with a smile. Sune was so sweet.

"Exactly. Let's make our life and home like Neverland."

I laughed. Sune smiled. "Then I want to be Tinkerbelle," I said. "At least she's not dirty like all those boys. Plus she's skinny and can fly."

"Deal," Sune said.

I chuckled lightly. Sune always had a way of making me feel better whenever I was down.

"By the way I heard on the radio on my way here that another person died in the camp," he said.

I gasped. "The screams last night. I completely forgot about them. What happened?"

Sune shrugged. "They said the police were investigating it, but it looks just like the first death. He was throwing up and just being really sick and then he died."

"Wow. That sounds horrible. Who was it this time?"

"Some member of the church. We read his statement last night. Hans Christian Bille. Not a public figure or anyone that people know. Probably wouldn't even have been mentioned if it wasn't because he was the second person in two days dying at that camp. Something weird is definitely going on up here."

"You can say that again. But they didn't say what they thought it was, what could have caused it?" I asked.

He shook his head again. "I guess they don't know."

"But don't they have the autopsy from the first death?"

Sune shrugged. "I don't know."

"It all sounds really weird. Could they be hiding something? They must have some theory as to what could have killed two people living in the same camp. Could they have eaten something? I hope it's not some disease that we all could be infected with."

Sune smiled.

"What? Why are you smiling?" I asked.

"You're worrying again. You worry way too much."

"Well then you tell me what you think this is," I said slightly offended.

He shrugged again. "Probably just the end of the world. Like Isabella Dubois said. It's the devil trying to take over and kill us all."

"Well if that's all then there's nothing to be afraid of," I said.

Sune chuckled. "We just need to drive the demon out. Command it to leave," he said and made a scary face.

I chuckled lightly. Then I went quiet thinking about Dad again. I spotted a doctor headed in our direction. I tried to analyze his face to see if he brought good or bad news. His face was like a stone. It had to be bad news, I thought and felt a huge pinch in my stomach. Please let it be good news, I thought. Please!

"Miss Rebekka Franck?" he asked as he approached us.

I stood up. Julie and Tobias stopped playing. I felt Sune's hand in mine. "Yes?"

"Your dad is stable now. We don't know what caused this, but he is still unconscious. His pulse is weak but he seems to be breathing on his own. He suffered a minor blood clot in his leg."

I exhaled deeply. "So he is going to be alright?"

"We're keeping him here for a couple of days just in case and to run some more tests, but yes. He'll need some rehabilitation over the coming weeks. I'll arrange for that. He'll need all the support he can get from his family. He had a stroke a few years ago, right?"

I nodded. "He fell from the stairs. That's why he uses a cane now."

"Good. These kinds of attacks are tough on the body. Take good care of him and don't let him get stressed out. If you could get him to cut down on the fat and salt in his diet it would help a great deal."

"I'll try. I have actually tried for years now."

"You can see him in half an hour," the doctor said. "A nurse will come and get you."

When the doctor left Sune put his arm around my shoulder and pulled me close.

"What a scare," he said.

"You can say that again." I exhaled deeply and sat in the chair.

Julie came up and hugged me for a long time. "Is Grandpa alright?" she asked.

I smiled and kissed her. "He'll be fine. But he needs to stay here a couple of days and we need to do a little more work around the house, so Grandpa doesn't get so tired and worn out, okay?"

"Okay," she said like it was the most natural thing in the world. "I'll start doing the dishes and bring out the trash." Then she jumped down from my lap and went back to play with Tobias. Just like that. It was that easy when you were a child. I on the other hand felt ripped apart on the inside, devastated. Was this my fault? Had I let him do too much work? Well that part was about to change. That was certain. I would start cooking and cleaning some more, or hire help to do the cleaning so we didn't have to worry about it. I was going to make sure of that as soon as we got back from this awful place. Suddenly I had no desire to stay here for the rest of my vacation. I wanted to go home. This place was horrible and had too many bad memories already. But Dad had to stay, the doctor had told us. That meant we had to stay too. Until he was better and ready to be transported the long way home. It was after all a long drive. I sighed and held Sune's hand. Some vacation, I thought. I was the one who was supposed to relax and not get stressed out. Now I felt more stressed than ever.

20

M ETTE GRITHFELDT WAS scared. She had always been a worrisome and anxious type, but right now she was more afraid than ever. She was walking in circles in her room at the camp where she had lived for twenty-seven years. Twenty-seven years in this room, at this camp where nothing changed and everything stayed the same. Suddenly her entire life had drastically changed within only two days. Her world had literally turned upside down. She was losing it, she thought to herself walking on the hard tiles. Finally her parents were right. They always told her she was crazy and tried several times to have her locked up in an institution, forcing her to leave "The Way" and the man she loved so dearly. Now she felt like she was about to give in and just go crazy once and for all. She paced the floors all night and morning ever since the police had talked to her and taken her statement after the second death in two days at the camp which she had witnessed.

Both of the deaths were devastating to her. First her great love of twenty-seven years had died before her very eyes without her being able to do anything, then her good friend

Hans Christian. With him it wasn't so much that he had faded away in front of her that had scared her, no it was what he had done in his dying moments. He had looked at her. Just before life finally disappeared from his eyes, they had looked at her. Then he lifted his finger and pointed at her and his last words had been for her. She could still hear them over and over again in her mind, no matter how hard she tried she couldn't escape them.

"... you ... you," he said. What was that supposed to mean? That he had a message for her from beyond the grave, from the pit of hell? Did the devil want to tell her that she was next? Was it time to pay for all of her sins?

Mette Grithfeldt grabbed a book from her dresser and stroked it gently. She turned and looked at the picture of the Priest on the back. He was smiling at her like he used to do when they were together. She recalled the stolen looks during meetings or in the dining hall, stolen kisses in the corridors, passionate sex in his chambers when everyone else were asleep. This was the book he had written just before Mette met him. He had handed it to her and whispered in her ear that this contained all the answers, that she should read it every day, meditate on the words, let them linger in her soul and change herself from the inside out. She had done exactly that and he had been right. The book had changed her life, her way of thinking, her way of looking at the world, at her own life and who she really was. The book had taught her to be a servant, to be obedient and it had saved her life.

See, Mette Grithfeldt was a mess before she met the Priest. At eighteen she ran away from home and met the wrong people who introduced her to drugs and parties. She had sex with so many different partners she couldn't even recall all of their faces. Just to get more drugs. Her father had looked for her, even put up a reward to anyone who could help find her. But Mette didn't want to go back to the mansion in Hellerup, north of Copenhagen where she had lived with her parents, where she grew up just waiting for the day when she would be old enough to get out of there. She hated that place and she loathed her parents and all their money and rich high-society friends. Yes, her dad was a very significant figure in the country, even friends with the Queen with whom he played secret card-games every third month along with other important people Mette never knew because it had to be all so secret. Oh how she loathed her parents and all they stood for. Buying people, exploiting people to make more money, to get more power. They had decided everything in her life. They had put her in the most expensive private school money could buy, they had bought her a horse to give her a healthy interest to attend to after school, they had hired a private teacher to teach her table manners and how to address people properly, how to speak like a lady to a gentleman and even to royalty since they expected her to be accepted as part of that circle and hang out with the two princes who were close to her in age. They found the right friends for her; they even made a plan for her education and career to keep on the family business. They had done all the right things a wealthy family would do for their child, they had just made one big mistake.

They never asked Mette what she wanted.

So on her eighteenth birthday Mette packed a backpack with clothes and some money she had hidden and left the oceanfront mansion on Hambros Allé after dark without looking back. She had taken the S-train into Copenhagen and laughed all the way enjoying her first time using public transportation like normal people did. In Copenhagen she had exited the train on the Central Station in the center of the city and never felt more alive. She had taken the exit towards Vesterbro and as soon as she stepped out on the street someone had approached her. A guy who had asked her if she was looking to have some fun.

"As a matter of fact I am. It is my birthday and I want to celebrate," she answered and then she followed him to an apartment not far away where he knew some fun people who 'would love to party with a nice girl like her.'

After that everything went very wrong for Mette Grith-feldt. The people in the apartment were nice enough once she got there. They offered her drinks and they played nice loud music. After an hour or so Mette felt very dizzy from the drinks and put her head down on the pillow on the couch and fell into a deep heavy sleep. When she woke up, she had no idea where she was.

Later someone told her it was Hungary.

21

I T WAS TOUGH for all of us to see my dad in the hospital bed. He was still unconscious and breathing through tubes. I cried and put my head on his chest, listening to his weak heartbeat and his heavy breathing. Julie had tears in her eyes when she hugged his hand tightly. Then she hugged me.

"He'll be fine, Mom," she said. "I just know he will."

Somehow that felt really reassuring coming from her yet disturbing that she was suddenly so grown-up trying to calm me down when it was supposed to be the other way around.

We were told by a nurse that Dad needed rest and we could come back later in the afternoon. We decided to drive back to Arnakke and find a decent place to eat lunch. The hospital was in Holbaek, the closest big city to Arnakke and it took fifteen minutes to get back to the small town by the fjord. We found a small inn located on a small hill with great views over Isefjorden. It was spectacular for such a small local place. The interior wasn't much to brag about, though. It was very old, had low ceilings and doors and it hadn't been renovated in many years. It was clearly a place where the locals hung out drinking beers. The heavy snow had driven more than usual to go there, the owner told us while she wiped a table clean so we could sit there.

"People drive each other crazy being buried in the snow like this on a Saturday," she said. "Then the men come here, to get out of the house. They cross snow and icy winds just to get away. It's either that or listen to the old wife all day. That's the way it has always been. Snow is great for business." She burst into huge laughter. "Who would have thought that, huh?"

We smiled and sat down at the table. Three guys stared at us from the pool table in the corner. They still wore hats to warm their ears. They were talking and drinking beer while shooting pool. At the bar I saw one woman sitting alone and two men sitting not far from her without uttering a word to one another. Four elderly men were sitting next to us still wearing their big winter jackets like they were leaving in a minute. A couple of younger guys entered just as we sat down, dusting off snow from their shoulders and taking off their jackets and hanging them on a rack on the wall. They had red noses and cheeks from the cold wind and had probably walked there from their houses. The owner who called herself Yvonne handed us menus.

"I'll be back to take your orders in a minute," she said and left us.

"I want a burger," Julie said.

"Me too," Tobias followed. "And fries."

I was about to argue that they might want to choose something a little healthier but stopped myself. This was not the time. This was the time to enjoy each other and be thankful that we were all still alive.

"I think I'll have the lunch-platter with fish and open faced sandwiches on rye-bread," I said and looked at Sune.

"I'm hungry. I think I'll grab a steak with fries."

Yvonne came back and we gave her our orders.

"Great choices," she said with a huge smile.

"Let's have a couple of beers with that," I said. "And sodas for the kids."

"Sure."

Sune looked at me and smiled.

"What?"

"Nothing. You just read my mind. That was exactly what I wanted," he said.

"Me too," I said and looked at Julie. I really needed a beer to calm my nerves down. I craved a cigarette to go with it but resisted the desire.

"So all the locals hang out here?" I asked when Yvonne brought us the food.

She shrugged. "Well the ones who drink beer, that is."

I chuckled. "Of course. So what is the word about the two people who have died at the camp?"

"I assume you mean what has happened at the Ranters' camp?"

"The Ranters?"

"That's what we call them around here. Because they like to run around naked like the Ranters did in sixteen-something in England or something. I don't know the exact story, but some people have seen them run around naked up there in the woods, so they got the name from that."

"Oh," I said. "What else do they do?"

Yvonne shrugged. "Who knows? Worship that Priest guy like he is some kind of God himself and then have sex with him. That's what I have heard."

I was startled. I hadn't heard the part about nakedness and sex before. That was new and a little disturbing to me.

"So what are people saying about the two men who have died?"

Yvonne sniffled. "That they had it coming, I guess. They all have. Running around in there acting like crazy doing stuff to each other. Driving out devils, screaming like only crazy people do. If you ask me they attract evil by doing all that stuff. If sin is a problem that only leads to hell like the pastor of our church - who by the way often comes in here - says, then they are in serious ankle-deep shit, if you want to know my opinion."

I drank some of my beer while wondering. "What kind of stuff are they doing to each other?"

She shrugged. "I don't know much. Just what people are telling me. But I guess God finally found out what they are doing and now he's wiping them out. About time, if you ask me."

"So you think it is some kind of divine punishment?" Sune asked.

"If there is a God, then them dying certainly proves it to me. We don't need people like that around here."

"Does anyone have any idea how they died?" I asked.

"No. But I might have," she said with a chuckle.

Sune and I both looked up at the big woman with the wild curly hair in front of us.

"You do?" Sune asked.

"Sure. Either God finished them off by letting them rot up from the inside - or the devil did and God didn't give a damn."

Yvonne left on that last sentence and I looked at Sune. We tried hard not to laugh. I ate with butterflies in my stomach. I wanted so badly to write the story about this place, about this sect. I wanted so badly to be the one, the first journalist to actually get in there and talk to some of the members. It would be a hard article to write because it would be a lot of speculation and rumors like the ones Yvonne had just presented for me. A closed community like this sect would always be surrounded by mystery and rumors. It would be hard to decipher what was actually the truth and what was just talk and gossip from the townspeople. If only I could get them to talk. I couldn't present a story based on rumors and talk, but if I could get some of them to talk to me - even just one person - then I could at least have their side of the story and I would have an article to write. Two people had died at that camp in the last two days, somewhere in there was a story hidden, one that was important and needed to be told.

After finishing my food I went to the bar and talked to Yvonne.

"Do you know anyone who has actually seen these things? Who has actually seen them run around naked or drive out devils or something like that?"

Yvonne stared at me with slight disbelief. Then she nodded.

"I might know someone who would talk to you," she said.

22

METTE GRITHFELDT SAT down at her bed feeling the anxiety grow strongly inside of her. She was looking at the crucifix above her bed in her small room which contained only a bed, a dresser and a lamp under the ceiling. There were no mirrors at the camp since the Priest believed mirrors were made for vanity and none of his disciples should ever care about what they looked like. He wanted to drive all these fleshly thoughts out of them that kept them in bondage. Vanity was one thing, greed another. Mette Grithfeldt hated greed more than anything. That was why she had donated all of her money to "The Way" when her parents died in a car accident in Southern France a couple of years ago. The Priest had told her that the money she inherited would only end up devouring her, leaving her always wanting more, never being satisfied.

"Aren't you happy here?" he had asked lying naked in his bed with her under him, tied to the bed with rope, while entered her with the same wildness and passion that he always did, slapping her across the face, holding her throat till she would almost suffocate.

Mette liked not having to look in the mirror ever again. The Priest was so right. They didn't need all this stuff and she certainly didn't need the money.

"Blood money," the Priest had called it while he beat the greed out of Mette till she broke down and cried for God to forgive her sin, her lust for money while the Priest entered her from behind and humiliated her by letting his semen wash all those sinful thoughts off her face afterwards. The night after she met with the lawyer, who told her about the millions and millions of dollars her parents had left her, the Priest punished her for hours for her impure thoughts. He smelled it on her skin, he said. She wanted that money for herself, and even worse she wanted to make more. She desired the money and let greed devour her.

"It will eat you alive, this desire," he yelled again and again while the strokes from the whip burned her back and blood started running down her legs. "The devil has taken a stronghold on you. These are impure thoughts coming from the devil. You must repent! Repent child before it is too late!"

"I repent! Please forgive me, please I don't want to be like this," she had cried almost falling unconscious from the pain.

Yet he hadn't stopped. He had continued for hours and hours, making her take his sex in her mouth, beating her with his belt, with a stick and then the whip again. Hanging her from the ceiling by her arms while he took her as he pleased and punished her as he willed.

Mette Grithfeldt didn't want to admit it but she had liked it. And she had liked the Priest. In fact she loved him. A lot. She enjoyed serving him and coming to his room when he told her to. She enjoyed the humiliation, the pain, the lust. She could even lie awake some nights thinking about it, craving it, lusting for the touch of his hands. But she never told him that. What if he thought it was a sin. What if it was a sin? Would she go to hell for this? For wanting to be with him? Even if she knew she had to share him with the other women in the camp it was all worth it. Was that why the Priest had died? Was that why she was going to be next? Were they in fact being punished? If so then by whom? God or the devil? Did it matter?

Mette Grithfeldt stood up and walked to her window. The sun was about to set behind the black pine forest. In an hour it would be pitch dark. She shivered in fear. She hadn't been this scared since the morning she first woke up in Hungary, in that filthy bed that she had to share with six other girls from countries all over Europe.

Mette sighed as she pictured Nadja. Nadja was from Russia and she was the only one who had taken care of Mette in that place where men came and took the girls as they pleased. Hundreds of men a day entered that door and chose one of them to have sex with on the filthy bed where roaches lived under the mattress. Nadja had taught her to close her eyes and think about being in another place, about leaving your body mentally to keep the mind sane. She had taught Mette to only accept the pure drugs, those they were certain weren't filled with all kinds of shit that every now and then killed one of the girls in the room. The next day a new girl would arrive and the body would be dumped somewhere.

"You don't want to end up like any of those girls," Nadja had told her. "When they give you drugs you take them and give them to me. I know how to see if it's pure or not. Never take anything without having me check it first, okay?"

Mette had nodded and done exactly what Nadja had told her. Nadja had kept most of the drugs to herself once she checked it, but Mette had gotten just enough to keep her from thinking too much about what was happening to her, just enough to be able to separate the body from the mind.

"They can have your body but they can never have your mind," Nadja had taught her. "It's the only way to survive."

So Mette had survived. While most of the other girls in the room eventually died and were replaced, she stayed alive. Three years she spent in the dark room in Hungary with the help from a Russian girl named Nadja.

Until one day when Nadja had told her it was time to leave. "We escape tomorrow," were her only words.

Those were the last Mette ever heard her speak.

23

S UNE STAYED WITH the kids while I drove out to meet with
the source Yvonne had arranged for me to talk to. He
lived on a farm on the south side of Arnakke about five
minutes by car from our rented cabin.

The farm was old yet well maintained. The man who
opened the front door was probably in his sixties. He was
wearing overalls and clogs. I noticed a smell of wet dog in the
hall as I entered the front door and took off my heavy coat.

The hall was decorated with heads and skins of deer and
foxes. As was the rest of the house. Antlers and rifles hung on
all the walls along with hunting trophies. I took off my boots
as well since they were filled with snow. I walked on my socks
into his living room where he asked me to sit on the couch in
front of the fireplace. He smiled a little shyly when he
brought cups and coffee in a pot. His hand holding the tray
shook slightly.

"Let me help you," I said and grabbed the cups before
they fell off the tray to the ground.

"Sorry," he said. "The wife is out visiting her sister, so I
feel a little lost here."

"It's okay. You really don't need to serve coffee," I said even if I could really go for a shot of caffeine right at that moment.

I grabbed a cup and poured some coffee in it from the pot. The man named Bjarne Larsen sat in a big chair in front of me. I handed him the first cup and then poured another for myself. Bjarne nodded and sipped his coffee.

"So Yvonne tells me you like to hunt?" I began in order to break the ice.

Bjarne nodded slowly. He was a man of few words, I thought. Maybe he just needed to be warmed up a little.

"Did you shoot all these yourself?" I asked and pointed at all the antlers and heads hanging on the walls. It felt creepy, like the black empty eyes were all staring at me.

"Every single one," he replied.

I sipped my coffee. It tasted horrible. Way too strong for my taste. I spotted milk on the table and poured some in. It helped a little. Not much, though. It was almost undrinkable.

"So I guess you must hear and see a lot of stuff in the woods when you're out there hunting?" I said.

"I have and I do. Lots of stuff through the years," he said.

"Well I'm interested in doing an article about the sect living up at the camp a little north of here. You know, where the members of 'The Way' live. The Ranters I believe you call them?"

"That's what we call them, yes."

"Why is that?"

Bjarne smiled widely and leaned over in his chair. "Because they like to run around naked, like they were a freaking nudist camp."

"Have you actually seen them?"

"I haven't but my son has. I never go on the other side of their fence, but the young boy likes to do it. It is private property so technically he is not allowed to go in there. I have told him a hundred times to not go in there, but you know how boys are."

"I won't tell anyone. This is just research. Could I speak to your son? Is he here?" I asked.

"Sure." Bjarne got up and went to the stairs, before he yelled. "Ole! There is some woman here to see you! Says she is from a newspaper."

Bjarne came back to me. "You'll have to excuse him. He's not all well up here." Bjarne pointed at his forehead. "My wife worries about him, but I tell her he is just fine. The teachers in his school think he is a little slow, but I tell them that he's just fine. Nothing but a slow learner just like his dad. I'm not book smart either but look how well I've done for myself. Ole is going to take over this farm one day, no need for him to sweat over homework if you ask me. He knows what he needs to know and the rest I will teach him. He'll work for me. That's how my dad taught me, and that's what I teach him. But these days everybody has to be alike, you know. Everybody must have the same education, they teach them the exact same things whether they're going to be a plumber or a professor. As soon as someone turns out to be a little different they want to put a diagnosis on his head and give him medicine."

Someone entered from the corner of the room. A face of a young teenager appeared in the light. He was tall and skinny with a shy look in his eyes that kept avoiding mine. I got up and reached out my hand.

"Rebekka Franck, *Zeeland Times*," I said.

He pulled his hand out of the pocket on his shirt and shook mine. His eyes dropped to the floor.

"Ole," he stuttered.

"Hi Ole. Your dad and I were just talking about hunting and he told me you like to hunt as well. Is that true?"

"I guess," Ole answered and came closer.

I signaled that he could sit down. He chose the couch opposite mine.

"Who do you hunt with?" I asked and sipped more coffee forgetting how bad it tasted.

Ole shrugged. "Mostly alone."

"And your dad tells me that you sometimes climb over the fence to the camp on the North side of the forest where the members of 'The Way' live?"

Ole dropped his eyes. Then he looked at his dad. Bjarne slapped him on the back. "It's okay son, she is not going to tell the police. She just wants to know about the things you have seen up there."

Ole nodded. "I do that sometimes."

"And what have you seen?"

Ole looked at his dad again. Bjarne nodded. "Go ahead. Tell her while I get some cookies to sweeten up that coffee." Then Bjarne got up and went into the kitchen.

Ole sniffed. He lifted his head and stared into my eyes. Something in them made me draw backwards. "Sex," he said.

"Excuse me?"

"I see them having sex. Orgies. They're dancing and screaming and singing. Then they take off their clothes and everybody touches each other."

There was something in Ole's voice that appalled me. It sounded almost like he enjoyed it, enjoyed talking about it. I wrote down what he was telling me.

"What else have you seen?"

"He is alone with them. One man and all these women," he said like he hadn't heard my question.

"Who is he?"

"The Priest." Ole started giggling. "One time he was

screwing three different women and they seemed to like it, man. They loved it. They screamed for more."

Ole could hardly sit still on the couch now. "Those women liked it. They liked him doing those things to them." Ole looked down, then he lifted his head and looked at me. "I like to do things too," he said.

I stared at him. I wasn't sure I wanted him to say any more. Ole leaned over while looking at me creepily. "I like to watch them when he punishes them. He whips them then leaves them outside, naked, tied up all night. I watch them."

Ole moved closer. I swallowed hard wanting desperately for the father to come back.

"So how often do these orgies take place?" I asked and moved a little backwards on the couch when Ole came closer. He looked at me with a tilted head. Then he put his hand on my thigh. I jumped and pushed it away.

"Do you like it rough like those women do?" Ole whispered. "I bet you do," he said and giggled. "I can give it to you, if you want. Pretty, pretty girl. I can show you. They come out when it is a full moon. I see them out there every full moon. Like the vampires," he said and snapped his teeth. I jumped again and Ole burst into a loud laughter.

"Are you behaving?" Bjarne had come back and was standing in front of Ole with his hand lifted in front of his face like he was ready to slap him. "Do I need to find the belt?" he asked.

Ole crouched and moved away from me. "No, no, not the belt," he whined covering his head with his arm like he was already protecting himself from strokes.

Bjarne looked at me. "You'll have to excuse him," he growled. "I need to keep an eye on him. As I told you he is a little slow."

Bjarne placed a plate on the table in front of me.
"Cookie?" he asked.

24

I HAD A strange feeling inside as I drove back to the cabin. Furthermore I felt like I had wasted my time. Ole's statements weren't something I could use for my article since it wasn't illegal to run around naked and have sex orgies on your own property. Also, Ole wasn't exactly what I would call a reliable source, I thought to myself as I parked the car in front of the cabin and got out. The house was quiet. It was getting darker. The heavy grey clouds above my head told me that it would snow again any minute now. I sighed and walked towards the front door. I really didn't want to be here anymore. I had a bad feeling about this place.

"I'm back!" I yelled and threw my bag on the kitchen table.

"We're in here!" Julie yelled. I could hear the sound of the kid's video games coming from the living room. I walked in and put my arms around Julie. I hugged her tightly and smelled her hair. Sune smiled at me from the couch. I sent him a finger-kiss. Tobias was concentrating on driving a car on the big screen TV. I let go of Julie and went to sit next to

Sune. He had been reading the paper that was scattered all over the coffee table.

"So how did it go?" he asked.

I shrugged with a sigh. "It's all just rumors and talk. I can't seem to figure out who is more crazy, the sect members or the townspeople. These guys sure were strange. I talked to some farmer and his son." I felt a chill on my back and snuggled up closer to Sune. "The son was really weird in a creepy way. I could never use him as a source."

"So you're not going to do the article?" Sune asked.

"Not unless something new opens up the story. I think it's too hard. There might not even be a story there."

"Has Jens-Ole even contacted you about the second death?" Sune asked.

"Come to think of it, no he hasn't," I said. "Do you think he knows?"

"It was on the news on TV earlier, but just as a small note. There is a debate about early retirement pension that the government wants to abolish that has taken up all the room in the news today."

"Again?" I laughed. "This happens every six months. The government wants to abolish it and then the people gets angry."

"I know," Sune said. "It's a circus."

"It's boring that's what it is. I am so glad I never became a political reporter. But it certainly explains why Jens-Ole hasn't called. It's just not a big story anymore. So what did they say about the death?"

Sune shrugged. "Just that there has been another death at the camp in Arnakke and then they showed pictures from the outside taken yesterday. They said the police still don't know what caused it but that it seemed to be the same that killed the Priest. Might be food poisoning."

I got up, found my laptop and turned it on.

"There is coffee in the pot," Sune said.

"Already ahead of you," I said and showed him I was pouring as we spoke. "Want some?"

"I've got."

It felt good to finally get some real coffee and not that thick stuff that mostly reminded me of tar.

"Any news from the hospital?" Sune asked.

I shook my head. "No, but I'm planning on going up to see him in like half an hour."

"Do you want us to come with you?"

I shook my head again while burning my lip on the coffee. "I think it would be best for Julie to stay here with you and have fun. He is not awake and it is tough to see a person you love in those circumstances. I'll bring her with me tomorrow morning if she wants to visit him."

Sune nodded. "Sounds good."

I sighed and looked at the screen. Then I Googled "Ranters." I had never heard the name before and was curious. Four hundred and fifty-five thousand hits. I opened the first link. Wikipedia. According to that article Yvonne was correct. The article stated that the Ranters were a sect in the English Commonwealth from 1649 till 1660 that were often associated with nudity that they used as a social protest as well as religious expression as a symbol of abandoning earthly goods. They were accused of antinomianism, fanaticism and sexual immorality and were put in prison until they recanted.

I leaned back and stared out the window. Big snowflakes were dancing outside as they slowly found their way to the ground. I wondered how the people of this town had even heard about the Ranters. Then I went back to Google and took the next link. It was a web-page describing the Ranters as some who embraced the concept of the 'indwelling spirit.' Whatever was done in the Spirit was justifiable to a Ranter. Apparently the Ranters were seen often parading naked in the streets at a time when nudity was a huge taboo. I went back to Google and found a definition of a 'Ranter' on the free online dictionary. According to it to rant meant 'to speak or to write in an angry or violent manner.' I sighed and opened one more web-page that stated that the Ranters were an Anarchic religious extremist group of the English Revolution that was often accused of sexual immorality, blasphemy and drunkenness.

I exhaled and closed the laptop. This was leading nowhere. It was nothing but a nickname.

"Well I'd better get going now before the roads are closed with snow," I said and emptied my coffee.

"You sure you don't want us to come with you?" Asked Sune.

"I'm positive."

25

M ETTE GRITHFELDT DIDN'T go down for dinner that evening. She wasn't feeling well and stayed in her room thinking about her past and if she was going to have a future after this night. Someone brought her evening tea that they always drank before bedtime. It was a soothing herb tea that always made her relax and get ready to sleep. The Priest had called it medicine for the soul and told them to drink it every night before bed in order to get closer to God. What was in it Mette didn't know, but it always did make her feel better. Right now she needed to feel better, she needed to calm down. She exhaled deeply and emptied the cup while thinking yet again about the Priest and how they first met.

Nadja had kept her word to Mette. The next day she woke her up by touching her hair gently. All the girls had just fallen asleep on the cold tiles in the room. They didn't know if it was night or day, they never knew since the men came at all times. Mette had woken with a start thinking it was another client, another man who wanted to use her. She was shaking and Nadja had held a hand over her mouth. Then she had signaled to her to be quiet. Mette understood. She got up from the floor, sore all over from all the men who beat her and taken her as they willed. Nadja held her by the hand and led her to the window that was covered with plywood behind a thick curtain that didn't let any sunlight get in to let them know it was day. Nadja looked at her with worn out eyes. Then she reached in her pocket and showed Mette something. A knife. A small pocket knife. Mette never knew where she had gotten it from but guessed that she had stolen it from some client. Maybe went through his pockets while he was on her. She didn't tell Mette since they never spoke in order to not let the people standing outside the door know they were awake. They would beat the women half to death if they knew they were talking. They had seen it and both felt it before. No one was supposed to talk. "Just lie still and be ready for next client," the men said. Punishment for not obeying was hard and often led to death. Mette was terrified of becoming their next victim. She knew she meant nothing to them and she had been there so long the clients were growing tired of her, they craved fresh meat and hers was growing old.

Nadja began working on the plywood with the pocket knife and Mette looked at her resignedly. This was her plan? This was it? There was no way they would be able to cut through the thick plywood with just a small pocketknife. Had Nadja lost it?

But Nadja didn't give up, with almost supernatural strength given their situation and circumstances she kept working on the plywood with her bony fingers, jagging the knife into the wood and chopping it. Her face was strained and almost manic as she kept hacking the knife into the wood again and again. Mette had no idea how long it took but it felt like forever, until suddenly a small ray of sunlight broke through the plywood. Mette looked at Nadja and suddenly realized that even if it seemed impossible then miracles did happen and might happen to her right there, right then. So she started pulling the edges of the plywood with all her strength while Nadja made the hole bigger with the knife. She was smiling, trying to make as little noise as possible to not alert the men on the other side of the door.

Suddenly more sunlight broke through when Nadja managed to make the hole bigger and Mette could put in a hand and with all she had she pulled it and some of it broke off. Mette froze when she realized how loud it had to have sounded. She stared at the door, her heart in the throat, but it didn't open. She turned and looked at Nadja who was staring out the hole with a paralyzed look in her eyes. Then she let Mette look through it as well. It hurt her eyes and she had to shield her face from the brightness. But what a sight. Houses and mountains in the distance. All that space and oh oh the sky, the blue sky right above her, leading to an endless limitless universe. If she ever managed to get out of that room, Mette promised herself she would never live in a small place again. She would sleep outside in the open whenever the weather permitted it, she would live in houses with high ceilings and she would never ever lock the door.

But to her surprise and disappointment Mette also realized that even if they had managed to make a hole in the wood big enough for them to escape, they were in an apartment many, many floors above the ground. Too many. They wouldn't be able to jump without killing themselves. She turned and looked at Nadja who had just realized the same thing. Together they stared at freedom right outside these windows knowing they would never be able to reach it.

That was when they felt a hand grab their necks from behind. Mette turned and looked into the eyes of the man she recognized as one of those guarding the door. He held them one in each hand, clutching her throat so she was almost choking. Behind him Mette realized he had forgotten to close the door. The other girls were awakened by the noise and saw the open door.

After that hell broke loose.

All the girls were on their feet and ran towards the door. Another guy outside tried to stop them, by beating them, hitting them, throwing them back, some fell to the floor but others managed to escape. They were screaming panicky, hysterically freaking the guards out. Scratching them, hitting them, taking chances, jumping from the top of the stairs, hurting themselves as they landed. The guy holding Mette and Nadja dropped them to the ground and pulled out his gun. Then he turned and shot Nadja. Mette screamed and kicked the gun out of his hand. Then he slapped her across the face till she landed on the tiles. Blood was running from her forehead. While the guard looked for his gun, Mette managed to get back up and run towards the door. The other guard was shooting wildly at all the girls swarming the place like bats, like wild animals who had nothing to lose. Then Mette jumped. She jumped over the banister and was in the air, falling towards the next floor and the stone stairs. She heard shots being fired behind her but it drowned in the screams from the other girls. Mette hit the stairs and heard bones break in her arm. Then she heard another shot fired and looked up. The guard who had killed Nadja was standing on the top floor aiming at her. Her heart was pounding in her chest. She managed to get on her feet and looked into his eyes once more before she was on her feet again and started running down the next set of stairs. She heard them yell and shoot after her but the fear and anxiety gave her the power to run faster and faster and finally escape

out the building into the open. Then she ran all she could
and never looked back.

After a while she ran out of strength and sank down on
the pavement. A woman approached her and took her hand.
She helped Mette get to a center where they took care of
young girls who had been sold as sex-slaves. At the center
run by a local church she met hundreds of girls with the
same story as hers.

She also met a man whose merciful eyes she would never
forget. His name was Anders Granlund and he was also from
Denmark.

26

M Y DAD WAS feeling better, a nurse said when I entered his room. He wasn't awake yet, but they were expecting him to wake up soon.

"Probably will happen tomorrow," she said just before she left the room. I pulled a chair up next to his bed. He looked so pale lying on the bed breathing through the tubes. I held his hand tight and squeezed it hoping he could feel it, hoping he knew I was there, that he wasn't alone. I had called my sister earlier and she was on her way, but the heavy snowfall on the south side of Zeeland had stopped her half way. The roads were blocked and she had called me and told me she had to turn around and go back home. I assured her I was taking good care of Dad and hung up. I felt tears piling up behind my eyes when I looked at my father. Suddenly I missed my mother like crazy. I didn't want to be alone with this. I needed my family around me. I needed us to be happy and laugh. Life was so short. Suddenly people were no longer there.

"I'm sorry, Dad," I mumbled. "I overburdened you. I should never have let you do all this work for us, taking care of the kids, always cooking when you should have rested instead. I should have known better after the stroke."

"Don't say that," a voice behind me said.

I turned and faced the doctor that I had spoken to earlier. Doctor Philipsen, his nametag said. "Sorry," he explained. "I didn't mean to eavesdrop. I was just checking in on my patient before I go home for the day."

I smiled and wiped the tears of my eyes. "It's okay. I'm glad you care," I said.

"Well I do," Dr. Philipsen said. "And I have to tell you that keeping your dad busy with work at the house, taking care of grandkids isn't why he ended up in here. On the contrary he needs it. He needs to keep his body working. Sitting still after a blood clot is the worst you can do. You need to move around, take long walks or whatever works for you. If house-work is what your dad likes to do he should keep it up, by all means. It is in his best interest."

"But ... I don't understand. Why did he get the blood clot then? If it wasn't because he overdid something?"

"I don't know, but the lab says they did detect something unusual in his blood sample that they want to look into," Dr. Philipsen said.

"What are you saying?" I asked, quite startled.

"I don't know anything for sure yet, but even after he wakes up we will need to keep your dad for a couple of days in order to run more tests."

"But what did they detect in the blood?"

"I don't know the details, just that they have to run more tests."

I sniffed. "Did they find cancer or something?"

"As I said I really don't know, just that they are asking for more time. Let's wait and see. It's probably nothing."

Dr. Philipsen gave me a not very reassuring smile. It felt

like all the blood inside of my veins froze. There was definitely something he wasn't telling me.

"I'll let you know as soon as we have the results," he said and left the room with a gentle "Goodbye."

I exhaled deeply and stroked my dad across the cheek. "Poor little daddy. What is happening to you?" I said while the tears rolled fast down my cheeks.

The snow fell thick and made the roads almost impassable when I tried to drive back from the hospital. The small roads leading to Arnakke had become slippery and hard to drive through. My car kept getting stuck in small piles of snow or slipping off to the side so I almost lost control. I texted Sune on my way that it was going to take a while for me to get back and he texted back that there was no need to hurry, he had started getting the kids ready for bed and they were all fine. Just be careful.

"That's easy for you to say," I mumbled while trying hard to see through my front window where the wipers had trouble keeping up with the big piles of snow that kept landing on it blocking my view. Even when I managed to wipe the snow away the visibility in front of me was like zero. I could hardly see the road and tried to focus on just not ending in a pile of snow not being able to get free or even worse hitting something.

Of course that was exactly what happened next.

27

S LOWLY AND GENTLY Anders Granlund managed to help
Mette get back on her feet again. He helped her regain
her self-esteem and her trust in people again. With love and
understanding he helped her get back to life and soon she
even found herself laughing. He could make her laugh.

Anders was only visiting Hungary on his trip around
the world visiting different churches, a trip he referred to as
his "spiritual journey." He told her he was trying to find
himself and God in a world destroyed by evil forces. Then
he taught her what he believed, that evil forces lived in
people, often even possessed people and made them sin
towards God and do evil things if they weren't stopped,
driven out of the body they possessed. Mette had never
heard anyone talk like Anders. She found him refreshing
and different, and she soon became very fond of him, and
later she fell helplessly in love with him, this savior who
wanted to save her from herself and the world surrounding
her. He told her he was starting his own church in
Denmark even if he didn't like the term "church" - he would
rather refer to it as a family. Mette had liked that. A family.

She had never had much of one and had always dreamt of having her own.

"If you come with me you'll get a big one," he said. "No matter where you come from, no matter what you experienced in your past, we will treat you as family, we will love you."

Mette had really liked the sound of that. So after a couple of months in the center Mette went back to Denmark escorted by Anders Granlund to meet her new family at the camp in Arnakke that they were restoring. At first they were so supportive and helped her in any way they could. She had a hard time staying in small rooms and they let her sleep outdoors since it was summer, at least for a couple of weeks. When it got colder she acquiesced to sleeping indoors in the big spacey common room and finally she felt comfortable enough to sleep in her own room. They were patient with her and very very loving. They even helped her at night when she woke up screaming and when she crumbled by human touch. They taught her that touching could be nice and filled with love.

It wasn't until later she realized that something was wrong. When her new adventure slowly turned into misery. After a while in the camp she realized that they never had anything else to eat other than vegetables and that they were all very weak from not having proper food, and not enough of it. Mette soon learned that it was used as a control tactic by Anders Granlund who now wanted her to call him the Priest and not by his name. He would feed them very little and sometimes drag them out to walk in the middle of the night. Mette remembered how she felt so exhausted she didn't even have the strength to protest when they came to get her. All night long they were forced to walk in circles in the court-yard. Mette loved the priest so much she was willing to endure anything for him. That quickly turned into him demanding her sexual favors which she provided and he returned the favor by letting her increase in rank and soon she was eating meat once a week at his table while the rest of the "family" were stuck with only vegetables.

The priest told them they needed to suffer, to deprive the body of its fleshly desires before they were ready to step up the next level like he had. It was vital for their survival that they fasted. It would starve the evil inside of them and soon it would be forced to leave. Then and only then they would be able to be closer to God. God demanded this of them, she heard the Priest say. The lack of sleep, the starvation and being engaged in intense physical activity during the day soon broke all of the members and Mette saw how they ended up worshipping the Priest and kissing his feet. So did she. Mette had only eyes for him and just the mention of his name could make her shiver. Shiver with a rare combination of fear and delight. The fear of losing him was worse than the fear of his rough treatment of her. Without him to guide her in her life where would she be? What would have become of her? That was why she gave him all of her money when her parents died, that was why she had devoted her life to serving him, to loving him and providing him the pleasure he needed, whenever he needed it. The Priest told her that she was "meant to serve" that it was a way to find "inner peace."

Mette tried to escape once. That was before she learned how to use her gender and sex appeal to have the Priest give her favors and make her one of the leaders. It was back in the beginning after only a few weeks in the camp when she had grown tired of all the hard work she was told to do. The members had told her to wash six of their cars and her hands were blistering and bleeding from scrubbing, but they told her to continue even if blood was smeared at the cars. So when no one was looking, she ran. Ran towards the exit and climbed the fence. She ran into the street and hid in a vacation house nearby that at the time was empty. Less than half an hour later she saw the six cars she had been forced to wash loaded with church members. They were driving on all the roads surrounding the house and knocking at all the doors, telling people they were looking for someone who escaped a sanatorium, asking if they could search their houses.

It didn't take them more than fifteen minutes to locate Mette. When they brought her back the Priest looked at her disappointedly. Then he locked her in a small closet without food, water or toilet for four days. Mette screamed hysterically for the first two days. Then she went quiet. When they finally opened the closet they found her shaking, covered in her own excrement, broken.

She never refused to obey again not even when the Priest asked her to participate in doing those awful things to that poor girl many years later.

Mette woke up with scream. She was lying on top of her bed still fully dressed. She hadn't realized she had dozed off. It had to be the tea, she thought and looked at the pot on the dresser. She hadn't wanted to fall asleep, she wanted to be fully awake all night and usually she slept with one eye open, something she had learned back at the room in Hungary. To survive, Nadja had told her. Now she woke up because she thought she heard a sound. Someone was outside her door, she thought and got up. Her heart was racing. Probably from that dream she just had. She had dreamt about the girl. She had stared at her just like Hans Christian had just before he died. She had pointed at her and yelled the same words:

"... You ... You!" then she had laughed that horrific laughter.

Mette stopped herself. Was the handle moving? She was certain it was. She reached over and grabbed her crucifix. Then she kissed it and started praying. Her heart was racing faster now and she felt almost suffocating. A burning sensation was spreading underneath her skin. Was this it? Was she coming for her? Was she finally going to pay for her sins? For what she had done? Suddenly it was like Mette heard voices in her head. The voices of the many men she had been with, the voices of her parents, the voice of the Priest yelling at her that she was impure. She threw herself to the ground holding her head between her hands, screaming. Where did all these voices come from? Where were they? Why were they yelling at her like this? Then suddenly it went quiet for a short while and Mette got on her feet again, panting, gasping for air. Was this it? Was she going insane before she died?

Next, she was certain she heard another voice. It sounded like it was coming from the other side of the door. Her heart was pounding hard in her chest. She recognized that voice. It was calling for her. Calling out her name. She whimpered as she reached out for the handle and opened the door.

Her heart stopped and Mette froze. There she was. Right in front of her stood the little girl with the crooked deformed head, looking at her with her green eyes, staring at her and pointing, while laughing a demonic laughter, her eyes almost like fire, like they were the very door to hell.

Mette screamed and backed up into the room. The girl stepped closer and Mette tumbled to the floor while trying to move away from her. Her laughter grew stronger, wilder, more manic. Mette crawled backwards, still while screaming. She reached the wall behind her and spotted her chance. Quickly she opened the hasp on the window and jumped out into the snow with a scream high-pitched enough to penetrate glass. When she got up she stared at the window, the girl was looking directly at her, still laughing manically. Then Mette turned around with a gasp and started running, just like she had run trying to escape the guards in Hungary, trying to cheat death for the second time in her life.

28

I HAD NO chance of seeing it coming. Luckily I was driving slowly on the slippery road when I hit it, whatever it was.

It was like had it come out of nowhere, I thought when I tried to regain control of the car that soon landed in a big pile of snow. I hurt my forehead as the car came to a sudden stop. I was breathing heavily trying to calm myself down and put the shock behind me, before I stormed out the door and ran through the heavy snow towards whatever I had hit. I hoped it was a big deer or maybe a fox, but I knew in my heart it was way too big in size to be just an animal.

"Oh my God," I stuttered holding a hand to cover my mouth. In front of me in the snow lay a woman. She was small, skinny and wasn't dressed at all to be outside in this kind of weather. "Oh my God," I exclaimed again when I realized the snow was colored red by her blood. She was moving, groaning, trying to pull herself forward in her arms.

"I'm so so sorry. Are you alright?" I asked.

The woman didn't answer, she groaned and looked up at me with weak eyes that seemed like they were about to cave in any moment now.

"You're hurt," I said. "Let me call for an ambulance." I fumbled, searched frantically in my pocket for my phone. Panic was slowly spreading in my mind. What if you have killed her? What if she is going to die out here while you're watching. Oh my God, oh please God don't let her die.

I called the emergency number and reached a woman who promised to send an ambulance, but told me to be very patient since the snow made it almost impossible for the paramedics to get out tonight.

"Just hurry, I am afraid she is really hurt," I said with trembling voice.

I put the phone back in my pocket and attended the woman who was still groaning and crying in pain in front of me. I had no idea what to do in a situation like this. There were no houses nearby and no other cars in the road. We were in the middle of nowhere. Where did that woman even come from? Did she just jump out of the forest? She was coughing and making noises that sounded like she was suffocating.

I walked closer. "Are you alright? Is there anything I can do for you?" I asked.

She lifted her head and looked like she wanted to say something but it wasn't words that came out of her mouth. Instead she threw up on the ground right in front of me. Yellow vomit mixed with a lot of blood in it. That was strange, I thought to myself. Could she have internal bleeding or something from the accident? But I didn't hit her that hard did I? I was driving pretty slow, no more than twenty miles an hour. Could I have caused that much damage? The woman tried to look at me again, then she groaned and looked like a wave of pain rushed in over her. Her face was strained in pain. Then she threw up again.

My phone vibrated in my pocket. It was the lady from the emergency number.

"The ambulance can't get through to you. The road is blocked with snow," she said. "It might take hours to clear it and get to you."

"Where is the ambulance now?" I asked.

"They're trying to get to you from the main road," she said.

I stared in the direction from where I had entered the small road. What was it, five to ten minute walk? Maybe twenty in the snow?

"I'll find them," I said and hung up.

I looked at the woman in front of me. I was on the verge of panic now. Damn it if I was just going to watch her die out here in the snow. The woman seemed small, not much bigger than Julie, a little taller but way skinnier. Then I reached down and grabbed her leg and arm and threw her over my shoulder. She was groaning and crying in pain while I started walking towards the main road in the deep snow.

It was much tougher than I anticipated. The deep snow made every step hard and being in the worst physical condition of my life I was soon completely out of breath. But I was determined to save this woman's life, so I struggled through the heavy snow, gasping for breath, until I spotted the lights from the ambulance in the distance. I forced myself to walk another step then fell into the snow. The woman landed next to me. She was in spasms now, her body shaking and her eyes rolling.

"Hey! I yelled desperately towards the lights. "We're right here! HELP!"

I looked at the light blinking in the distance while foam and drool came out of the woman. We were almost there. All

I had to do was to lift this woman up again and carry her for a few more steps.

"Come on, Rebekka," I told myself. "You can do this!"

I took in a deep breath then pulled myself up from the deep snow that had grabbed my leg and made me fall. Her body was cramping, convulsing and it made it almost impossible to hold on to it. I grabbed her arms and with great strength and effort I managed to pull her over my shoulder. Two more steps through the snow, then one more and I fell in a deep hole again and dropped the woman. I screamed as we both fell face flat into the icy snow.

I groaned and fought the heavy snow while yelling. Suddenly I heard voices in the distance yelling back.

"We're on our way. Stay where you are!"

A burst out in relieved laughter as I saw flashlights and heard the voices approach. I waved my arms in the air and soon we were surrounded by men and women in yellow suits.

29

T HEY BROUGHT THE woman to Holbaek Hospital where my dad also was. After being examined by a doctor they told me I was fine except for a bump on my head that they put a bandage on. I went to see Dad while waiting for news about the woman. He looked so peaceful, I thought and sat in the chair next to him. Then I called Sune.

I started crying when he answered the phone.

"What's wrong Rebekka?" I heard the anxiety in his voice. "Did something happen? Why are you not home yet? Where have you been? Has something happened to your dad?"

"I ... I," I had a hard time getting the words across my lips. It all kind of came back to me, all the emotions having piled up inside of me during the last couple of days. I just needed to let it out, to cry it all out.

"Please talk to me Rebekka," Sune pleaded. "What happened? Are you okay? Is your father okay?"

"I'm fine," I finally managed to say. "My dad is fine too ..."

"Phew," Sune exclaimed. "You had me scared there for a second."

"I know," I sniffled. "I'm sorry ... I didn't mean to scare you."

"Okay," Sune said. "I'm calmer now. Just tell me why are you crying? Where are you?"

"I was in an accident."

"What?" the desperation was back in Sune's voice. "But you're okay, right?"

"I am," I sniffled again. "But I hit someone, a woman, with my car and now I'm afraid I might have killed her. She was in a really bad shape, bleeding from her mouth and throwing up, then her body started having spasms while I had to carry her to the ambulance that was stuck in the snow and couldn't get to us. It's just been a really awful night."

"Wow," Sune said. "Where are you now?"

"Back at the hospital. I decided to check in on Dad while they're taking care of the woman in ER. Oh Sune I just hope she is going to be alright. What if I killed her? I can't live with that."

"I understand that, but you have to. It wasn't your fault. It was snowing heavily, you probably didn't have a chance to see her. Accidents happen. I know you Rebekka you're not a bad person because of this. This is just something that happens in weather like this. What was she doing out in this weather? Was she walking?"

"I don't know. She didn't have a jacket on or anything. Seemed like she just came out of nowhere. I wasn't even driving that fast because of the snow. They tell me that the police will arrive later to get my statement and I'm really dreading having to do that. What if they think I did something wrong?"

"You need to relax now. No one will ever say this was your fault. If she was walking in the middle of the road. You couldn't have avoided it no matter what you had done. Did you say she was vomiting?"

"Yes she kept throwing up in the snow and some of it had blood in it. I'm afraid it might have been internal bleeding or something awful."

"Why would she be throwing up because she was hit by a car? It doesn't add up," Sune said.

"Well I don't know anything about all that but she was really sick afterwards and now she is in there and maybe she is ... maybe she will ... She might even have kids or something and maybe I'm about to make them orphans."

"You need to calm down Rebekka. If you drove slowly then she will definitely not die from being hit by you. She is not going to die, you hear me?"

I sniveled again. "Okay," I whispered. "It's just everything right now, I guess. My dad is still unconscious and I am afraid he will never wake up again."

"Everything is going to be just fine," Sune said, sounding very reassuring.

"How are the kids?" I asked.

"Both sleeping in their beds. I gave them a long warm bath before bedtime and that made them sleepy. They're just fine. What happened to the car?"

"It's still out there. Maybe you could call for a tow truck to get it tomorrow? I'll take a cab home if possible."

"Sure. Now keep me updated, alright. And Rebekka?"

"Yes."

"Don't worry."

I chuckled lightly. "I'll try not to."

I sobbed while putting the phone back in my pocket.

"He's right, you know."

I jumped at the sound of his voice. I couldn't believe it. I looked up and stared at Dad. His eyes were still closed and he hadn't moved. Was I hearing voices all of a sudden? I stood up from the chair and looked at him. No nothing had changed. Then I sat down in the chair again. I had just been imagining things.

Suddenly his eyes opened and he stared at me. "Sune is right," he said. "Haven't I always told you that everything will be just fine?"

"DAD!" I jumped up from my chair and threw myself at him. "You're awake!

My dad chuckled. "That I am," he said with a strained smile.

"Are you in any pain? Should I get the nurse to give you something?"

"Nah. I'll be fine. The old body is just a little tired, that's all." Then he smiled. I hugged him and held him tight feeling the tears roll down my face.

30

THE NIGHT AT the hospital became quite busy for me. First the nurses came running as soon as I told them Dad was awake, then a doctor examined him and told me that they wanted to keep him for a couple of days more to make sure everything was working the way it was supposed to. Then they told me he needed to rest and I went back to the ER to see if there was any news about the injured woman. In the waiting room the police came to talk to me. They took my statement and were soon on their way telling me this was a very busy night with the snow causing many accidents.

"Will I be charged with anything?" I asked just before they left.

"We'll be in touch," was their not so satisfying answer.

Of course they needed to look into the circumstances of the accident before they could determine if I had done anything wrong. I knew that perfectly well, I was just hoping for a more comforting answer.

I had a strange feeling inside sitting in the waiting room staring out the window or flipping through old magazines without even looking at the pictures. Part of me was happy, thrilled even, that Dad had woken up and was feeling better, but then I was overwhelmed with guilt since it was after all my fault that this woman was laying in there while the doctors fought for her life.

I texted Sune and told him that my dad was awake and he replied with an annoying "Told you everything would be fine." Then I laughed as I read the text again. Had I in fact found a guy who was just like my dad? They did both have the same calm nature, they were both like rocks and they always chose to stay positive even when things looked awful. It was a wonderful quality in a guy and something that often made me forget how young Sune was.

I put the phone back in my pocket when I spotted a nurse walking past the waiting room. I approached her.

"Hello, nurse? Excuse me."

She stopped and turned to look at me with a smile clearly indicating that she was busy and did not have time for this, but she did it anyway.

"Yes?"

"I was wondering if there was any news about the woman I brought in a couple of hours ago. She was hit by a car."

"Let me get a doctor for you who can answer that," she said and walked away still smiling widely and forced.

"Okay, thanks!"

I went back to the chairs and waited for another half an hour before someone finally approached me. He sat down in the chair next to me. His eyes were serious. The nametag said Dr. Wad.

"Are you the driver who hit the woman with her car?" He asked.

I swallowed hard feeling my stomach turn into a knot. "Yes. How is she?"

"I'm afraid she is not doing too well," he said.

I felt my heart pounding in my chest. My cheeks flushed and I gasped for air. "Will she ... is she ..."

The doctor sighed. It wasn't a nice sigh, it was deep and worried. "She is very sick and we are having a hard time finding out what is causing this. Plus we don't know who she is. She didn't carry a wallet or any identification. Do you have any idea who she is or where she is from?"

I shook my head. "No. She just jumped right out in front of my car. Like she was running and was surprised that there was a car. It was really strange. You said she was really sick, did that come from being hit by the car?"

"No, no. She keeps vomiting blood and having seizures. This has nothing to do with the hit. She has a few fractures on her left arm from bumping into the car, but that is not what is making her sick. She has also ripped her arms and legs on what may have been barbed wire."

"Then what is making her sick?"

He looked at me and our eyes locked. "If only we knew," he said with heavy voice. "If only we knew."

"Will she survive it?"

"We don't know yet."

I gave the doctor my number and told him to call me if there was any news about her condition. He promised to do so. Slightly dazed and startled I walked down to the reception and asked her to call a cab for me.

"In this weather it might take awhile for them to get here," she said.

"It's okay. I'll be right over here," I said and pointed at some chairs in the lobby. Then I walked to them and took off my jacket. I folded it into a pillow and laid my head on it. Soon I was sleeping heavily.

31

S OREN SEJR HAD a happy morning. He was thankful he was still alive but even more thankful that no one else had died at the camp during the night. Two people in two days was enough to drive them all into panic, and that was exactly what the devil wanted them to do. He always used fear to prevent them from accomplishing anything, to paralyze them.

Well, he would never get to Soren Sejr. Not again, not anymore.

He ate his breakfast consisting of only boiled carrots and oatmeal while studying the new young ones who arrived at the camp just a few days ago. Like all newcomers they looked scared and insecure, trying hard to fit in into this new life that had been given to them. Trying hard to grasp this new chance to start over in life that had been handed to them. Until now they thought they were only supposed to be here for a short period of time, which was what they were told.

Soren Sejr had recruited the four of them himself.

He found one in the nightlife of Holbaek right outside of a club, lying drunk on the ground alone, abandoned by his friends who didn't care enough about him to even help him, leaving him in the hands and fate of complete strangers like Soren Sejr. Soren had talked to him and realized the boy had nowhere to go since his parents had thrown him out and now he stayed with a friend in his apartment but since the friend had found a girl that same night, the young boy had to sleep outside in the freezing cold. Soren had told him he knew a place they could go and get a nice meal and somewhere to sleep for the night. The young boy had said he thought it sounded wonderful and followed Soren Sejr into his van.

The second youngster he had found among the drug addicts in Copenhagen. He always knew where to look, in a stairway in Vesterbro next to the Central Station. The young kids would sniff glue or take the needles left there by the real drug addicts and take the leftovers in them and inject them in their veins with the risk of getting all kinds of diseases.

The third was a girl he rescued from the hands of a violent boyfriend. They were arguing in an alley, both of them very drunk and he was slapping her across the face. Soren parked his van and grabbed his baseball bat. Then he rescued the girl by beating the boy senseless.

He told the girl he would take her to a place where she could meet friends and people like her. Drunk and high, she accepted his invitation not knowing what else to do or where to go. She fell asleep in the backseat immediately after Soren had started the van.

The last one had been a lot harder to get to go with him in the van. This girl had been quite resistant when he approached her at the train station where she was on her way home after a night in town. Soren sat on the bench next to her and started talking to her, asking her where she was going. She had gotten up and left telling him that it was none of his business and to leave her alone. Soren didn't like to be too pushy so he stayed in his seat trying to figure out what to do to help this poor girl find the true purpose to her life. She was so beautiful, he thought to himself. So young, with skin so tight and smooth. Her short dress showed her long legs in panty hose and her low-cut shirt revealed her fleshy breasts, so juicy and sensational. Soren loved the young girls the most and even more he loved to help them get away from this horrific world that only wanted to exploit them and use their young bodies. This was his calling in life, to change the course of these youngster's lives. It was his mission and he adored it, he thought as he approached the young girl from behind with a cloth of chloroform holding it against her face while she struggled to get free. He loved the power, the strength that the good Lord had given him to help these people. He knew that even if they tried to fight him now they would eventually end up loving him. Like a slave learns to love her master. Some day they would thank him for what he had done; thank him for helping them get away from this world and all its atrocities.

Yes Soren Sejr was a happy man this morning, happy because he was alive and no one else had died last night, and happy because this was the day when he started training his new recruits. Today was the day he started shaping them into real servants of God.

32

S UNE LET ME sleep in the next morning and took care of the kids. I heard them downstairs but still managed to get an hour or so more of sleep. Around eleven the kids couldn't keep out any longer and came into my room.

"Mom? Are you still sleeping?" Julie whispered.

"Not anymore," I said and opened my eyes. I smiled when I looked into her deep blue eyes. Then I grabbed her and pulled her into the bed where I started tickling her.

"Stop!" she laughed.

Then I kissed her and held her tight. "Grandpa is better," I said. "He woke up yesterday and talked to me. Do you want to go with me to the hospital today and see him? I think he would like that."

Julie's eyes smiled. Then she nodded. "I miss him, Mom."

I sighed and kissed her again. "Me too sweetie. Me too."

"His breakfast is better than Sune's."

I laughed. "What did he give you?"

"He tried to make oatmeal but it tasted horrible. I had some cornflakes instead," Julie said.

I chuckled. "I could go for one of his big breakfasts right now. I'm starving."

I had a bowl of cornflakes when I got downstairs and ate it while letting my mind wander. Sune grabbed another cup of coffee and sat at the table while reading the newspaper.

I looked at him and felt suddenly emotional. "I'm scared, Sune," I whispered.

He put down the paper. "Of what?" He said.

"That woman dying. I'm not sure how to live with myself if she dies."

He reached out and grabbed my hand. "She'll be okay."

"I keep thinking about her and wondering where she came from, who she was. They said she didn't have any papers or even a wallet. Who walks around in the middle of the forest on a snowy night without anything, not even a jacket?"

"Sounds weird to me too," he said and sipped his coffee. "Maybe she is a psychiatric patient? Maybe she escaped from somewhere?"

I nodded pensively. "Or maybe she was running from something."

"Are you thinking what I'm thinking?" Sune asked.

"I might be. If you're thinking she came from the camp. I was driving right past it at the moment. I didn't see what direction she came from, but she could have come from up there."

"That was exactly what I was thinking," Sune said.

"She had also ripped her arms and legs on barbed wire, the doctor told me. Sounds like she climbed the fence." I felt a pinch in my stomach. "She was sick," I continued. "She was throwing up. Wasn't that what the Priest was doing before he died? According to the statements we read he was vomiting blood. So was she."

"What about the other guy that died?" Sune said. "According to what I heard on the radio then the police were investigating it like it was some kind of food poisoning."

"Could it be some kind of collective suicide pact?" I asked. "Could this woman be trying to escape from it because she didn't want to do it?"

Sune shrugged. "Sounds plausible. Lots of sects commit collective suicide. Maybe she regretted it at the final moment."

"Isabella Dubois did keep talking like it was the end of the world or something. Like an apocalypse. Maybe they believe that and now they all want to die before the end is coming."

"Like the religious group Heaven's Gate who committed suicide in the late nineties?" Sune asked. "Remember them?"

"Yes. They killed themselves following the comet Hale-Bopp. Wasn't it in order to reach some spaceship or something? I don't remember the details, but you get the picture."

Sune nodded. "It could be something like that. Lots of religious sects have done similar things."

I finished my bowl of cereal and put it in the dishwasher. "I think we should go to the hospital right away," I said and wiped my mouth on a paper towel, then finished my glass of orange juice. "I promised Julie to take her to see her granddad today and I really want to talk to Dr. Wad about that woman and make sure she is still alive. I might have to contact the local police as well and tell them my theory. There might be a lot of people in that camp who are forced to participate in this if so it needs to be stopped immediately."

I stopped on my way to the living room. Then I turned and looked at Sune.

"I know," he said. "You don't have a car. I called the towing company but they have a lot to do today, so they couldn't promise that they would be able to bring it back today. Maybe tomorrow, they said."

"We'll take a cab then."

M Y DAD WAS sitting up in his bed when we entered the room. It made me smile. Julie ran to him with a shriek.

"Grandpa!" she yelled and hugged him.

He chuckled and hugged her back. I kissed him on the cheek. "How are you feeling today?" I asked.

He shrugged. "Still a little weak, but definitely better. But enough fussing about me. How are my munchkins?"

Julie and Tobias looked at each other then they laughed. "Sune made breakfast," Julie said. "It was really bad. And yesterday he tried to make dinner, pork chops, but he screwed that up too."

"Don't say that Julie," I said. "It was really nice of Sune to take care of you. Tell him you're sorry."

Julie looked at Sune. "Sorry," she said.

Sune smiled. "It's okay. I'll try harder."

Dad laughed. It felt nice to see him happy again. He had even regained a little color in the cheeks. "It's nice to know that I have been missed," he said. "How long do you think I need to lay around here? I really want to get out now."

"I don't know," I said. "I haven't talked to the doctor today."

"It sounds like you need me at the house, so if you could, tell him I really want to go home today."

"I will, Dad. But once we get you home you have to remember to rest too, okay?"

"I have a feeling you're going to be really annoying about this," he said. "I'm not dead yet, you know."

"No, but you could have been."

Dad ignored my remark and concentrated on the kids. They talked about the snow that hadn't stopped falling since yesterday. They told him what they had been doing and about the snowman in the yard that was now covered in so much snow they were thinking about making him into an igloo instead. Dad enjoyed listening to them. I looked at Sune.

"I'll go talk to the doctor. Be right back," I whispered.

"Okay," Sune said and kissed my cheek.

"Ew," Julie exclaimed.

I shrugged and sighed. Then I left the room. I went into the hallway and found a nurse who didn't seem to be busy. "Excuse me, do you know where I can find Dr. Philipsen?" I asked.

"Actually I just saw him attending another patient. If you wait here he'll be out in just a minute."

"Okay, thanks."

"No problem."

I only had to wait for a few minutes before a door opened and Dr. Philipsen showed his face. He spotted me immediately and as soon as he had talked to a nurse and given her what looked like instructions he walked towards me.

"Rebekka Franck," he said. "I just told my secretary to call you a minute ago and tell you to come in."

"Well here I am. Hopefully you have good news for me?" I asked with a knot in my stomach fearing that he didn't. "I mean my dad is already much better. He was sitting up when we came in this morning."

"That he is," Dr. Philipsen said but his face remained serious. A little too serious. It scared me. I couldn't figure out if that was just his professionalism, this distance, or if he was about to tell me some bad news. I hated that about doctors. You could never read their faces.

"We're all very pleased to see his improvement," he continued.

"Why do I feel like there is a 'but' coming up?" I asked nervously.

"Because there is," he said.

I froze. I really couldn't bear any more bad news. I was an emotional wreck already.

"Remember how I told you that the lab needed to run more tests on your father?" he asked looking at me over the top of his glasses. It made me feel like a child standing in front of my teacher.

"Yes. You told me they detected something unusual in his blood sample that they wanted to look into," I said my voice trembling slightly. I was already imagining the worst kinds of things that could be wrong with my father.

"Well yes. They did and I just received the results. I have to say that what they came up with is quite unusual and slightly disturbing."

I swallowed hard. What was he saying? Was my dad seriously ill or something? Was this the moment where he told me my dad only had a few months to live? Or maybe just a few weeks?

Oh please don't say something like that. Please let it be good news, please.

"What kind of result?" I managed to ask while a knot of tears was growing in my throat making my breathing troubled. Many thoughts ran through my mind. It doesn't have to be bad news. He only said it was disturbing and unusual. It doesn't have to mean he has to die, does it?

"Well it is quite strange, I might add, but it appears they found small traces of polonium in his blood. It was almost microscopic but still traceable."

I stared at the doctor with wide eyes. Had I heard right? "Polonium?" I asked. "Isn't that some sort of radioactive material?"

"I'm not an expert on chemistry, but yes it is. Normally, radioactive polonium is almost impossible to detect because - forgive me if I get a little technical here - it does not emit gamma rays. Therefore it doesn't show up when using gamma ray detectors as you'd normally do in the lab if it is suspected that a patient has been exposed to radioactive material. But someone in the laboratory was clever enough to try and test your dad's blood for alpha-emitters using special equipment. Apparently the test was positive. What we found in your father's blood is far below a deadly dosage, keep that in mind. But still enough to be able to cause damage to the tissue and we believe now that it has caused the blood to clot in his leg."

I was staring at the doctor in great disbelief. "What are you saying?" I said while shaking my head slowly.

"That your father somehow has been exposed to a radioactive material. We will need to test you and your family as well to see if any of you have been exposed to this as well. It is very deadly if a person is exposed to polonium in a higher dose than what your dad has been. Especially if it is ingested or inhaled."

"But having it in the blood, will that kill him eventually?"

I felt my heart racing rapidly now. What the hell was going on here?

The doctor shook his head. "We don't believe it will. The dosage is - as I said - very very small."

"But you don't know," I stated.

"No. We don't know the long term effects of this. It might give him other health issues like more blood clots. Radioactive isotopes are absorbed via respiration and with food and water. These very small particles are transported throughout the body via the blood and lymph systems. While in contact with the lining of the vessels – and incidentally the gut – the isotopes cause damage to the cells via release of radiation. Whether that will happen to your father or not, I don't know. I'm sorry I can't tell you more. But we need to find the source of this and I have contacted the proper authorities. They will begin an investigation as soon as possible. The center for radiological protection, SIS, will be here soon and will check all of you for any exposure and determine if they need to check the place you live. I believe you're only here on vacation, right?"

"Yes," I said not believing a word the doctor was saying. So much information at once that was hard to comprehend.

"The authorities need to make sure there hasn't been a spill somewhere. There is radioactive material in many things in our lives. Like smoke detectors, chemistry labs in our schools and even here in this hospital and so on. Maybe something was spilled into the water around here, if so they need to detect it so no one else is exposed to it."

"So what are you telling me?" I asked.

"We have to keep your dad for a few more days in the hospital and you need to stay here at the hospital too until SIS arrives and tells you what is going to happen. They'll take it from here."

"Do we need to be afraid?"

Dr. Philipsen exhaled. "I don't know Rebekka, I honestly don't know."

34

S OREN SEJR STARTED with the girl from the railroad
station. She had been locked in the isolation room for
three days now and it was time to break her. He had been
listening to her kick and scream on the other side of the iron
door. He knew she would eventually become quiet. They all
did sooner or later. This morning as he walked towards the
dining hall to eat his breakfast, he realized that the time had
come. He hadn't heard a sound from her room. She had
gotten tired and now it was time to start breaking her down.

There was a fuss at the camp since they realized that one
of the church members had gone missing during the night.
Mette Grithfeldt, one of the members of the leader group
that Soren Sejr was also a member of, had vanished from her
room. Rumors went that she had escaped; surveillance
cameras had shown her climb the fence ripping her arms
and legs on the barbed wire. How she had managed to get
out was beyond Soren's understanding. But he knew that it
would only be a matter of hours before the search group
found her. They always did.

Like they had done with Soren Sejr when he tried to

escape once. Then she would be punished just like he was. Like it was proper for someone who tried to bail on the rest. They had to be punished, to set an example. At least that was what the Priest had told Soren when he had tried to get out of there.

Only twenty years old Soren Sejr had first met Anders Granlund at a get together for UFO aficionados in Hamburg, Germany. Anders had brought enlightenment to Soren's life. He had invited him to his hotel room where he stayed during the convention. They came here every year, he told Soren Sejr. "To find the lost people and bring them back to their purpose in life." Anders explained that his group believed that people like Soren who were fascinated by UFOs and anything extraterrestrial had "lost their way and needed help to get back on track." There was nothing wrong with believing in these things or being fascinated by them, he told him, because they didn't know what they were doing. That was why Anders was there, to teach the lost souls that God wanted them to come back to him, He wanted them to know that it was the devil putting up obstacles - or distractions - so they couldn't hear God's voice, God's guidance in their life. Soren had thought Anders was a nice guy and listened to every word he had told him thinking it made perfect sense. Later he had said goodbye and Anders had given him his card. "Stop by our camp anytime, even if you just need a place to spend the night," Anders had said. Soren had kind of liked that but never thought he would actually use the offer. Not until two years later when he found himself on the street after a bad break-up with his girlfriend that ended in financial turmoil. Not knowing where else to turn, he found a phone booth and called Anders Granlund asking him if he could 'spend a couple of nights' at his place.

Less than half an hour later a van had parked next to the phone booth and two people stepped out of it with huge smiles on their faces. One was Anders, the other Hans Christian Bille. They had greeted Soren and told him he would never have to be alone anymore. They were going to take him in and help him get back on his feet again. He was to consider them as more than friends, they said. They were family now. Soren had liked the sound of that. He needed friends and he desperately wanted a new family. He had turned his back on his own many years before. Tired of them always being drunk and never taking care of anything, least of all him. He was sick of being their doormat that they used in any way they wanted. Tired of being the only grown-up in that house, tired of never having had any childhood, tired of being embarrassed by them and living a life scared to death of coming home from school to a house full of drunks who would amuse themselves by slapping him around or ordering him to go and get more beers and cigarettes.

Now Soren Sejr had found a new family and they would never treat him like that, he remembered thinking on his way to the camp in the white van.

Soren Sejr touched the iron door where he knew the young girl was waiting for him on the other side, waiting for him to enter and begin her training. She was his now, his slave and he would make her do whatever he told her to, he thought laughing to himself while humming the lyrics to *Hotel California*.

"You can check-out anytime you like," he sang while finding the key to the door in his pocket.

"But you can never leave."

35

"R ADIOACTIVE MATERIAL? In your dad's blood?"
Sune stared at me like had I told him I had just
seen the Pope walking around in his underwear. He simply
didn't believe a word of it. I had asked him to come out of the
room and told him what the doctor had told me. Now he was
shaking his head in disbelief. "How? Why? What about
our kids?"

I shook my head as well. "I don't know, Sune. The doctor
told me he didn't know much either. Only that the lab had
detected polonium in my dad's blood sample and that it
might be the cause of his blood clot."

"You've got to be kidding me," he exclaimed. "So now
we're all exposed to it, I guess?"

"That's what they need to find out. SIS is on their way
here to start the investigation. I guess they'll check our blood
as well."

"Well that's just perfect, isn't it?" he said stretching out his
arms resignedly.

"Hey we're all in the same boat here," I said.

Sune looked at me. "Yes, well that's just the way it always

is, isn't it? Your boat, your problems. You always drag the rest of us with you into all your trouble without even asking us if we want this, if we want things to be like they are. Maybe, just maybe people want something different than you do," he said. Then he turned around and went back into the room.

I was shocked. Mostly by his reaction. So much for that calm always positive-thinking guy that I was in love with. Who was this?

I wondered if he was going to tell everybody what was going on or if he wanted me to do it. It wasn't exactly a pleasant message to have to deliver to your family. How was I supposed to do it without scaring the kids senseless? I sighed deeply and rubbed my forehead. It was moments like these we were supposed to stand together, I thought. As a couple we were supposed to support each other in difficult situations. Not fight about it looking to blame each other. I felt tired. I stared at a clock on the wall. It was past noon. I needed to get away from my family for a little, away from Sune.

I knew exactly where I wanted to go.

Dr. Wad wasn't easy to locate, but with a little help from several nurses I managed to find him sitting in the waiting room talking to some poor relatives who were waiting to hear news about a loved one. I waited till he was done then I approached him.

"Dr. Wad?" I said.

"Rebekka Franck," he answered and shook my hand. "How is the head?"

I felt the bandage from yesterday. I had to admit I hadn't thought about it all day. "Great," I said.

"Good."

"How is the woman?"

Dr. Wad nodded slowly. "Stable," he said. "Or more like status quo. Still unconscious but we managed to stop the bleeding. We still can't seem to figure out what is wrong with her."

"Will she make it?" I asked feeling slightly nervous about the answer.

Dr. Wad shook his head. "I don't know. My hopes are not high. But I do know that if she doesn't make it then you hitting her with your car has nothing to do with it. I already told that to the police. They told me they will not be investigating this any further. This woman was already sick when she ran into you. It might be something she has eaten. She kept throwing up even after you brought her here and she has some kind of internal bleeding that we can't seem to stop. We hope to know more once the lab is done with her blood work. But being hit by a car couldn't have put her in this condition. That's the only thing I'm certain of in this case."

I felt huge relief in my entire body. I was still worried about her and felt somehow connected to her, but now I had the doctor's word for it. It wasn't my fault. It really wasn't.

"Have you identified her yet?" I asked.

"As a matter of fact we have," he said. "Well the police did. Dental records helped them. Her name is Mette Grithfeldt."

"Is she in any way related to the late Asger Grithfeldt?" I asked.

"The finance mogul, yes. It's his daughter."

"I thought she disappeared many years ago. I remember they searched for her everywhere and even had a reward out to anyone who would bring information about her to them. That was back in the beginning of the nineties."

Dr. Wad nodded. "Yes that's her. Her parent's lawyer managed to find her when the parents died and she inherited all their money. The police talked to him earlier today and

explained the situation. They asked him if she had any relatives that we needed to inform, but he said they were all gone
except for a few distant cousins that she had no contact with."

"Did she live at the camp?" I asked. "Is she a member of
'The Way'"?

Dr. Wad looked at me with surprise. "As a matter of fact
she is," he said. "How did you know that?"

"Just a hunch."

36

THE SIS ARRIVED later in the afternoon. Men wearing heavy suits and masks entered Dad's room where we were all waiting. They examined us, using small hand held detectors and taking blood samples. They took our clothes off and put them in sealed containers, after giving us a bath they gave us hospital clothes to wear.

I thought they were exaggerating and was worried about how much they scared the kids. I managed to explain to Julie and Tobias that we were going to be checked out to make sure that we weren't sick, but that there was nothing to be scared of. Julie knew me way too well to fall for that. She looked at me with frightened eyes.

"It's going to be just fine," I repeated to her. "They're just checking us, like the doctor checks you up every now and then," I told her.

It didn't calm her down. Once they were done with her examination she ran to me and hugged me tight. She was crying silently not wanting to let go of my leg.

"They took samples from my hair, Mommy. I'm scared. Are we going to die? Are we Mommy?"

"Shh, it'll be all over soon, sweetie," I said while stroking her hair. "Don't worry. It'll be just fine."

I sincerely hoped I was right.

We were told to stay in Dad's room to wait for the results. The SIS told us they would go to our vacation rental next and search to see if they could detect the source there. While we waited I did what any sensible worried mother would do. I grabbed my iPhone and started searching radiation exposure and how it affected the human body. It wasn't exactly calming to put it mildly. Sune sat next to me and read over my shoulder.

"Loss of hair, brain damage," he started reading out loud. "Radiation kills nerve cells and small blood vessels, and can cause seizures and immediate death."

Sune sighed and looked away. I felt how afraid he was, it was almost like he was struck and paralyzed by the fear inside of him. Still, he kept reading out loud, feeding the fear growing in all of us.

"Data from Hiroshima and Nagasaki show that symptoms may persist for up to ten years and may also have an increased long-term risk for leukemia and lymphoma. Intense exposure to radioactive material would do immediate damage to small blood vessels and probably cause heart failure and death directly. The radiation will begin to destroy the cells in the body that divide rapidly. These including blood, GI tract, reproductive and hair cells, and harms their DNA and RNA of surviving cells. Wow. That's festive," he continued. "If it doesn't kill us now it will give us a slow and painful death, like cancer or leukemia instead."

I sighed and looked at him. He was scared. Naturally. I was too. I grabbed his hand. I looked into his eyes. "It'll be fine," I said with my most reassuring voice. "You told me it will, remember?"

Sune scoffed. Then he smiled. "Yeah. I know. Sorry about that. I'm just panicking slightly."

I squeezed his hand. "I am too. But we're in this together. We need to keep it together - for them," I said and nodded in Julie and Tobias' direction. "We need to be strong and not lose it for their sake, alright?"

Sune exhaled and nodded. Julie and Tobias were holding hands while sitting quietly on Dad's bed. He was trying to cheer them up by putting on a puppet show with a pair of socks. It made me chuckle. If Dad was not panicking then there was no reason for us to be, I thought. So far he was the only one we knew for sure had been exposed to anything and that was such a small dosage that it might not affect him further at all. This was not a time to panic. I looked at Sune again. He was pale and scared. He suddenly reminded me of a little child. I stroked his cheek.

"It will be fine," I repeated. "Trust me."

He grabbed my hand and kissed it. "I sure hope you're right. I really truly hope you are."

On my phone I Googled 'polonium' thinking I remem-bered hearing about it somewhere before. I was right. In November 2006 the former officer of the Russian Federal Security Service, FSB and KGB - Alexander Litvinenko - was allegedly killed by polonium poisoning. According to the article in Wikipedia Litvinenko "suddenly fell ill and was hospitalized. He died three weeks later, becoming the first confirmed victim of lethal polonium-210 induced acute radi-ation syndrome. According to doctors, 'Litvinenko's murder represents an ominous landmark: the beginning of an era of nuclear terrorism.' "

Furthermore polonium was suspected to have killed the

French scientist Irène Joliot-Curie. She was accidentally exposed to it in 1946 when a capsule exploded in her laboratory. Ten years later she died from leukemia.

Rumors also had it that Palestinian leader Yasser Arafat's clothes had unusually high concentrate of polonium, but that was never confirmed.

I looked up and stared at Julie and Tobias. This thing could have long term effects like it had on Irène Joliot-Curie. If Julie had been exposed to it could it cause health issues for her later on in life? I couldn't bear thinking about it. It was obvious that none of us had suffered from any short term affects, so I wasn't scared that we were about to all die here and now, but what was this going to mean to all of us in the long run? I felt a pinch in my stomach, a pinch of fear.

37

S OREN SEJR LOOKED at the young girl in the corner. She was curled up, staring at him with fierce eyes, a fierceness he would soon get out of her. He always did no matter how long it would take.

Soren approached the girl, she was trembling, hissing trying to keep him away, covering her face with her arms. He kneeled in front of her and reached out his hand. He put it on her arm. She pulled it away with a loud hiss.

"Let me out of here," she groaned. "You have no right to keep me in here."

Soren Sejr smiled. Like he always did in this situation. Smiled with compassion and empathy, but not without displaying authority and letting them know that they were at his mercy, and he was the one to decide what would happen to them. He liked them like this, just before they were broken down. It was these moments he enjoyed the most, when they still believed they could fight him, when they still thought they could resist and get away, but knew deep down inside that they would eventually cave in and give up. They all came to that point when they realized that it was no use fighting this. Once they gave up he could begin to fill their minds with the right thinking. The kind of thinking that would make them obey his every word.

"You will get out of this room. When you're ready," he said with deep assuring voice. "But right now you're not well, we need to help you get back on your path with God. It's God's will. He brought you here."

Soren stroked the girl's cheek gently while smiling. Oh the smoothness and freshness of young skin. He always enjoyed touching it especially the new ones. It excited him so.

"Don't worry. I'm here to help you. You'll thank me one day."

The girl was sobbing now, first sign of the brokenness starting in her. She was about to give in now. This one wasn't going to take long. She was feisty still, but Soren had seen worse cases. He had taken care of them all.

Just like the Priest had taken care of him.

Just arriving at the camp Soren had thought he was only going to stay there for a few days and nights - just until he found a place to live and could take care of himself again. He probably only needed a few days to recover he thought as they showed him a small room at the camp with nothing but a bed, a dresser and a huge wooden cross on the wall over the bed. On the dresser lay a book that Anders Granlund had written and a silver cross that Soren still carried with him wherever he went. Toilet and bathroom was shared with the others in the camp and was down the hallway, they told him. Then they let him alone, let him settle in and get some sleep.

Never in his life had Soren slept better and heavier. This was really a nice place and the people were so nice to him it was almost unbelievable, he thought when he woke up and looked outside the window onto the deep dark pine forest surrounding the camp. Underneath his window was a huge courtyard where he saw people walking and talking, some were alone praying while holding a book out in front of them.

It was nice to know that he always had a place to turn, where friends would welcome him with open arms if he ever found himself in trouble again. He was beginning to think that this God-thing maybe wasn't so bad after all. The love for your neighbor and the forgiving part, he really liked. Maybe he would look into it some more. If these people were representing God then he wanted God in his life as well. He wanted to be good like them, good to others, taking care of them.

So Soren Sejr stayed at the camp for a few more days than planned and studied the ways of the church members and was very impressed by the way they labored and worked for the community without complaining, without murmuring about the hard work. And they never expected anything from him. Not once did they tell him that he had to do anything. For the first time in his life no one bossed him around, no one told him what to do, no one asked him to take care of them like his girlfriend had done, like his parents had done before her. For the first time the heavy weight of responsibility was lifted off his shoulders. It filled him with relief and great peace at mind.

"Just enjoy yourself and let the love of God fill you," they said.

So he did. He enjoyed the food, the friends, the beautiful surroundings and on his long walks through the forest where he often talked to God and asked him for direction, he never thought once that the high barbed-wired fence could be meant for anything else but keeping people out of the camp.

It never occurred to him that it might be there to keep him and the others in.

After two months Soren Sejr thought it was time to move on. He had been living of their generosity long enough he told his new friends. But now he was feeling great and ready to start over. He would never forget their hospitality and all they had done for him and if he ever could repay them, he would.

"Just let me know. You're my friends and I really see you as my family."

Anders Granlund whom Soren had learned to call the Priest like the rest did in the camp looked at him while shaking his head slowly, closing his eyes, exhaling deeply.

"Well here you go again leaving people," he said. "Isn't that what you always do, Soren? Leave the people you love? I know you've done it in the past, first your parents, next your girlfriend. Isn't it about time you broke that pattern and stayed for once? We feel it is time for you to break those bad behavior patterns in your life and we're here to help you."

The Priest had looked to the other three from the leader-group that was present and they nodded in agreement.

"I don't understand," Soren said and looked from one face to the other of the camp leaders. He smiled and chuckled insecurely thinking it was like they didn't understand what he was saying. He felt a little overwhelmed by their love for him, thinking they exaggerated slightly and acted a little overly dramatic. "I mean I will definitely be back to visit every now and then. I just think it's time for me to get out and get a job and take care of myself for once. I think I'm ready to stand on my own two legs again."

"Well that's where we disagree, Soren. We don't think you're ready for that world. It'll just tear you apart again. What kind of a family would we be if we didn't protect you against such a failure and disaster? We think you should stay," the Priest said.

"We really think you should," one of the leaders repeated.

"But ... I don't want to be a burden anymore. You guys have already done so much for me," Soren said.

"True," the Priest replied. "We have done much for you. That's what families do. So why are you repaying us by leaving us?"

"We are very saddened by your decision to leave us," another leader stated.

Not knowing what to say to not hurt their feelings further, Soren Sejr had stuttered and looked at their faces with helplessness. "I didn't know you felt this way," he said. "But I have friends on the outside that I miss and I want to get an education. It's about time I start taking responsibility for myself and move on with my life. I have decided I want to be a carpenter. I want to start my own business. Maybe I want to find a girlfriend and have children and start a small family of my own."

The Priest and the three others around the table had stared at Soren Sejr while shaking their heads in disbelief.

"I have to say you really disappoint me, Soren," the Priest said. "I'm sorry to have to do this, but it is for your own protection. You will never make it out there in the world. You belong here with us now. We're your family. We only want the best for you."

Then the Priest signaled the three others and they stood up and grabbed Soren by the arms and dragged him inside, into a bathroom where they locked the door and left him for five days without food or toilet paper. He survived by drinking the water from the tap. Every day the Priest would check on him. He came into the bathroom with a stick in his hand and a crucifix in the other. Then he beat the fierceness out of Soren until he pleaded him to stop.

When they finally unlocked the door and let Soren come out, he knew he had lost. He was defeated and he never talked about leaving the camp again. The humiliation had done him good, just like it would do this girl good too, Soren thought to himself as he slapped her across the face till she fell onto the tiles, bleeding from the mark his ring had made on her cheek. Then he held up his crucifix and kissed it before he pulled off her panty hose.

"I'm so sorry I have to do this to you," he said as he took out his sex and she screamed. "It's for your own protection. I only want what's best for you."

38

I T HAD BEEN a full day, Soren Sejr thought to himself as he prepared for bed. He said his Latin phrases that the Priest had written in his book and told them to say before going to bed, then he repented and asked God to forgive all of his sin and finally he kissed his silver crucifix ninety-nine times like the Priest had taught him to do.

Soren wouldn't say he actually missed the Priest but he did feel kind of sad that he was gone. He had taught Soren so many valuable lessons and nothing would ever be the same with Isabella Dubois as the leader. Soren knew that much. But luckily for Soren he had been around so long that he had nothing to fear from her. He wasn't a threat and he had always treated her nicely, always obeying her orders. Even if she was much younger, she had a higher rank than him and Soren had been smart enough to respect that fact from the beginning. He never questioned the Priest's methods or orders and he wasn't going to do that with Isabella either. He was way too smart for that. Soren Sejr minded his own business and never got in anyone's way. As long as he could have his, taking care of the youngsters and newcomers, he was satisfied. As soon as he had broken them he would hand them over to Hans Christian Bille who would begin rebuilding them. That wasn't Soren's thing. He enjoyed breaking them. The rest he didn't care much about. It was beating the resistance out of them, beating their willfulness out of them that was the fun part. That was what he loved and was good at.

But now Hans Christian Bille was no longer there either and that upset Soren. Who was supposed to take over where he left off? Soren sure wasn't going to do it. He didn't have it in him to be gentle. That wasn't his strength.

Well that was Isabella's headache now, wasn't it? He thought to himself as he put the head on the pillow and closed his eyes.

That night Soren Sejr had a dream. He was walking towards the isolation room when he realized the iron door was open and someone had escaped. He ran to the courtyard outside where someone stood with their back turned and bent over the ground. He looked down and realized the person was drawing circles in the gravel. Carefully inside of them she placed objects, one in the middle of each. As he slowly approached he saw what it was she was placing inside of them. It was human parts. In one it was teeth that had fallen out, in another hair that looked very similar to his own, in a third it was a finger bearing his ring, then an eyeball that was staring back at him resembling very much his own eye, finally in the last one she placed a drop of something greenish, some liquid that glowed in the dark night. Soren looked at her not understanding what all this meant. Then she turned her head and he staggered backwards. He recognized her crooked face and glowing green eyes.

Then she laughed. A manic hysterical laughter while the

green stuff in the circle grew and turned into a huge flood that soon drowned him. Under the surface he felt hands grabbing his feet and pulling him down.

Soren Sejr woke up with a scream.

He gasped for breath and tumbled out of bed, still wheezing, panting breathlessly. Even if the dream was over he still felt like he was drowning, his lungs filled with water. He coughed and coughed trying to get it up and be able to breathe again and soon he spurted blood out all over the floor. He tried to scream again, to call for help, but no sound left his body. Half-choked he reached to the dresser and grabbed his crucifix. He held it high in the air and prayed with spurts and gushes of blood spraying out of him. He felt the skin burning on his fingers and arms and soon he noticed it started to fall off along with his teeth and hair. He squeezed the cross praying, asking God why this was happening.

"Oh but you already know, don't you?" a voice in the room said.

Soren turned his head and while vomit spurted out of his mouth he tried once again to scream. But not a sound left his body. The little girl with the green eyes standing in front of him smiled and laughed like she had done in his dream.

Yes, Soren Sejr knew perfectly well why this was happening in the seconds before he died.

He only wondered why it hadn't happened until now.

39

W E ENDED UP spending the night in Dad's room at the hospital. The nurses rolled in more beds for us and made sure we had enough to eat. When we woke up the next morning and finished our breakfast the director of the SIS, Gunnar Moll, came into the room and asked to talk to me and Sune.

I told him I appreciated that he spared the kids unnecessary worry as we walked into a small office he had borrowed to the occasion.

"Well, I have kids of my own," he said.

Gunnar Moll sat behind a desk and looked at the both of us. I felt nervous and grabbed Sune's hand.

"First of all I'm very sorry that we had to put you all through this, but I do hope you understand that we have to be very cautious with this kind of thing," he said nodding.

I couldn't quite detect if he was about to give us good news or bad news. I hoped for the first and expected the last.

"We're glad you're thorough," Sune said.

Gunnar Moll stared down at the papers in front of him for a little too long for my taste. It made me feel sick and uncomfortable. It seemed like he was finding the courage to tell us the results.

"It doesn't appear that any of you - except for your father - have been exposed to any radiation, I'm pleased to tell you," he finally said.

A huge sigh of relief came from the both of us.

"Yes I understand you're feeling relieved. But the fact that we haven't been able to detect anything in you or on your clothes doesn't mean that you are completely in the clear. You might have been exposed to something that we can't detect or you might be exposed to it otherwise later on. Since we haven't found the source of your dad's exposure, that doesn't mean it's not there. Therefore you all be aware of the following symptoms of radiation sickness." Gunnar Moll lifted a piece of paper and started reading: "fatigue, fainting, bruising, hair loss, diarrhea, weakness, bloody stool, dehydration, mouth ulcers, vomiting blood, sloughing of skin, nausea, open sores on the skin, skin burns, redness, blistering, ulcers in the stomach, bleeding from the nose, mouth, gums or otherwise, inflammation, swelling, bleeding of the skin. Be aware that early symptoms of radiation sickness mimic those of the flu and may go unnoticed unless a blood count is done."

He put the paper down and looked at us. "Again any of these symptoms should in your case be a cause to visit a doctor immediately. And remember we there is a difference between external contamination and internal contamination. External contamination happens when radioactive material in the form of powder, dust or liquid comes in contact with a person's clothing, skin or hair. People who are contaminated externally may become contaminated internally should the radioactive material get inside of them. Internal radiation contamination happens when people either breathe or swallow radioactive materials, or when these materials enter their bodies through open wounds or get absorbed through their skin. Some forms of radioactive materials remain in a person's body and get deposited in various organs. Other forms of radioactive materials are eliminated from a person's body through urine, blood, feces or sweat. If someone who has been exposed to radiation vomits less than an hour after being exposed, it usually means the dose of radiation they received is very high and they will most likely die. Please see a doctor if any of you have severe symptoms or even if you're in doubt. Now as far as we know we are talking about Polonium 210 here and luckily for you it acts slightly different than other radioactive materials. Polonium 210 is a highly radioactive and chemically toxic element. But it represents a radiation hazard only if taken into the body. It's important to note that alpha particles do not travel very far - no more than a few centimeters in air. They are stopped by a sheet of paper or by the dead layer of outer skin on our bodies. Therefore, external exposure from Po-210 is not a concern and Po-210 does not represent a risk to human health as long as Po-210 remains outside the body. Most traces of it on a person can be eliminated through careful hand-washing and showering. It might leave a rash but it is no further risk to the person's health if not ingested. Po-210 can enter the body through eating and drinking of contaminated food, breathing contaminated air or through a wound. Internal contamination with Po-210 is however very dangerous. It is more than 250,000 times as toxic as cyanide, and is very hard to find in the body. Polonium 210 has a half-life of about 138 days, making it thousands of times more radioactive than the nuclear fuels used in early atomic bombs. It is considered to be one of the most hazardous radioactive materials known and if ingested, it is lethal in extremely small doses. Less than

1 gram of the silver powder is sufficient to kill. Once deposited in the bloodstream, its potent effects are nearly impossible to stop. A poisoning victim would experience multiple organ failure as alpha radiation particles bombard the liver, kidneys and bone marrow from within. The symptoms - nausea, hair loss, throat swelling and pallor - are also typical."

"But ... but my dad has internal contamination, then," I said feeling slightly confused on the verge of panicking. "Will he die? What is going to happen to him?"

"We will need to monitor his blood count and white blood cells. So far it all looks fine, but we don't know if it will affect him further. The dose that was found in his bloodstream is far less than the lethal dose and only slightly higher than what is normally found in the human body. I can't say for sure that it won't have any effect on his health along the road, I wish I could, but I can say that I'm very optimistic."

"You don't know where he was exposed to it?" Sune asked.

I felt his frustration. It was great to know that we were in the clear but since we didn't know where Dad had been exposed to this radiation we had no chance of avoiding it in the future. For all I knew it could just as well have happened here than back at home.

"We have examined the cabin you have been living in and found nothing. At first we suspected it might have been a transport accident nearby that might not have been reported, contaminating the ground and maybe the water, but that didn't seem to be the case. The dose your dad has been exposed to is very very small and it is only because he was weak and had previous health issues before it happened that his blood clotted."

"But it's internal? Won't it destroy his tissue eventually?" I asked.

"We do have treatments. We will give him Dimercaprol right away and I have great confidence that it will prevent just that," Gunnar Moll said and accompanied the statement with a small yet quite reassuring smile.

I felt somewhat relieved but still disturbed as we said goodbye to Gunnar Moll. A doctor came to our room and told us we could leave the hospital if we wanted. My dad was to stay however since they wanted to monitor his development further. Plus they were about to begin a new treatment on him and wanted to make sure he didn't have a bad reaction to it. Given his age and earlier health issues it was vital to keep him under observation.

I wasn't happy about leaving Dad behind again, but he assured me he was fine and if I could just bring him some of his favorite salty licorice that he always ate, then he would even be very fine.

Julie grabbed my hand on our way down the elevator. I kissed her head and stroke her cheek.

"Everything is going to be fine now, isn't it Mommy?" she asked.

I looked into her eyes. I wanted to tell her that I believed it would be, but I couldn't. I was determined to find the source to this and protect my family from it. I couldn't rest until it was found. Somehow. Some way.

"I think we should move into a hotel while we're here," I said looking at Sune. "Just in case."

He nodded. "That sounds like a good idea. We'll go home and pack all of our stuff."

"Yeah!" exclaimed both kids.

I smiled, then looked at Sune again. When the doors to the elevator opened and we started walking out, I stopped.

"What's the matter, Mom?" Julie asked.

Sune and Tobias looked at me. "What's going on Rebekka. You look like you've seen a ghost," Sune said.

"Radiation sickness," I stuttered. "Why haven't I thought about that before? It struck me when the director of the SIS mentioned all of the symptoms. But I didn't see the connection until now. They fit. They all fit."

"What do you mean?" Sune asked.

"I'll explain later. Take the kids. Bring them to a hotel, text me once you've found a place, I'll get a cab later to join you. Then I'll go back and get our stuff later, alone. I don't want the kids in that cabin again in case the contamination source is still there. I don't want any of you to risk being exposed to it."

"Okay, Sune said. "But where are you going?"

All three stared at me waiting my response with anticipation. I didn't have time to clarify.

"To talk to a doctor about a patient."

40

I RAN INTO Dr. Wad in the ER. He was coming out of a room looking frustrated, then he discussed something with a nurse. I approached him.

"Ah Rebekka," he said then lifted his finger to let me know to wait a second. I listened as he directed the nurse and instructed her in how to medicate a patient. Then he turned and looked at me with a tired, long face.

"I'm sorry," he said. "I don't have any news for you. I really wish I had. Mette Grithfeldt had a seizure last night and we fought to keep her alive for hours. Her heart gave up but we managed to get it beating again. Now she is finally stable. She woke up for just a minute or so and she kept screaming. Said she was dying and that some girl was after her. 'Don't let her drag me to hell with her, don't let her take me with her to hell,' she kept repeating. I don't know what it was all about. Probably just a dream." Dr. Wad sighed. "It's been a long night."

"For you and me both," I said. "I think I might have an idea to what is happening to her, to Mette Grithfeldt."

Dr. Wad looked at me with astonishment. "You do?"

"Well it might be nothing, but I had the thought this morning when I talked to the director of the SIS. They were examining us for radiation exposure. See my dad had traces of polonium in his blood, that's why his blood clotted."

Dr. Wad didn't seem to see where I was going. I could tell he was anxious for me to get to the point. He probably had another place to be right now, other patients to attend to. "The bottom line is," I said. "Maybe she is suffering from radiation sickness. I mean the bloody vomiting, the seizures. When I heard all of the symptoms, I thought of her immediately."

"She does have swelling of the skin and rashes several places on the body," he said. "And the ulcers in her stomach and throat could be caused by something like that. You said your father was exposed to radiation, to polonium? From where?"

"We don't know where it comes from yet, SIS checked our cabin and the areas surrounding but didn't find the source. But our cabin is very close to the camp where Mette Grithfeldt lives."

Dr. Wad nodded. He suddenly seemed to be in a rush. "I think you might be on to something. Thank you," he said and shook my hand. "Thank you so much!"

Then he ran off.

I had a taxi take me back to the cabin. I texted Sune on the way and let him know where I was. He had found a nice small inn in Arnakke, he wrote. They were waiting for me and missing me. I looked forward to spending a few hours in a safe hotel room with my family as well. But first I had to pack all of our things.

I opened the door and went inside the small cabin. It was strange how everything had suddenly changed, the same place I had enjoyed spending time with my family in felt suddenly uncomfortable to be in. No matter where I went I couldn't stop thinking about the radiation and where it could come from, especially when I went into Dad's room and began packing his stuff. I couldn't escape the thought that there might be something in that very room that made him sick. That the source could be in there after all - even if the SIS hadn't found it. I mean he had been with us all the time, hadn't he? We had eaten the same things, drank the same water. How come he was exposed to something and we weren't? The only place he had been that we hadn't, was in this room where he had slept.

I hurried and picked up his pants and shirts from the chair and put it all in the suitcase on the bed. I threw in his book, his socks, his underwear. My movements were slightly frantic and desperate. I didn't want to spend one second longer in that room than necessary. I didn't like being in there at all. When I picked up his brown cardigan that he loved to wear I felt something strange in the side pocket. I stuck my hand inside and pulled out a package of cigarettes and a lighter.

I exhaled and sat on the bed with heavy heart. We had quit smoking together my dad and I - two and a half years ago. He needed to do it since the doctor told him to after he had the stroke a couple of years ago. Was he still smoking behind my back?

I threw the package in the garbage can and continued packing. I was saddened that he insisted on destroying his body with things that caused him to have health issues. I knew I was a hypocrite since I had been smoking too with

Sune, but I didn't have health issues like he did. I felt even sadder that he felt he had to keep it a secret from me. I stared out the window while wondering. How could he have managed to keep this a secret from me? When had he been smoking? Maybe he just kept the package in case he wanted to smoke, maybe he didn't even take them out? I glanced at the package in the garbage can next to the bed. It was half empty. My dad would never be able to resist the temptation, I thought. He was that type. If he had a package like that then he would smoke it. It was the same reason why I always hid the chocolate. If he found it he would eat all of it. Not just one piece. That was just the way he was and always had been.

So assuming he had been smoking while we were here in the cabin, where would he have done it? I looked out at the white landscape again and glanced towards the pine forest.

Could he have been sneaking out without us seeing it? I guess he could. He could have done it at night, when he told us he was going to bed, I thought. He had turned in very early every night while we had been in the cabin. Maybe he had sneaked out. I looked towards the forest. Did he go in there? In the darkness? Sune and I had been sitting outside on the porch on the first night we had spent in the cabin. Maybe my dad had sneaked out the front door and walked into the forest to make sure we didn't see him? I looked at the brown cardigan in the suitcase. Then I grabbed his grey pants and lifted them in the air. Something was in the pocket. I put my hand inside and pulled out a small flashlight. I couldn't help but chuckle lightly. That clever bastard. He had gone in there to smoke with his flashlight. Well I could hardly blame him, could I? He never had much time to himself and never had much privacy with both me and Julie in the house. On a vacation like this there wasn't much room for privacy either.

I sighed and stared at the forest. Then a thought entered my mind. Could he have been exposed to the radiation in there? Had he encountered something or somebody in there at night?

41

I SEFJORDEN INN WAS a small cozy place in a timbered house with thatched roof, small windows and low ceilings that had tall people like Sune bent over constantly to not knock their head. It was located right across from the town's church. A typical Danish Lutheran church, white with red roof, placed on a small hill overlooking the fjord. The people at the inn seemed nice and helped me with getting the suitcases and bags out of the trunk of the taxi when I drove up. In the room I took a shower then changed into my own clothes and soon I almost felt like myself again. Still I had the weird almost eerie feeling inside about this town.

We ordered room service and ate in the beds. The kids were watching TV lying on one of the beds while Sune and I found two beers in the mini-bar. We opened them and drank while we ate.

I filled Sune in on the latest news, the talk I had with the doctor and my dad's cigarettes.

"I think it is all somehow connected," I said and drank.

Sune looked pensively. "So you think people are being

killed at the camp by radiation sickness and somehow your father was exposed to it in the forest as well?"

I nodded. "Basically that sums it up, yes."

"So the deaths in the camp are not a mass suicide? It's an accident?" Sune asked. "Shouldn't we tell the police so they can get people out of there before more get sick and die?"

"We can't make the connection before they confirm that Mette Grithfeldt is in fact suffering from radiation sickness. It's in the hands of Dr. Wad now. I expect he will inform the police and the SIS if it turns out to be radiation. The police should be able to connect the dots themselves."

"I guess you're right. Glad we got away from the forest though," Sune said. "If the radiation source is there."

"Me too. I never want to go back there again. This radiation stuff is scary, I tell you."

"But where does it come from? Radiation doesn't just appear out of the blue. There has to be a spill or something, right?"

I shrugged. "I guess."

We both went quiet for a long time. The eerie feeling was back as my thoughts went back to the first night when we heard the Priest's scream in the night. I shivered and cuddled up closer to Sune. He stroked my hair gently while drinking his beer.

"It is a little weird, though ..." he said.

"What is?"

Sune shook his head. "No my imagination is running too wild here. Nothing. Forget it."

I lifted my head and looked at him. Then I kissed his lips. It felt wonderful. Waves of pleasure shivered through my body. It had been too long since we had been together as a couple. I missed it. I missed the closeness.

"I am afraid it's not only your imagination that is running

wild here. I have a feeling I've been wondering the same thing over and over again. It's that girl, right? The Chernobyl-kid?"

Sune looked at me and smiled. "Good to know I'm not the only insane one here. Yes, I have been wondering constantly ever since the first talk of radiation. The old lady who told us about the Chernobyl-kid said that people kept dying around her. She was in that camp, used to live there, now she has disappeared according to the rumors?"

I exhaled trying to sort this out. Right now it was nothing but a feeling, some strange sense that there could be a connection. "Why are people dying from radiation-sickness in the camp? The doctor told me that Mette Grithfeldt kept saying that 'some little girl was after her and wanted to drag her to hell with her'. It is a little too coincidental," I said. "How was the story again? Her parents worked at the plant when the accident occurred and the radiation was spilled. The father died right away but the mother didn't die until years later when they had both moved here."

"The girl was still unborn when it happened and came out deformed and acting weird," Sune continued. "After several accidents and deaths in her trail no one wanted her in the end so the church said they would take her."

"The question is what happened to her after the church took her in. Where is she now?"

"That's what we need to find out," Sune said.

42

I SABELLA DUBOIS LOOKED at her face in the reflection of the window and realized she had aged. It was dark outside and inside she felt a darkness of her mind as well. Today the third person from her church had been found dead in the camp and one was still sick in the hospital. Not that Isabella was sad to see them all disappear one by one. No she wanted this to happen to them, she needed them to be gone in order to make the generation change she wanted for the church. The leaders had all become weak in their older days, she thought. They had deviated from their own beliefs. Especially the Priest whom Isabella had adored so much and whose ideas she had worshipped from the first time she heard of them. But the last couple of years even he had turned soft on her. His ideas had weakened and he was no longer the strong leader she had believed him to be.

It was time for a change, she had thought to herself. It was finally time for someone else to take over.

Isabella had been famous all of her life. At only four years old she had taken the entire Danish population by storm when she had played an adorable young kid in the hit family movie *My sister's children*. She had been loved and adored all of her life and never lacked anything - except a life that she could call her own.

From only four years of age she had belonged to someone else. She had absolutely no say in her own life, it was all decided by agents and moviemakers. All she could do was what was expected of her and smile her cute smile whenever she was told to. They would all sigh and clap their hands while the newspapers and magazines called her the 'most adorable child-actress of the century.' She had offers constantly to be in movies, commercials and walking runways in children's outfits. She made tons of money to her parent's great satisfaction. Having struggled most of their lives just to make ends meet her parents could now buy anything they wanted and live the life they had always dreamt of. Never once did they ask Isabella if she wanted this life, never did they wonder why she always cried in her bed at night before she fell asleep. Isabella knew how to act, how to put on the right face at the right moment. That was what made her famous, that was what made her parents rich beyond their wildest dreams.

But that also made Isabella's childhood years incredibly lonely and desolate. The only friends she had were make-up artists and other actors who were so star struck in her presence that they were no fun to be around. Her life was lived in the endless spotlight and flashing cameras no matter where she went. Her life was lived at the red carpet, on the cover of magazines, but as soon as the lights were turned off and the cameras stopped flashing, Isabella felt dead inside.

The loneliness tore Isabella apart growing up and she wondered if there was more to this life. She sought out answers to life's big questions about life and death, heaven and hell. As a teenager she declared she was a Buddhist and the hungry journalists ran the story in all of the magazines and newspapers. But not even here did she find something to fill that growing hole inside of her, that emptiness inside of her ever since she could remember. Isabella sought fulfillment elsewhere and studied all kinds of religions, even flirted temporarily with Scientology.

Still she felt the vast emptiness in her grow bigger and it wasn't until she had turned eighteen and starred in the latest hit movie, the last one she ever did, that she heard about "The Way" and met with the leader who called himself The Priest, that she finally found peace and fulfillment. The Priest told her about his beliefs and they clicked immediately. He opened her eyes to the evil growing inside of her that left her heart empty and unfulfilled. He told her the demon of greed and pride lived inside of her and needed to be driven out before she could finally find peace and joy.

She liked what he told her. She agreed to join them at the camp and soon after she arrived the exorcism of her demons began. The Priest had taken care of her case personally, making sure that it was done properly. Night after night she had been on her bleeding knees for hours repenting her sins, rebuking the demon living in her, commanding it to leave her body, asking God to clean her body, soul and spirit of anything demonic. The Priest whipped her, causing her to fall to the ground, but she fought her way back on her bleeding burning knees, while the church members chanted and sang, filling themselves with God and speaking in tongues. After eleven sessions of forty-eight hours on her knees she was finally cleansed. Beaten, broken and crying they dragged her to a room and let her sleep for days. When she was feeling better and finally ready to walk again, the Priest came to her room. He told her there was one last thing he needed to do. He explained to her how he believed that semen had a cleansing effect and that Isabella had to let him fill her with his cleansing juice to make sure every part of her inside was cleaned and ensure the demons wouldn't come back. He talked to her about her inner dreams, about her past, her future and what she wanted out of life. She had felt confused when he began opening her blouse and touched her young breasts. She felt disordered when he forced her down on the bed and tied up her hands so she couldn't move. She felt even more puzzled when he forced his sex inside of her while screaming his pleasure out.

But if there was one thing Isabella Dubois knew how to do it was to put on a face when it was expected of her - she could smile her adorable smile even in uncomfortable situations - so that was what she did. She smiled and acted like she enjoyed his rough touches, because she knew in the end that it was to her own benefit. Some day she would be the one in power, she would be the one ordering others to do things against their will.

She also knew she was going to enjoy it.

43

I WENT TO visit my dad at the hospital alone later in the evening. I didn't want him to feel alone and I needed some answers.

He was in a grumpy mood when I entered his room.

"Rebekka!" he exclaimed. "Finally a friendly face. Those nurses ... I'm sick and tired of them. I don't trust them. They are so sloppy. They keep asking me the same questions. They're new ones almost every day so I have to explain everything to them over and over again. It's annoying, really."

I kissed his cheek and smiled at him. "How are you, Dad?"

He grumbled. "Getting tired of the food. Tired of just lying in this bed. Don't you think you could get me out of here soon?"

"I'm trying hard," I said. "But they need to see how you react to the new medicine first. They need to monitor you for at least a couple of days more."

Dad exhaled. "Well I guess I could do a day or two more, if that's what's best for me, but then I'm definitely going home. We're going back to Karrebaeksminde. I miss my own house and bed."

"I brought you these," I said and threw a bag of Piratos, salty licorice, on the small table next to him.

"Oh you're a darling!" he exclaimed and picked them up.

"I found them in your room. I also found something else when I packed your things," I said.

He blushed. "Ah what the heck, I can't keep it a secret forever," he said. "So what if I enjoy a cigarette every now and then?"

I sighed and patted his shoulder. "It's okay, Dad. I just feel hurt that you hid it from me."

Dad laughed. "Are you kidding me? The way you have been fussing about me and talking about my health the past two and a half years. How could I tell you? It would have killed you before it killed me. Either that or you would have taken away the last of my privileges and started escorting me everywhere making sure I wasn't tempted again. I enjoy my freedom and you keep taking it away from me."

I chuckled. "Point taken," I said. "Guess I have been treating you like a child."

"You have," he said with a smile. "Please don't ask me to slow down, stop cooking or stop taking care of the kids. I love those things, you know it. It keeps me sane."

I nodded. "I won't, Dad. I will get better at not fussing over you. I promise." I sighed deeply and stared at him. I was so scared of losing him. "It's just that I don't know what will become of me if you die."

"If I die? Sweetheart, there is a little thing you need to know. You will lose me someday. You will have to go on with your life without me some day. You will be just fine. You're a big girl." Dad smiled widely, chewing a big round licorice.

"I know you're right," I said and sat in a chair. I smiled at him eating his candy. "There is another thing I would like to know."

"Yes?" he said, mouth full of the black candy.

"When you sneaked out to smoke did you go into the forest?" I asked.

He nodded while still chewing. Some licorice was stuck to his teeth and he had to loosen it with his finger. "Go on," he said.

"Did you meet someone or something in there?" I asked.

He looked flabbergasted. "What do you mean? Someone? Who?"

I shrugged. "I don't know. A little girl maybe?" I knew how stupid it sounded as soon as it had left my lips.

Dad laughed out loud. "I would think I'd remember that! A little girl in the dark forest late in the evening. I don't think so."

"Well maybe she is an adult now. Did you see anyone in there?" I asked knowing that it didn't make any sense to my father.

"Rebekka. What are you talking about? Girls running around in the forest at night. Why are you asking me this?"

I exhaled and sat on his bed. "The people in the camp, the members of that sect, 'The Way' they're dying from radiation sickness, at least that's what I think. It hasn't been confirmed yet. But I have this idea that maybe you were exposed to the same thing, just a much smaller dose. That's why I'm asking you to tell me if you saw anything in there while you were smoking, did you encounter anything? Did you touch anything?"

Dad inhaled. "Well I only went into the forest on one occasion, on our first night here, since you and Sune were sitting outside on the porch. I was afraid you might see me or smell the smoke so I grabbed my flashlight and went for a walk in the forest. I guess I mostly just walked around. It was very cold so I couldn't stand still for long. I did at one point pass a water post, one that was set up for the joggers in the summer. I was happy to see it wasn't frozen, water could still flow through it, not much but a little bit. I was thirsty so I drank from it."

"Did you do anything than that?"

"I don't think so. To be honest Rebekka I really don't remember. But come to think of it I have had a rash on my hand ever since."

"You poured the water in your hand and then drank from it?" I asked.

"Yes. It was too low for me to bend all the way down."

"Can I see the rash?" I asked.

Dad lifted his hand and showed me. It was a little swollen and reddish, but didn't look like much. "We have to have the doctor look at that," I said. "Why haven't you told me you had a rash before?"

"Rebekka. I'm seventy-eight years old. I have rashes all the time all over the body. I thought it was just psoriasis like your mother had. It looked just like it."

I nodded slowly trying to put together the pieces one by one. Dad had been contaminated by drinking from that water post, I was almost certain. Something had to be in that water at the water post. That was the source.

44

D AD WAS TIRED and wanted to go to sleep early so I left him around nine. I was about to go home, but wanted to make a stop first.

The door to Mette Grithfeldt's room was open and a nurse was inside looking at a monitor, adjusting something.

"Excuse me?" I said and knocked at the open door.

The nurse turned and looked at me with a smile. "A visitor?" she said. "Are you a relative?"

"I'm afraid not."

"A friend?"

"Something like that."

The nurse smiled widely. "Well isn't that nice. Mette hasn't had a visitor ever since she got here. I was beginning to think she was all alone. It's good to know that at least someone cares about here."

I smiled briefly and nodded. "So how is she?"

"Better. Much better. Ever since the doctors found out that it was radiation sickness, we have been able to give her the right treatment. It has really improved her condition. She was even awake for a few minutes this afternoon. That's huge progress."

I exhaled deeply. It felt good to have at least been able to help her a little. Plus I was glad to realize that I had been right.

"So it was polonium poisoning?" I asked.

The nurse nodded. "God only knows how she came in contact with such a lethal material. I mean it's not something you come across every day around here."

"I bet it isn't."

The nurse sighed and put the blanket over Mette's body. Then she looked at me. "Well I guess I'll leave you two alone." The nurse smiled at me and walked towards the door. Then she turned and looked at me. "Talk to her. It might do her good to hear your voice."

Then she left.

I walked closer to Mette. Her skin was so pale and she looked so tiny in the big hospital bed. I felt bad, couldn't escape the feeling that it was still partially my fault she was laying there, even if I knew it wasn't true. She was sick when I hit her with the car. Sick with radiation poisoning. I turned my back at her and walked to the window. Lights from cars were flickering in the night.

"What on earth happened to you before you ran into that street," I murmured. "If only you could talk to me. Tell me why you were running."

I heard a noise and turned around. At that same moment Mette opened her eyes and looked at me briefly. I froze.

"Are you awake?" I asked.

She nodded slowly. Then she closed her eyes again like she was trying to regain her strength. A second later she looked at me again.

"Do you want me to call a nurse?" I asked.

"No," she said with a weak hoarse voice. She cleared her throat. Tubes through her nose helped her breathe. It caused her to make a hissing and wheezing sound when she spoke. "Who are you?" she asked.

"Oh. I'm sorry. Can't blame you for wondering. I'm Rebekka Franck. You don't know me. I brought you here. I ... kind of hit you with my car. It was snowing. I couldn't see you."

Mette nodded. She seemed groggy.

"Why were you out in the forest in the middle of the night in a snowstorm without even a jacket?"

Mette Grithfeldt opened her eyes big and wide. She looked frightened, scared to death. I approached her reaching out my hand but even if it looked like she was staring at me, she wasn't looking at me. It was as if she saw something completely different. I wondered if it was the memory of what had happened. I grabbed her hand and held it. She came back to me, looking directly at me.

"She was there ..." she stuttered. "She came back to get me, to drag me with her back to burn up in hell. But I ran. I escaped. But she won't let me go that easy. I will die. I know I will. I have to pay for what I've done."

Mette put her other hand on top of mine. I looked into her eyes. They seemed darkened almost obscure.

"Who is she?" I asked.

"Edwina."

"Is that the girl they used to call the Chernobyl-kid?"

Mette grabbed my shirt and pulled me closer. She lifted her head. Then she whispered. "She has come back. They say if you dream about her it means she will come to kill you."

"Did you dream about her?" I asked confused.

She let go of my shirt and put her head on the pillow again. "Yes. I did. When I woke up she was still there. She was in my room. She was laughing at me like she did ... like when ..." Mette shook her head slowly. "Then I fell sick. Just like the others. I knew it was over but I ran anyway. I couldn't let her get me."

I swallowed hard looking at Mette's strained face. A wave of pain rolled in over her, she groaned and crumpled up in the bed. "Do you want me to call for someone?" I asked.

"No. It's no use. They can bring me all their medicine but it's no use. I'm already dead. Maybe it's for the best anyway. I guess I deserve it. I guess we all do."

"Who? Mette, who deserves it? And why?" I asked.

The pain seemed to be easing off now. Mette's face seemed less tense. "We do," she mumbled. "Me and all the others who killed her."

I swallowed. "You killed Edwina?"

"We all did. Trying to save her from herself. She was possessed. The demon made her do crazy things. She was completely out of control. She would scream, tear off her clothes, eat spiders and coal; she would even lick her own urine off the floor. The Priest didn't know what to do about her. He tried all kinds of treatments but nothing helped."

"What kind of treatments?" I asked. "Exorcism?"

Mette nodded. "The Priest had driven out demons from all of us and freed us, so naturally we all thought it would work. We all believed anyone could be freed from their demons if they were cast out. But it didn't work with her. The demon had too solid a stronghold on her, or maybe she didn't want it to leave, I don't know. But I do know that the Priest tried everything. Days and nights he worked on her, trying to cast out the demon from her body. The rites were performed for about ten months in 1993. Seventy-six exorcism sessions were held in our courtyard, one or two every week, some lasted up to nine hours. During those sessions

Edwina demonstrated almost superhuman strength; sometimes it took three grown men to hold her down. It was like
she grew stronger as time passed. Later they used chains to
hold her body down, as they tied her to her bed in her room.
She spoke to us, cursed us, using different languages and
even different voices. But most of all she just laughed at us.
This weird, shrill almost manic laughter. One thing she kept
repeating I can't forget. She kept saying 'I'm the one who
dwelled within Cain' in an eerie voice. During the exorcisms
there was screaming in the camp and breaking of things.
Edwina had an aversion towards religious objects. She would
break pictures of Jesus and pull apart rosaries. The Priest
tried everything, but nothing worked on her. Edwina
endured seventy-six rites of exorcism over a period of ten
months. Over time, the ligaments in her knees ruptured due
to the hundreds of genuflections that she performed obses-
sively during each exorcism session. You know what that is,
right? A genuflection?"

"Sure. Kneeling of some sort?" I answered.

"It's an act of reverence consisting of falling onto one or
both knees. During Edwina's last rite of exorcism, she was
too weak and emaciated to perform the genuflections on her
own. The Priest and Isabella stood by her and helped carry
her through the motions. Her knees were ripped to shreds
and bloodied. They forced her to fast because they believed
that it would rid her of Satan's influence. At the end, she
weighed barely forty pounds."

"Then what happened to her?" I asked.

"The Priest and the rest of the leader group had this idea.
Isabella Dubois had heard of the use of a re-birth as a way of
cleansing a body."

"A re-birth?"

"Yes, the idea was that the demon was supposed to be

born out of Edwina." Mette's eyes teared up suddenly. "Naturally not all of us thought that was a good idea. Several of us tried to protest, but the Priest loved the idea and he always had the final word. No one ever spoke up against him. Hans Christian Bille tried, but ended up being excluded from the leader-group and the Priest hardly ever spoke to him again."

I exhaled deeply. "So what did they do to Edwina?"

Mette looked at me while fighting her tears. "They had sex with her."

Now Mette was crying, letting the tears roll across her cheeks. "They had this ceremony in the courtyard at night where they all wore masks and we were chanting these hymns while watching all the men have sex with that little girl. One after the other they raped her for hours and hours." Mette sobbed. "She was only twelve for Christ sake. I knew then that it wasn't right, but it was too late. No one would listen anymore. Me and Hans Christian kept close after that, trying hard to avoid trouble and the others. I know I should have done something. We all should. It just wasn't right." Mette sighed profoundly. "But I didn't. I have regretted it ever since."

"So what happened to her after that?"

"She became pregnant, right after the plan. The Priest told us the child was the demon that had become flesh. Being pregnant actually did seem to calm her down. She no longer acted crazy and possessed. She almost seemed like a normal little girl except for the growing stomach of course. She was carrying the devil's child, they kept telling her, but I think she didn't believe them. I think she finally found peace within, I could tell in her glowing green eyes that she was looking forward to becoming a mother. Even if it was at a very early age. It was like she grew along with the stomach."

"Did she have the baby?"

Mette dropped her eyes. She seemed weak, tired. I knew I shouldn't keep pushing her, but I really wanted to know.

"She had the baby, yes. They prepared for weeks for the ceremony," Mette said with a feeble voice. "When the contractions began they brought her to a stone altar they had built." Mette sighed and closed her eyes, trying to regain strength. "You have to excuse me," she said. "I haven't spoken about this to anyone before. It's hard to find the words."

I grabbed her hand. "Take your time," I said.

"Edwina screamed as the baby was delivered. It was a perfect little baby boy. They let her see him and she was so happy to see that he didn't have any deformities or abnormalities like she had. He looked perfectly normal. Ten fingers and ten toes just like he was supposed to. The Priest cut the umbilical cord and Edwina was so happy. Right until they took him away from her."

"They took the baby?" I gasped thinking about the time when I had given birth to Julie. I still remembered so vividly that moment when they put her on my stomach. I wanted her to stay there forever, I wanted nothing more of this life at that moment. It was so perfect. I couldn't imagine having her taken away from me like that.

"Yes. They took him and removed her. Then they asked me to clean him up and put him in a small blanket. I did as ordered, but had a horrible feeling inside of me. I didn't know what the plan was or what was to happen to both of them but I had an idea. And I didn't like it one bit."

"What did they do?" My stomach was in a knot now.

Mette sighed. She closed her eyes as she spoke. "They told me to put him on the altar. It took five men to hold Edwina down. They tied her in chains to a pole where she could watch the baby on the altar. I will never forget her screams. I still think I hear them at night sometimes."

"Please tell me they didn't do something to the baby." I was almost in tears now. I wasn't even sure I wanted to hear the rest of this story.

Mette looked at me. She didn't have to speak. I knew the answer.

"Oh my God," I exclaimed heavily.

"They chanted a lot of words in Latin while the baby cried and screamed. They rebuked it as being the devil himself and then they left it to die. It was a February night just like tonight, they snow lay heavy on the land. It was freezing outside. They told us to go back to our rooms and pray while holding on tight to our crucifix cause there was going to be a battle tonight and we were going to win. I shall never forget that night. I lay awake listening to the screams of Edwina and the cries from the baby. I thought so many times of doing something, but I was so scared. I knew they would kill me accusing me of helping the devil. Part of me thought the Priest was doing the right thing. I wanted so badly to believe him. I guess I was nothing but a coward. We all were."

"So they both died that night?"

Mette shook her head. "The screaming died out at some point during the night. We don't know what happened and no one ever dared to speak of it. When we woke up they were both gone. The Priest declared that Edwina had been taken to hell by the devil along with the baby. He looked upon it as a failure. He had not managed to drive the demon out of her body; it had taken both of them with it instead. He wanted us all to be prepared for its return someday. It was going to kill all of us. I guess he was right. It is killing us now."

"Do you believe that?" I asked.

Mette nodded. "I think they both died that night and Edwina has come back from hell to take us all with her."

"So you think that's why some of you are dying?" I asked.

"Because as far as I know you're suffering from radiation sickness. You have somehow been exposed to polonium 210."

She nodded with her eyes closed. I could tell the pain was back. She moaned slightly. "She did it to me somehow. I don't know how, but it is her. She won't stop till she has killed all of us who hurt her back then. The Priest, Hans Christian, Soren, Isabella and me. We all put this on ourselves. We deserve no better."

I searched in my purse and found a notepad and a pen. Then I noted the names she had told me. "Were there others?" I asked.

"No," she said still strained. "Wait. Yes there used to be another man in the leader-group. He left after the first ceremony when Edwina became pregnant. He told the Priest he didn't want to be a part of it anymore."

"What was his name?"

"Bjarne Larsen."

Mette's face became suddenly torn in agony as a new wave of pain rolled in over her. She was gasping for breath and bending forward. Her body was shaking in convulsions, gagging and soon bloody vomit spurted out of her.

I ran to the door and yelled for a nurse to come in. Soon the room was filled with nurses and doctors. The seizure continued and they frantically tried to stop it. I heard them yell as I slowly backed outside to not be in their way.

From behind the door I heard Mette scream. "I see her, I see her. She's here to get me! Don't let her take me!" Then her voice drowned in the sound of her vomiting again. I closed my eyes and bowed my head. The sound of her fighting for her life was horrific. I knew it was a fight she would eventually lose.

A few seconds later Mette Grithfeldt was declared dead.

45

I CRIED DESPERATELY when I finally threw myself in Sune's arms at the inn. I cried for Mette Grithfeldt, for my dad and I cried for Edwina and all the cruelty she had met in this world.

Then I told him the whole story, every little detail that Mette had told me. Sune teared up as well as I spoke. I was sitting in his arms on our bed, talking with a low voice in order to not wake up the kids. Sune opened a small bottle of red wine from the mini bar and poured us each a glass.

"Do you want to go onto the balcony and smoke a cigarette?" he asked his voice thick with grief.

I nodded. I felt like a hypocrite, but I didn't care. It didn't matter right now. I really needed a cigarette, I craved it.

Sune brought a pack and held the lighter for me as I lit it. It was irritating how much I enjoyed it. Especially since I knew I was going to regret it the next day, I always did.

"So what is really going on here?" asked Sune, glass of red wine in his hand. We had put on our big jackets. His finger-tips were already red, as was the tip of his nose. I could see his breath in the air as he spoke.

"I have no idea," I said. "But something is definitely going on. Something really strange."

"We have four dead people in the church - or sect - whatever you want to call it," he stated.

"Four?"

"Yeah. I forgot to tell you. There was another one. They found him yesterday morning. I checked the police report earlier today that's how I know. It's not a story the media care about anymore apparently. His name was Soren something."

I went inside and found my notepad in my purse. "Soren Sejr?" I asked when I came back out.

"Yes. That's him." Sune inhaled his cigarette.

"Another of the leaders from back then," I grumbled. "Now they're all dead except Isabella Dubois and Bjarne Larsen."

"Bjarne Larsen? Wasn't he the guy you visited a couple of days ago and talked to his son?"

"I think so, but I don't know. It's a pretty common name. It could be someone else, but then again, I don't believe in coincidences. Besides it would explain how he knew so much about religious sects. He called them 'Ranters' which isn't something everybody knows what is. I know I didn't until I looked it up."

"Could Edwina still be alive?" asked Sune.

"I have thought about it," I answered. "It's definitely possible. Maybe she came loose from her chains somehow and took the baby and disappeared."

"So maybe she's getting her revenge?" Sune said.

"It is one of my theories. It is after all quite suspicious that it is all of the leaders from back then who are being killed. One of them, Hans Christian, wasn't even in the leader group anymore. He left after the birth of the baby, or was thrown out because he tried to stand up to the Priest. Today the leader group has lots of new members. I remember from my research about them that they are nine leaders now, but only people who were part of the group back then, have died. That's a little too coincidental if you ask me."

"I agree," Sune said. He drank from his wine and stared at the church across from the street. "But Edwina must be what? Twenty-six, twenty-seven?"

"Yes, that's about it. But I don't understand why Mette kept saying she saw the girl in her room the other night. She told me she jumped out the window and ran from her. That's why she ran out in front of my car," I said. "When she died I even heard her scream that she saw her again."

"That is strange," Sune said. "Maybe she was dreaming?"

I sipped my wine. "Maybe," I said.

"So what do we do now?" Sune asked.

I leaned over and kissed him. "Tomorrow I'll call the SIS and tell them about the water post. Then I think I'll pay Bjarne Larsen another visit, I fear that he might be the next victim. Either him or Isabella Dubois, but she is harder to get in contact with."

46

ISABELLA DUBOIS WAS kneeling on the floor. She was clinging on to her silver crucifix asking God to help her and lead her, guide her in the right direction. She wanted to help this church walk in the right direction.

"Forgive us father for we have disappointed you, we have strayed from the path you have given us to walk in. We have been weak and let evil in among us."

Then she stripped off her shirt and took the whip and began whipping her own back leaving big bloody stripes. She moaned in pain but continued undaunted. Pain came before gain. If anyone knew that it was Isabella.

"Please God forgive us, have mercy on our souls for not obeying your commands," Isabella pleaded while crying.

Then she swung the whip once again and moaned in pain and agony. She bent over crying, groaning.

Then she put down the whip and smiled while she kissed her crucifix again and again. She fell to the tiles on her knees in praise of the good Lord, and then kissed the crucifix again and again showing her love and humbling herself to the Lord of Heaven's Armies whose battle she had devoted her life to fight. The battle against all evil here on earth. The battle to outcast the devil.

"I am not worthy, dear God. I am nothing but a humble servant. Please anoint me and grant me the grace to teach my people and direct them," she said while crying and kissing her crucifix. "They are lost in this world, they are like lost sheep who need to be found and directed."

Isabella had heard from God for the first time on the night the Priest had taken her virginity. When he was panting and puffing on top of her she had heard a small still voice inside of her mind. It spoke to her and told her to not be afraid. "One day, one day soon I will exalt you," it said. "I will make you a great leader of this church."

All God wanted Isabella to do was to endure the trials put upon her and wait patiently, and then he promised to guide her to victory, to glorification. She was going to lead all these people, she thought every day looking at all of them filling herself with pride, because God had a special plan for her. She might have to endure pain and humble herself right now, but soon, soon she would taste the sweet taste of triumph.

God hadn't let her down. He had been there through all of her trials, every night when the Priest came to her room, He was there with her, holding her hand, whispering comforting words in her ears, telling her that soon, soon she would be lifted up, soon they were all going to obey her commands and worship her instead.

Her loyalty and obedient behavior had soon paid off. The Priest had grown quite fond of her and soon she was elevated to sit at his table when they ate and she was allowed to have meat and wine with her food. Soon she became a part of the leader group and helped make the important decisions. God showed his faithfulness because she did what he told her to, she obeyed every word and she endured hardship with a happy mind and attitude, because she knew the reward was coming one day. When that thing happened, when that girl, that Chernobyl-kid, arrived at the camp Isabella had sought God's wisdom. She had prayed and heard from Him that now it was her time to flourish. She needed to take over and guide the Priest and the rest of the group in what to do.

"There will be resistance," God had told her. "Some won't like it. But that's the Christian life. You will always be persecuted and ill-treated. But know that I am with you. Know that I am your God."

So she had told the others what she believed God had told her they should do about the girl, to save her from the evil inside of her. Just like God had prepared her for, some of the leaders didn't like the ideas she presented. Some even protested, but not for long. The Priest had understood Isabella's vision and he was behind it right away. He too believed it came from the mighty God himself. So he had listened and Isabella had managed to remove her worst competition from the position as the Priest's right hand. She had managed to remove two of those closest to him, the very two who were supposed to take over once the Priest wasn't there anymore. One left the church completely and the other was disowned by the Priest. Now Isabella was the sole heir to the throne.

Yes, God had been good and faithful in Isabella's life and now he was being faithful again. He was slowly helping her by removing the last competition and resistance in the church that was left. She had no use for them anymore. She was ready to take the throne and claim her right.

Soon she was going to have her victory. What a sweet victory it was going to be. All thanks to the good Lord who would never abandon her and never forget his promises to her.

Isabella was interrupted in her praises when someone knocked at the door. She snorted in irritation and got up to open it. Outside stood one of her loyal leaders, one of those she had trained herself when he arrived at the camp as a teenager. He looked at her and bowed his head in respect as she had taught him to.

Behind him stood two police officers.

47

BJARNE LARSEN STILL thought of himself as a man of God. Even if he had left the church many years ago he still believed in God and in doing good to others. But he had long ago lost his belief in man.

People were in his opinion permeated and poisoned by evil. Especially religious people. They were by far the worst. That lesson had Bjarne Larsen learned many years ago. Religion was the worst thing mankind had ever come up with. It was the cause of most wars and most of the misery found in this forsaken world. Therefore Bjarne Larsen stayed far away from anyone who called himself or herself a religious person. But he hadn't turned his back on God. Not entirely. He still believed in Him.

He just didn't believe He cared about people.

"God decided to leave us all alone many years ago," he told himself as he put water in the kettle and placed it on the stove. "Guess He just had enough of all of our nonsense and cruelty towards each other."

There was a time when Bjarne Larsen believed that God

cared about him and the rest of the people on this earth. Back when he was young and searching for meaning in life he had been part of the Danish Tvind empire - a left wing experiment founded by the mysterious Mogens Amdi Petersen. They were hippies and founded schools in Denmark and traveled to India and created The Necessary Teacher College. They drove in a bus following "The Hippie Trail" through Afghanistan in the late seventies where Bjarne Larsen had met many interesting people among them some who had introduced him to LSD. Bjarne decided then to jump off the bus and stay there a couple of years, but when the Russians invaded the capital Kabul in Seventy-nine he had to go back home to Denmark. By then he was an addict and he continued like that for a few years and thought he was going to be addicted for the rest of his life until he met Anders Granlund. They met at a concert in Copenhagen. Bjarne Larsen was high on drugs yet Anders Granlund had talked to him and started discussing the facts of life and death and suddenly brought the concept of God into the picture. Up until then Bjarne Larsen had never thought about God or even decided if he believed He existed or not. At this point in his life Bjarne Larsen didn't believe in any kind of divinity except for the divine fix of a drug. Suddenly this guy was telling him about how he believed that the devil used things like drugs to keep people from living out their true God-ordained destinies.

Bjarne Larsen had liked that. He liked the idea that there was a plan for his life and suddenly he realized that he was in fact wasting his life away. Even if it was his favorite band playing at the concert, he had at that instant decided to go with Anders Granlund.

Back then "The Way" was an idea and Anders Granlund was nothing but a man with a vision, a dream. There was no camp and no church members. It was just him and a small apartment in Copenhagen that Bjarne followed him into. Anders locked him into a room for a week in that apartment and only provided food and water and a silver crucifix. Every day for hours and hours Anders sat outside the door and read from the bible while Bjarne knocked and banged on the door screaming for a fix, yelling that he needed drugs, but Anders never gave in to his demands and soon Bjarne was clean, the evil was driven out of him. Anders opened the door and brought Bjarne into the kitchen where he made a meal for him and congratulated him on his accomplishment. They prayed for Bjarne's healing and Bjarne asked God to forgive his sins.

Later Anders told Bjarne that he needed people like him. If Bjarne wanted to he could help him start a new movement, what he believed would be a new wave in Christianity in this country, maybe even the world. Anders had visions of saving people all over the world and reaching out to the lost ones.

Bjarne really liked that too.

So Bjarne told him about his childhood town of Arnakke where his parents owned a big property. He told them most of the land had been used as a campground for schools but it had been closed off for years now. Bjarne told him his parents owned that land and that they could move in there and begin rebuilding it for a small monthly payment.

So the next day they had gone to see Bjarne's dad who was so thrilled to see his son again and see that he was free from the bondage of drugs and now had found Jesus and wanted to become a Christian and help others.

"You can stay in the camp as long as you want," his dad had told them. "I'll help you rebuild it. I'm just so happy that my boy is finally back," he had cried.

That's how "The Way" ended up in Arnakke and now

since Bjarne had inherited the property he was now also the rightful owner of the camp. That was how he managed to leave the church again after almost fifteen years. That's why the Priest had to let him go without stopping him like he normally did.

When and where it all went wrong at the camp, Bjarne Larsen couldn't tell, but somehow along the way they all got lost. Bjarne Larsen tried on several occasions to point out that he disapproved of the way they treated the young people, how they were used as forced labor, of the way they weren't allowed to leave and especially how they treated that young girl who couldn't help it.

"She is mentally ill. She needs medication," he kept telling them. But no one listened. He tried everything to help her and got the idea that maybe she suffered from some sort of brain damage caused by the exposure to radiation while she was still in her mother's womb. But he couldn't get them to listen to his arguments, and then they came up with that horrendous idea to impregnate her.

Bjarne Larsen sighed when he heard the water boil. He got up from his chair and searched for the coffee in the cabinet. He never liked thinking about what had happened back then, but it wasn't healthy to keep things like that bottled up inside. That they all had sex with the girl wasn't the worst part for him, the worst part was that he had participated. Bjarne hadn't said no and he had regretted that all of his life. You could call it peer pressure, you could call it fear, but Bjarne knew the real reason why he hadn't said no.

Because he wanted to. He wanted to have sex with that girl. Oh, the realization of your own weakness, it hurt so bad, so deeply. The pain and the anguish of regretting your past had almost eaten him up afterwards.

Once the night was over he had cried and punished

himself with the whip again and again, punishing himself for this secret pleasure, this desire that could be born from nothing but evil.

That was when he realized that they were in fact the ones that had evil living inside of them. All these religious hypocrites were in fact pure evil. He was evil. That realization made him leave the church and the camp during the night.

He had only been back once since. To reclaim was what rightfully his.

48

I CALLED GUNNAR Moll at the SIS first thing in the morning and told him about the water post and how I suspected it was the source that had contaminated my dad. Gunnar Moll was very happy to hear from me and told me they would send a team out there immediately to seal it and examine the area.

"If it's in the water at the post then it might be the source of what has contaminated the people in the camp."

"That's what I thought," I replied. "But what I wonder is how it got into the water in the first place?"

Bjarne Moll cleared his throat. "Well that is a good question, since polonium-210 is not something you come across every day. It's very difficult to get a hold of. Polonium in large quantities can only be used by the government of a country that has military or civilian nuclear facilities. Only a few countries produce polonium. One of them is Russia because the country produces polonium for industry."

"So that's why they think the Russian government was behind the death of Alexander Litvinenko?"

"Precisely," he answered.

"So what you're telling me is basically that this can't be an accident? It can't accidentally have spilled into the water?" I asked.

"No it can't. Someone must have put it there for some reason. Someone poisoned that water."

"But if the water is contaminated then why didn't anyone else in the area get sick? Why is it only the people living in the camp? And why only some of them?" I said.

"That's a also a good question. We'll have to look into all that. I alerted the police after the doctor discovered that they had a patient who was killed by polonium and the forensic lab is now testing the bodies to learn if the three others also were killed by it. They decided to evacuate the camp and I have a team at the hospital in Holbaek right now cleansing all of the church members. That'll give us time and room to investigate the water up there as well."

We drove the kids to the hospital to be with my dad who was thrilled to have some "intelligent company for once," as he put it. After talking a little with Dad we drove to the local police station and told them all we knew. They were very interested and Officer Frederik Knudsen who was in charge of the investigation listened carefully and wrote everything down on a notepad. We told him that we thought the church members were being killed and that we feared that Bjarne Larsen would be the next victim. Isabella was already in a safe place at the hospital so I wasn't worried about her.

"Those are the last two who were part of the leader group back then," I said.

Officer Knudsen nodded slowly and pensively. I got the sense that he didn't quite believe us even if he wanted to.

"Listen," I said. "We know it's a strange story, but polonium 210 is not something that appears by a coincidence.

Someone has put it in the water up there to kill those people. Four are dead already."

Officer Frederik Knudsen leaned backwards with a deep sigh. "I am very interested about the story about the girl Edwina and we will certainly look into that. If what you're telling me is true, then it is very serious. About the other stuff, I hear all you're saying, but the problem I'm facing is I just received a phone call a minute before you stepped into the police station from the SIS telling us the water is clean. There is no contamination of the water in the camp. Not of polonium 210 or anything else. The water is clean."

I looked at Sune. He shrugged. "I don't understand," I said. "I was so certain."

"Well, all I can do is look at the facts and they're telling me that if these people were killed by polonium 210, they didn't get it through the water. The SIS did find some by that water-post you told them about. But only very little and it was on the post, on the handle, not in the water."

"It had to have come into the camp from somewhere else," I mumbled. "I still feel we should talk to Bjarne Larsen."

Officer Knudsen nodded. "I have a few questions for him of my own. I'll go with you."

49

BJARNE LARSEN'S HANDS were shaking slightly when he pulled out the cups from the cabinet. He wanted to use the nice ones like his wife always did.

It had been hard the last couple of weeks, trying to get by on his own since his wife Elisabeth had left him. He was still wondering why she had chosen to leave him like that after thirteen years of marriage. He had met her two years after leaving the church and had considered the years following as the happiest years of his life. But Bjarne had refused to tell Elisabeth about his past and questions kept popping up in her, even if she knew he would get mad and sometimes even violent when she brought up his past, she would do it anyway from time to time. Bjarne had no answers to give her, only that he wasn't very proud of his former life, but that was his past now. Yet she kept asking.

Then finally seven weeks ago he had decided to tell her everything. He told her about Afghanistan, the drugs, about Anders Granlund, the church and even what they had done to that girl.

Elisabeth had looked at him with tears in her eyes. She

hadn't spoken a single word for almost half an hour. Then she had gotten up from her chair and gone upstairs only to return with a suitcase in her hand. She hadn't even told him she was leaving. She just looked at him with wet eyes, touched him gently on the cheek, then walked out the door and never looked back. Bjarne hadn't heard anything from her since. Not a phone call, not a postcard or an e-mail. Not even a message on Facebook where he had tried to track her down by constantly checking her account. But she hadn't posted anything, not a status, not even a whereabouts. Bjarne didn't know where she was or if he was ever going to see her again.

That was when he had decided it was time to do something. He had thought about it for years, but like the coward he had always been, he hadn't done anything. Now he became determined. It had already ruined too much for him. It was time to get rid of the past.

Eliminate it.

Bjarne put down the cups from Royal Copenhagen that they had inherited from Elisabeth's mother. His hands were still shaking, something they had done a lot lately. Bjarne feared it might be beginning of Parkinson's disease that his dad had suffered from until he died more than ten years ago. He kept postponing the inevitable visit with the doctor. He was afraid of what the doctor was going to tell him. Bjarne focused on keeping them still. It helped sometimes if he was really concentrating. At other times it only made things worse.

Bjarne sighed deeply while remembering his dad. How he had high hopes for Bjarne. He had tried to teach him about farming and wanting him to take over the farm. But Bjarne didn't want to. He wanted to change the world, he told him, just before he left for Afghanistan. Little could he have known that the people he met in Afghanistan were nothing but scum, introducing him to drugs and later on weapons. They wanted him to fight with them to take back their country, they said and promised him lots of opium and LSD if he decided to go with them. Then they showed him an arsenal of weapons and bombs and told him they were going to overthrow the king and make way for the country's first president. The king was about to leave on a trip overseas and that was when they were going to do it. Bjarne ended up helping them, fighting for what he believed was their freedom. They managed to do it and changed the history of Afghanistan. Later when the Soviets and the Americans both began spreading their influences in Afghanistan, Bjarne and his friends fought for the Soviets and were heavily provided with weapons and artillery from the Russians - along with all the drugs they wanted of course. Once the Soviet soldiers invaded Kabul Bjarne was forced to leave even if he had been on their side. It was all good the same, he had thought back then. Drugs had become harder to get a hold off and he was tired of fighting a war that wasn't his.

Bjarne's hands were steadier now and he managed to pour the coffee into the pot without spilling. He found the bowl with sugar and warmed some milk in the microwave. There were still a few cookies left that he placed neatly in a circle on a platter. It all looked nice, almost like when Elisabeth had prepared it for guests coming to their home. Bjarne felt a pinch in his heart. Boy, he missed having her around the house. He even missed her nagging. Was he ever going to see her again? He thought as he took off the lid of the small transparent vial carrying the expensive silver powder. Almost without shaking he poured some into a spoon and poured it all into the pot with the burning hot coffee.

"Tasteless and odorless," he mumbled when he turned it with the spoon. "Impossible to trace before it's too late." That was what his Afghani friends had told him when he travelled back to see them and asked for help. It was probably stolen from a Russian nuclear reactor, he suspected. It cost him a huge fortune, but it was worth it. It was even more concentrated and a larger dose than what was used to kill that KGB agent, Litvinenko, they said. Even so he had certainly been surprised at how fast it had killed his old friends. The choice of poison was genius in that polonium, carried in a vial, could be carried in a pocket through airport screening devices without setting off any alarms. His friends had assured him that once ingested, the polonium would create symptoms that didn't suggest poison. It would target the spleen and liver first since those organs were much smaller than the rest of the body. Once concentrated in those vital organs there was no turning back. It would soon bring severe damage to the nervous system. Within minutes, the patient was going to suffer severe vomiting, dizziness and headache before falling unconscious. Seizures and tremors were common as well and they would also lose control of muscle movement. The victim would certainly die within hours of these symptoms.

Bjarne Larsen felt more confident now that it was done. He put the lid back on the pot and wiped away a drop of sweat from his forehead. Then he put the vial back in the cabinet and closed it.

He lifted the tray and began walking towards the living room where his guests were waiting for him by the fireplace.

50

U NFORTUNATELY THEY HAD brought a police officer with them. Bjarne Larsen had at first been a little taken aback by it, but then felt it left him with no choice. They all knew too much and it was only a matter of time before they figured everything out.

He couldn't have that. Not now when he was almost done. He had almost gotten away with it and they weren't going to spoil that. There was no way he would let them.

Bjarne Larsen smiled and tried to put down the tray on the table in front of them. His hands had started shaking again and he almost dropped everything, but luckily the young man with the Mohawk got up and grabbed the tray for him.

"Let me help you," he said and together they put down the heavy tray with the cups from Royal Copenhagen.

The young man set the cups in front of the guests. Bjarne Larsen was sweating heavily now.

"I'm sorry," he said. "The wife's out of town and it's hard to try and do it all on my own."

Officer Knudsen that Bjarne had known for years nodded

and smiled. He grabbed a cookie from the platter and started eating. The crouching sound was loud in Bjarne's head and he felt his heart race faster. His eyes remained fixated on the officer's mouth where crumbs landed on his lips and he used the tongue to remove them. His mouth looked dry when he chewed with it half open. Bjarne sat down with a sigh. Then he nodded slowly.

"Have some coffee," he said.

The young reporter woman, Rebekka, leaned over and grabbed the pot. Bjarne Larsen felt a pinch of excitement. This was the first time he was actually present when the powder was ingested. He wondered how long it would take for them to have actual symptoms. Minutes? Hours? Days? He didn't know and neither did the people who gave him the powder. They just knew it would kill, painfully eating the victim's internal organs one by one. The best part was that it only killed if you inhaled or ingested it. It wasn't dangerous to you if you accidentally touched it. That was very unique for a radioactive material. Bjarne had found it perfect to kill by using a radioactive material when revenging Edwina. Oh the joy he had felt when he realized that the church members actually had thought that it was the devil that had possessed the victims. He had wanted so badly to be present to watch their faces trying to rebuke the devil, he wanted to feel their fear when they thought it might have been Edwina coming back from hell to take them. He didn't doubt for one second that all four of them had seen her when they died. His Afghani friends had told him they would have hallucinations once the polonium attacked the brain. Some might even have experienced paranoia, seeing and hearing things, thinking someone was after them. If there was anything Bjarne knew about, it was hallucinations and paranoia caused by drugs. They would always show your worst fear, displayed like a living nightmare. Bjarne almost laughed out loud just by thinking about it. Served them well, he thought to himself. For doing what they did to Edwina.

"So given the circumstances of the deaths we are naturally worried about you and your son, since you used to be a part of the leader group at the time," Officer Knudsen said.

Bjarne hadn't been listening to what the officer said. He didn't have to. Bjarne nodded and smiled and told them to drink some coffee or have another cookie. Still none of them had touched it.

It will come, he calmed himself down. He sensed how his hands and legs were shaking heavily now. It will come. They have to drink at some point. The cookies are making them thirsty.

Bjarne smiled while he watched the officer lean over and grab another cookie. "These are really good," he said.

Bjarne smiled and nodded. "The wife's recipe." He watched as crumbs landed on the officer's chin. His mouth looked so dry now. It would only be a matter of seconds before he would drink some coffee. Then the others would follow. Of course they would. They had to. They weren't going to leave this house alive. Bjarne would make sure they didn't.

A sigh of relief burst out of him as he watched the officer lean over and lift the cup between his fingers. Then he smiled and nodded as the officer dragged it closer to the mouth and tipped it. Bjarne Larsen felt a thrill inside as he watched the black liquid disappear into the officer's broad mouth. It almost made him want to clap his hands in excitement.

One down, only two more to go.

51

I FELT STRANGE sitting in Bjarne Larsen's couch watching Officer Knudsen tell him about the killings and our concerns. It was like Bjarne Larsen wasn't listening at all. It was like he was in a world of his own and wasn't interested in what we were telling him. It worried me. His manic eyes stared at Officer Knudsen drinking his coffee troubled me. It was like he enjoyed watching him drink his coffee a little too much. What about the sweating and the shaking? Something was off here, even for him. I looked at Sune. He didn't touch the cookies nor the coffee. I had warned him in the car driving there, following Officer Knudsen in his police car.

"Whatever you do, don't drink the coffee," I said. "It's horrible. Almost killed me the last time I was here." Then we laughed. If there was one thing Sune and I agreed upon it was that life was too short for bad coffee.

"Thanks for the warning," he said as we left the car.

Now I kind of regretted it looking at Officer Knudsen drinking it and slurping it. Maybe it was better this time? Maybe he was getting the hang of it? I thought. I stared at the cup. It looked just as thick as the last time. I poured in some milk and started turning my spoon. I was really in the mood for coffee. I could really go for it, I thought, but then again I really didn't want it if it tasted anything remotely like what I had the first time I was there. I put in a teaspoon of sugar and turned again. It still looked bad. Bjarne Larsen was watching me. His eyes were strange, almost feverish. I couldn't quite figure him out.

"Do you have any idea on who would want to kill all the members of the leader group from back then?" I asked him thinking maybe he could shed some light on the case that we hadn't thought of on our own. "Did you make any enemies?"

"I guess most people never cared much about us," he answered. "The locals wanted us out, especially back when the Priest was very active in the media and often appeared on TV. They thought we brought bad publicity to the area."

"So why did you leave the church?" I asked.

"I guess we went in different directions. I wanted something for this church. Anders, the Priest wanted something else. We had to part ways."

He didn't want to talk about what had happened, that was fair enough, but I wasn't going to let him off the hook that easy, I thought. He could provide me some of the answers I was missing.

"There was a girl," I said. "Edwina, I believe she was called. She was at your camp, but then disappeared. Do you have any idea what happened to her?"

Bjarne's face froze. He stared at me with agitated eyes. Sune leaned over. "It's okay. We know the story about what they did to her," he said. "We also heard that you left the church because of what they did to her."

"We're not interested in your part in this," Officer

Knudsen said. "But your testimony could turn out to be very important to us and I'm sure you could make a deal if you chose to talk, a deal so you wouldn't be prosecuted if you told everything. We're extremely interested in the leader, Isabella Dubois and her involvement in what happened."

Bjarne stared, still frozen solid.

"What happened to the girl?" Officer Knudsen asked. "Where is she?"

Then something truly awkward and weird happened. Bjarne Larsen began to laugh. Not a normal laughter, but a frantic, hysterical one. I was beginning to think he was losing it.

"Well it seems you know everything, don't you?" he said. "I might as well tell you."

"That would be nice," Officer Knudsen said.

"First let me pour you some more coffee," Bjarne said and grabbed the pot. He filled up Officer Knudsen's cup. I declined stating I still had enough in my cup. Sune didn't want anything either. Officer Knudsen drank more from his. We all waited expectantly for him to begin talking.

Bjarne Larsen exhaled deeply. His eyes dropped to the ground, then he looked at me. "She died," he suddenly said. "On the night that she gave birth to the baby I went back to the forest to save her. I knew what their plan was. I had decided not to interfere anymore, but as the night progressed and I heard her screaming through the forest I realized I couldn't let this happen. I had to do something. But when I arrived she was dead. She had lost a lot of blood from the birth. There was a pool underneath her. Apparently she hadn't stopped bleeding after giving birth, so she bled to death."

"So she is dead?" I asked quite startled. I was so certain

she was alive and revenging herself. "But what about the baby?"

Bjarne looked at me. That was when it finally clicked.

"Ole is the baby, isn't he?" I asked. "Ole is Edwina's son."

"I went back and got him. Edwina was dead. I threw her body in the fjord thinking she would turn up eventually and the police would come after the church members. If I had left her they would have just buried her and no one would know what they had done. I had hoped that they would get what they deserved once the body was discovered. But it never turned up. I have gone down there often to see if I could find it, but it's gone."

I leaned back in the couch. "So you have been killing them, haven't you? You're the one trying to get rid of all the group leaders from back then. You're avenging Edwina and Ole?"

"Someone had to do something before they did it again. I waited for years for the police to discover the body but that never happened. I waited for them to screw up otherwise, but they never did. I realized I had to get rid of them on my own."

I looked at Officer Knudsen. He was pale and didn't seem well. A fear struck me. Sune leaned over and grabbed his coffee cup and lifted it up to his mouth. I pushed it out of his hand, causing it to tumble on the carpet.

"It's in the coffee," I said.

Sune gasped and wiped his mouth on his sleeve. Officer Knudsen looked at me with fear. He was even paler now, almost greenish in his face.

"We need to get you to the hospital," I said and got up from the couch.

Then I heard steps on the stairs behind us and turned around. Ole was walking down slowly with a rifle pointing directly at us. My heart started racing.

"The doctors say he has a slight brain damage," Bjarne said. "They don't know why, but I know. I have talked to specialists about it. His mother had it too. It's from the radiation Edwina was exposed to when she was in her mother's womb. Ole won't get old. He'll probably die from leukemia in ten or fifteen years. He is not going to spend them in jail. He is the only thing I've ever done right in this world. When I asked God to forgive me after that night when we made Edwina pregnant, he told me to go and make things right again. That's what I've done. I've taken care of Ole and now I have avenged his mother."

Ole walked closer still pointing at us with his hunting rifle.

"He is a very skilled hunter," Bjarne continued. "He never misses a target, so I wouldn't try anything if I were you."

"You had Ole do it, didn't you?" I continued. "He knows how to climb the fence and get into the property. He knows his way around and how to avoid the surveillance cameras. He put it in something, the food or something they drink. He did the dirty work."

Bjarne nodded. "He wanted to. I had to let him do it. My hands are not what they used to be." He lifted his hands. They were shaking heavily.

I turned and looked at Ole. "You spilled some didn't you? You got it on your fingers and were scared of what it might do to you, you ran through the forest and found a water post. You washed it off there, am I right?"

Ole nodded. "I spilled some on my finger where I had a wound. I was afraid it would penetrate the skin through it and get into my bloodstream. So I washed it off. All it left was this small rash," he said and showed his finger.

"What do you want to do with us?" I asked Bjarne. "We

need to get officer Knudsen to the hospital immediately. He will die if we don't."

"I'm afraid you all have to die," Bjarne Larsen said. "As much as I want to, I can't let you leave here knowing the things you do. I just can't."

O LE CAME DOWN the stairs still pointing at us with his rifle. Officer Knudsen tried to stand up, but felt too sick and had to sit back down. I spotted his weapon in his belt. He tried to grab for it, but had to bend over and throw up on the couch. Bjarne approached him and took his gun. Then he put it to his head and fired. I screamed as Officer Knudsen sank onto the couch, dead.

Then I looked at Sune. His eyes were suddenly filled with fear like I've never seen before. These people were serious, I realized. They weren't bluffing. Killing a police officer in cold blood like that meant they had no remorse in killing us as well. I turned and looked at Ole. I was breathing frantically now. I knew I had to react within seconds or they would shoot us. Frantically my eyes searched across the room, the dresser, the stairs, the hallway. I spotted the switch behind Ole's back. Then I grabbed a lamp and threw it as hard as I could towards Ole. He bent his head and as he did I sprang for the light switch. When I flipped it the entire room went black. Long live the dark Danish winters, I thought as I felt Sune grab my arm and we ran up the stairs. Bjarne was

standing near the main entrance so up was the only way out
for us. We jumped the stairs and heard shots being fired
behind us. Then we turned the corner and ran into a room.
Sune found a dresser and blocked the door with it.

I was hyperventilating, finding it hard to even draw in a
breath. My head was pounding with fear. There was one
window in the room, that seemed to be an office of some sort.
And underneath it stood Bjarne pointing the sheriff's gun at
us. When he spotted me he fired a shot that hit the roof right
above us. I jumped backwards. Then I heard knocking.

Ole's voice was right outside the door. "There is no way
out," he said almost giggling.

I gasped and clung to Sune. "Don't answer him," he whispered. "We'll find a way out." He began searching the room
desperately. "There has to be something in here we can use,"
he said going through closets and looking under the desk.

"Can't we call for help? We have our phones," I asked.

"I'm afraid we'll be dead before they get here," Sune said.

"I'll try it anyway."

I found my phone and just as I was about to dial 911
Bjarne fired another shot that went straight through the glass
and left a perfect little whole through the shattered glass. I
screamed and dropped the phone as I watched the bullet
land in the wall and leave a small but deep hole.

Ole started banging on the door causing it to start cracking. A loud noise followed and a huge crack was made in the
wooden door. The blade from an axe went through it, then
disappeared until it returned after another loud noise and
another crack was formed in the door.

I screamed. "He's getting in!" I yelled and picked up my
phone. "Sune, he is destroying the door with an axe!"

I fumbled with the phone again trying to call when Ole

was able to stick his head through one of the cracks and peer through it.

"Here's Johnny!" he screamed, impersonating Jack Nicholson.

Soon the hole in the door was so big Ole could manage to get his body in and pull himself up on the dresser. He smiled widely while he stared at us. We were trapped. Then he jumped into the room and knocked Sune over with the end of his rifle.

I screamed as I watched Sune tumble to the floor unconscious. I approached Ole but he hit me in the face and caused me to fall backwards. My phone landed on the floor next to me.

He walked slowly towards me with the rifle loose in his hand. Then he leaned over and grabbed my face clutching it between his fingers.

"I thought I would get my way with you some day," he said. "I knew you would be back for me. I knew you liked it rough. Am I right?" Ole licked his lips. Then he giggled. He put down the rifle and began opening his pants. He pulled off his belt. Then he swung it and slapped it across my chest. I screamed. He kept beating me with his belt while laughing.

"Feisty one, huh? I like them feisty. Like the Priest in the forest. He liked them wild. I do too. I liked to watch him with them."

Ole tied my hands with his belt, while I kicked and screamed. Then he began pulling his pants down and taking out his sex. He touched himself while moaning. "I'm almost ready for you," he said. He looked like he was feeding off my fear.

I heard Bjarne yell from outside, but Ole never answered him. He started fumbling with my jeans. I tossed and writhed my body trying to kick him but it was no good. He was too strong.

Dear God please don't let this happen. Please don't let him do this to me.

I let out as huge scream but he covered my mouth with his hand and got on top of me. He pulled down my pants and stuck in his hand and started touching me. I groaned, tried to get my mouth free, tried to bite him, but had no luck. I moved desperately. I tossed and screamed, but nothing but a muffled sound came out.

I began crying, almost giving up when I saw movement behind Ole's back. I watched Sune as he got to his feet, grabbed the rifle and hit Ole with the shaft so hard it made a cracking sound when it hit his head. Ole fell to the ground bleeding. Sune removed the belt and grabbed my hand and after I had picked up my phone he helped me climb the dresser. We sprinted to the stairs and jumped down the steps. When we reached the bottom, Bjarne came walking in the door, pointing the gun at us.

"Lose the rifle," he said to Sune.

Sune obeyed. Carefully he bent to the floor and put it down.

"Now kick it over here to me," Bjarne said.

Sune did as he was told. I felt rage growing inside of me. Exploding rage. Bjarne moved closer and picked up the rifle. He put it in the corner.

"Don't you understand that I was only doing you all a favor?" he asked walking closer to us. "You should all be thanking me."

I was breathing heavily while a million thoughts ran through my mind. I remembered having taken a self-defense class once. If only he would come close enough, I thought and stared at him while he walked. Just a few more steps.

Bjarne kept talking about how they had all deserved it for doing what they did to that poor girl. Just one more step. As he came closer and closer he lifted the gun towards my head, ready to pull the trigger as soon as he was done talking. I calmed myself down by breathing steadily, thinking only of getting back to Julie. Then I lifted my hand as fast as I could, stuck out my pointer finger and jammed it as hard as I could directly into Bjarne's eye. When he recoiled while whining I kicked him as hard as I could in the crotch. While Bjarne bent over and dropped the gun Sune managed to hit him on the jaw and the blow forced him to the ground, unconscious.

Then we ran to our car as fast as we could.

53

W E CALLED THE police from our car and told them to go to Bjarne Larsen's house immediately. There was a dead police officer and two unconscious murderers. I told them we were going to the hospital and they could find us there for our statement later.

"There is something important we need to take care of first."

Soon I heard sirens wailing in the distance and for the first time in many hours my heart calmed down. I just hoped they would get to Bjarne's house before he and his son woke up.

Arriving at the hospital I ran straight to the reception and asked for the Director of the SIS, Gunnar Moll. I pulled out my press-card. I knew he was there to clean the church members and check them for radiation exposure, I told her.

"He knows who I am. You can call him if you want."

"Fourth floor, department 5432," the receptionist told us.

We ran for the stairs, jumped them and burst into the hallway. A nurse tried to stop us.

"This is restricted area," she said.

"I need to talk to Gunnar Moll immediately," I said, panting from running up the many stairs. "It's very urgent."

"I'm right here. What's going on?" I heard Gunnar's voice behind the nurse. "Rebekka Franck? What happened to you?"

That was when I realized I probably looked like a homeless person. My clothes were torn, my face beat up by Ole.

"I don't have much time. I might even be too late. Isabella Dubois. Where is she? We know who the killer is, who gave them the polonium, and we know she is his last victim. We need to stop her before she gets sick."

"She's in her room," he said. "She has refused to participate in any of this. We haven't even been able to wash her let alone take her blood test."

"I need to see her," I said. "I need to warn her."

"Sure. I'll show the way." Gunnar Moll started walking. He stopped in front of a door. "She's right in here. If you could get her to cooperate with us then I would be very grateful. She has this idea that she doesn't need our help."

"I'll try," I said.

Carefully I pushed the door open and entered her room. Isabella was kneeling on the floor with her head bowed. She looked pale and weaker than last time I saw her. Between her hands she was holding her silver crucifix. She lifted it and was about to kiss it.

"Stop!" I screamed.

I ran towards her. She turned her head and stared at me. "It's on the crucifix," I said breathing heavily. Isabella looked at her silver crucifix then dropped it to the floor. Gunnar Moll came in behind me.

"It just struck me now," I said. "They all carry these crucifixes and they kiss it several times a day. Bjarne knew that, so he had Ole dip the crucifixes in the polonium 210 powder.

That way he could control who was exposed to it. When they kiss it, it enters via the mouth when they lick their lips. Every day they received a small dose, just enough to one day make their bodies sick, but not enough to make it easy to trace."

Gunnar Moll put on a plastic glove then picked up the crucifix. "We'll have it checked right away," he said and gave it to a nurse who sealed it and left the room in a hurry. Gunnar Moll put his hand on Isabella's shoulder. She looked at him with fear in her eyes. "We need to have your blood checked immediately," he said.

Isabella Dubois nodded heavily. Then she started crying.

54

O NLY A FEW days later we were all back home in Karrebaeksminde again. Dad was feeling better and the doctor told him that the medicine, the Dimercaprol, seemed to be working on him. They still couldn't guarantee that he wouldn't eventually get sick from the exposure to the polonium, but so far his body seemed to be doing fine.

My dad accepted that and decided to live like every day was his last.

"Well I always do that anyway," he said laughing on the way home in the car. "Cause when you pass seventy, every day could be your last, right?"

"I'm so happy to have you back," Julie said and hugged his arm.

The house and the town hadn't changed, we were happy to realize. We hadn't been gone long, but it felt like forever, like everything had changed in us with all we had been through. If nothing else, then it had certainly brought us closer together. Even Sune and I who enjoyed each other even more than before. I decided to stop over thinking everything and just live life.

I talked to Jens-Ole as soon as we got home and had unpacked. I told him I had a great story for him, unlike anything he had ever published in his paper. He listened very carefully as I explained what had happened to the sect and the members.

He was in a state of shock when I was done, I could tell by his long silence.

"So do you want it or not?" I asked.

"Are you kidding me?" he answered.

I laughed. "Thought so. I'll write it tomorrow. Today we're unpacking."

"That's a deal," he said.

Then we hung up. I stared at my wonderful family who were already playing some board game in the kitchen, very loudly discussing a rule that Julie and Tobias weren't agreeing upon. Sune sneaked up behind me and hugged me tight. I closed my eyes and enjoyed it.

"It's good to be back home," I mumbled.

Sune kissed my neck. "Mmm," he said.

"Case is closed," I said while enjoying his kisses and touches. "Ole and Bjarne are in the hands of the police now."

He stopped and looked out the window. "I do still wonder what happened to the body of Edwina, though," he said.

"Yeah. Me too," I answered.

We both went quiet for a little while. Sune was staring out the window at the snow that was still falling slowly from the sky. It had been snowing all day, it felt like it wasn't going to stop. They had just managed to clean the roads enough for us to be able to drive home. By the next morning they would be blocked once again if it continued.

I thought about Isabella for a second. The doctors didn't know if she was going to make it or not. She had been exposed to a big dosage of polonium, the test results showed, but how severe it was they didn't know when we left the hospital with my dad. Time would show if she could survive it and if she would be healthy enough to be prosecuted for what she had done.

"Say, do you still want that baby?" I asked. I was surprised to hear the words come out of my mouth so I really couldn't blame Sune for being astonished as well.

He froze completely. Then he looked at me. "Why are you asking this now?"

I shrugged with a laugh. "Don't know. Guess all this made me think."

"Think about what? Having babies?" Sune looked at me like I had gone mad.

"No. About how short life is, silly. About taking the chances life gives you."

"Ah, a little like 'Life gives you lemons so make lemonade,' is that it?"

I pushed him gently." I'm serious here," I said. "Maybe we should do something. Maybe we should embrace our love by making our family bigger."

Sune grabbed me and pulled me closer. "I have an idea," he said.

I kissed his arm holding me tight. "Mmm?"

"How about we try and move in together first? Then see what happens from there? What do you say to that?"

I smiled widely, then I kissed him on the lips. He closed his eyes and tasted the kiss for long after it was over.

"I say it is a wonderful idea," I whispered while our faces were still close together.

Sune kissed me again. Then Tobias called him from the kitchen. Sune kissed me one last time then went in there to help him. The kids were discussing wildly. It made me chuckle. I looked at my phone. I had changed the picture to one of my dad holding the kids. Still having him in my life was truly a gift. I sighed and shut off the phone when someone suddenly knocked on the door. It was a heavy knock, not a gentle one and made me jump slightly. I looked through the peep hole then opened the door.

"Peter?"

Peter smiled and gesticulated. "I'm back," he said. "In a better shape than ever." He sighed deeply with a wide smile. I felt confused, startled. He looked great.

"I'd like to see Julie if I may?"

EPILOGUE

ESTHER PETERSEN was walking through the forest. Why she didn't know but she knew she was searching for something, maybe even someone. It was pitch dark between the pine trees yet she knew how to find her way. She followed a trail on the ground. It looked like small footsteps, made by someone with small feet, maybe a child. They were glowing in the dark night, casting a green light for her to follow. Deeper and deeper she went into the dark forest. She felt scared when she heard an owl in a tree and when she thought she heard a dog bark in the distance. It was full moon and every now and then she could see it through the moving clouds in the sky, and every now and then it would peek through the trees and light her way. She didn't know why she knew she was supposed to follow these glowing footprints, only that she knew she had to. She had this urgent feeling that this was very important, it was crucial even - that she followed them till the end.

Now Esther Petersen was an elderly woman but she had always kept the old body in great shape. Even though, she was quite impressed with the endurance that she displayed

almost running through the pine forest. She felt something
she hadn't done in years, she felt light on feet, and filled with
an energy that seemed to never run dry. She ran through
piles of snow, through almost impassable paths, she ran but
couldn't even hear her own heartbeat or her panting breath.
She stayed focused on the footprints in front of her and
where they led her until she finally reached the end of the
forest. Then she stopped. She was standing in front of the
fjord. It was right beneath her and the hill she was standing
on. The glowing footprints continued all the way into the
water and she followed them as far as she could, down the
hill and into a small rocky beach. Then she froze. A huge
spot in the dark water in front of her was glowing green.
Something was in there. She leaned over and gasped. A small
face was looking back at her. The face of a little girl. Two
green eyes were staring at her from underneath the water.
She had seen the face before and knew those eyes and the
crooked face. The girl smiled, then she laughed, causing the
water to bubble. Esther backed up, falling over small rocks as
she watched the girl elevate from the water and walk towards
her pointing at her with a glowing green finger.

"You!" she yelled, still pointing.

Esther Petersen woke up panting and gasping for air in
her bed. Her heart was beating faster and faster and she
could hardly catch her breath. The door to her room opened
and her daughter walked in. Her sweet beautiful daughter
that had stayed the night with her mother because Esther
hadn't been feeling well the night before. The daughter
looked at her and stroked her hair gently.

"She's coming to get us," Esther finally managed to say
while panting. "She's coming!"

"What are you talking about?" the daughter said desperately trying to make sense of her mother's words.

Esther stared at her daughter. Then she froze. She gasped for air a few times, her body shaking like in a seizure.

Then she drew in her last breath and died.

THE END

Want to know what happens next? Get *Seven, Eight ... Gonna stay up late* **here:**

Seven, eight ...Gonna stay up late

Want to read Edwina's story? Get it here:

Edwina

AFTERWORD

Dear reader,

Thank you for purchasing *Five, Six ... Grab your crucifix.* I hope you enjoyed reading it as much as I did writing it.

If you liked the settings and the creepy parts, then you might as well enjoy the series of scary short-stories that I've written. *Horror Stories from Denmark* . They all take place in Rebekka Franck's hometown and are related to this series.

I also put in an excerpt of my new series that takes place in Cocoa Beach, Florida.

Don't forget to check out my other books as well. You can buy them by following the links below. And don't forget to leave reviews if possible. It means so much to me to hear what you think.

Take care,

Willow Rose

Connect with Willow online and you will be the first to know about new releases and bargains from Willow Rose:

Sign up to the VIP email here:
http://eepurl.com/vVfEf

I promise not to share your email with anyone else, and I won't clutter your inbox. I'll only contact you when a new book is out or when I have a special bargain/free eBook.

Follow Willow Rose on BookBub:
https://www.bookbub.com/authors/willow-rose

BOOKS BY THE AUTHOR

MYSTERY/HORROR NOVELS

- In One Fell Swoop
- Umbrella Man
- Blackbird Fly
- To Hell in a Handbasket
- Edwina

7TH STREET CREW SERIES

- What Hurts the Most
- You Can Run
- You Can't Hide
- Careful Little Eyes

EMMA FROST SERIES

- Itsy Bitsy Spider
- Miss Dolly had a Dolly
- Run, Run as Fast as You Can
- Cross Your Heart and Hope to Die
- Peek-a-Boo I See You
- Tweedledum and Tweedledee
- Easy as One, Two, Three

- There's No Place like Home
- Slenderman
- Where the Wild Roses Grow

JACK RYDER SERIES

- Hit the Road Jack
- Slip out the Back Jack
- The House that Jack Built
- Black Jack

REBEKKA FRANCK SERIES

- One, Two...He is Coming for You
- Three, Four...Better Lock Your Door
- Five, Six...Grab your Crucifix
- Seven, Eight...Gonna Stay up Late
- Nine, Ten...Never Sleep Again
- Eleven, Twelve...Dig and Delve
- Thirteen, Fourteen...Little Boy Unseen

HORROR SHORT-STORIES

- Better watch out
- Eenie, Meenie
- Rock-a-Bye Baby
- Nibble, Nibble, Crunch

- Humpty Dumpty
- Chain Letter
- Mommy Dearest
- The Bird

PARANORMAL SUSPENSE/FANTASY NOVELS

AFTERLIFE SERIES

- Beyond
- Serenity
- Endurance
- Courageous

THE WOLFBOY CHRONICLES

- A Gypsy Song
- I am WOLF

DAUGHTERS OF THE JAGUAR

- Savage
- Broken

ABOUT THE AUTHOR

The Queen of Scream, Willow Rose, is an international best-selling author. She writes Mystery/Suspense/Horror, Paranormal Romance and Fantasy. She is inspired by authors like James Patterson, Agatha Christie, Stephen King, Anne Rice, and Isabel Allende. She lives on Florida's Space Coast with her husband and two daughters. When she is not writing or reading, you'll find her surfing and watching the dolphins play in the waves of the Atlantic Ocean. She has sold more than two million books.

Connect with Willow online:

willow-rose.net
madamewillowrose@gmail.com

WHAT HURTS THE MOST - AN EXCERPT

For a special sneak peak of Willow Rose's Bestselling Mystery Novel *What hurts the most,* turn to the next page.

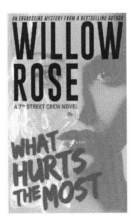

PROLOGUE

They're not going to let her go. She knows they won't. Holly is terrified as she runs through the park. The sound of the waves is behind her. A once so calming sound now brings utter terror to her. She is wet. Her shirt is dripping, her shoes making a slobbering sound as she runs across the parking lot towards the playground.

Run, run! Don't look back. Don't stop or they'll get you!

She can hear their voices behind her. It's hard to run when your feet are tied together. They're faster than she is, even though they are just walking.

"Oh, Holly," one of them yells. "Hoooollllyyy!"

Holly pants, trying to push herself forward. She wants desperately to move faster, but the rope tied around her feet blocks them and she falls flat on her face onto the asphalt. Holly screams loudly as her nose scratches across the ground.

Get up! Get up and run. You can't let them get you.

She can hear them laughing behind her.

You can make it, Holly. Just get to A1A right in front of you.

Only about a hundred feet left. There are cars on the road. They'll see you. Someone will see you and help you.

She tries to scream, but she has no air in her lungs. She is exhausted from swimming with her legs tied together. Luckily, her arms got free when she jumped in the water. They have pulled off her pants. Cut them open with a knife and pulled them off. Before they stabbed her in the shoulder. It hurts when she runs. Blood has soaked her white shirt. She is naked from the stomach down, except for her shoes and socks. Holly is in so much pain and can hardly move. Yet, she fights to get closer to the road.

A car drives by. Then another one. She can see them in the distance, yet her vision is getting foggier. She can't lose consciousness now.

You've got to keep fighting. You've got to get out of here! Don't give up, Holly. Whatever you do, just don't give up.

Their footsteps are approaching from behind. Holly is groaning and fighting to get a few more steps in.

So close now. So close.

"Hurry up," she hears them yell. "She's getting away!"

Holly is so close now she can smell the cars' exhaust. All she needs to do is get onto the road, then stop a car. That's all she needs to do to get out of there alive. And she is so close now.

"Stop her, goddammit," a voice yells.

Holly fights to run. She moves her feet faster than she feels is humanly possible. She is getting there. She is getting there. She can hear them start to run now. They are yelling to each other.

"Shoot her, dammit."

Holly gasps, thinking about the spear gun. She's the one who taught them how to shoot it. She knows they won't hesitate to use it to stop her. She knows how they think. She knows this is what they do. She knows this is a kick for them, a drug.

She knows, because she is one of them.

"Stop the bitch!" someone yells, and she hears the sound of the gun going off. She knows this sound so well, having been spearfishing all her life and practiced using the gun on land with her father. He taught her everything about spearfishing, starting when she was no more than four years old. He even taught her to hold her breath underwater for a very long time.

"Scuba diving is for tourists. Real fishers free dive," she hears his voice say, the second the spear whistles through the air.

It hits Holly in the leg and she tumbles to the ground. Holly falls to the pavement next to A1A with a scream. She hears giggles and voices behind her. But she can also hear something else. While she drags herself across the pavement, she can hear the sound of sirens.

"Shit!" the voices behind her say.

"We gotta get out of here."

"RUN!"

1

SEPTEMBER 2015

B lake Mills is enjoying his coffee at Starbucks. He enjoys it especially today. He is sipping it while looking at his own painting that they have just put up on display inside the shop. He has been trying to convince the owner of the local Starbucks in Cocoa Beach for ages to put up some of his art on display, and finally Ray agreed to let him hang up one of his turtle paintings. Just for a short period, to see how it goes.

It is Blake's personal favorite painting and he hopes it will attract some business his way. As a small artist in a small town, it is hard to make a living, even though Blake offers paintings by order, so anyone can get one any way they want it and can be sure it will fit their house or condo. It isn't exactly the way the life of an artist is supposed to be, but it is the only way to do it if he wants to eat.

Blake decides to make it a day of celebration and buys an extra coffee and a piece of cake to eat as well. He takes a bite and enjoys the taste.

"Looking good," a voice says behind him. He turns in his chair and looks into the eyes of Olivia.

Olivia Hartman. The love of his life.

Blake smiles to himself. "You came," he whispers and looks around. Being married, Olivia has to be careful whom she is seen with in this town.

"Can I sit?" she asks, holding her own coffee in her hand.

Blake pulls out a chair for her and she sits next to him. Blake feels a big thrill run through his body. He loves being with Olivia and has never had the pleasure of doing so in public. They usually meet up at his studio and have sex between his paintings on the floor or up against the wall. He has never been to her place on Patrick Air Force Base, where she lives with her husband, a general in the army. Blake is terrified of him and a little of her as well, but that is part of what makes it so wonderfully exciting. At the age of twenty-three, Blake isn't ready to settle down with anyone, and he isn't sure he is ever going to be. It isn't his style. He likes the carefree life, and being an artist he can't exactly provide for a family anyway. Having children will only force him to forget his dreams and get a *real job*. It would no doubt please his father, but Blake doesn't want a real job. He doesn't want the house on the water or the two to three children. He isn't cut out for it, and his many girlfriends in the past never understood that. All of them thought they could change him, that they were the one who could make him realize that he wanted it all. But he really didn't. And he still doesn't.

"It looks really great," Olivia says and sips her coffee. She is wearing multiple finger rings and bracelets, as always. She is delicate, yet strong. Used to be a fighter pilot in the army. Blake thought that was so cool. Today, she no longer works, not since she married the general.

She and Blake had met at the Officer's Club across the street from the base. He was there with a girl he had met at Grills in Cape Canaveral, who worked on base doing some contracting or something boring like that; she had invited him to a party. It was by far the most boring affair until he met Olivia on the porch standing with a beer in her hand overlooking the Atlantic Ocean. She was slightly tipsy and they exchanged pleasantries for a few minutes before she turned and looked at him with that mischievous smile of hers. Then she asked him if he wanted to have some fun.

"Always," he replied.

They walked to the beach and into the dunes, where they enjoyed the best sex of Blake's life.

Now it has become a drug to him. He needs his fix. He needs her.

"Congrats," she says.

"Thanks. Now I just hope someone will grab one of the business cards I've put on the counter and call me to order a painting. I could use the money. I only had one order last month."

"They will," she says, laughing. "Don't you worry about that." She leans over and whispers through those pouty lips of hers. "Now let's go back to your place and celebrate."

"Is that an order?" he asks, laughing.

"Is that an order, *ma'am*," she corrects him. "And, yes, it is."

2

SEPTEMBER 2015

Being with Olivia is exhilarating. It fills him with the most wonderful sensation in his body because Blake has never met anyone like her, who can make him crazy for her. Not like this. But at the same time, it is also absolutely petrifying because she is married to General Hartman, who will have Blake killed if he ever finds out. There is no doubt about it in Blake's mind.

Yet, he keeps sleeping with her. Even though he keeps telling himself it is a bad idea, that he has to stop, that it is only a matter of time before he will get himself in some deep shit trouble. Blake knows it is bad to be with her. He knows it will get him in trouble eventually, but still, he can't help himself. He has to have her. He has to taste her again and again. No matter the cost.

Their lips meet inside Blake's studio as soon as they walk in. Blake closes his eyes and drinks from her. He doesn't care that the door behind him is left open. Nothing else matters right now.

"I thought you couldn't get out today," he says, panting, when her lips leave his. "Isn't the general on base?"

"He is," she mumbles between more kisses.

It has been two weeks since they were together last. Two weeks of constantly dreaming and longing for her. They communicate via Snapchat. It is untraceable, as far as Blake knows. Blake wrote a message to her a few days ago, telling her about the painting being put up in Starbucks, knowing that she probably couldn't come and see it. He even sent a picture of the painting. It is also her favorite. She messaged him back a photo of her sad face telling him she didn't think she could get out, since her husband was home. Usually, she only dares to meet with Blake when her husband is travelling. Even then, they have to be extremely careful. General Hartman has many friends in Cocoa Beach and his soldiers are seen everywhere.

"I told him I was seeing a friend today. It's not like it's a lie. I don't care anymore if he finds out about us. I'm sick of being just the general's wife. I want a life of my own."

Blake takes off his T-shirt and her hands land on his chest. He rips off her shirt and several buttons fall to the floor. She closes her eyes and moans at his touches. His hands cup her breasts and soon her bra lands on the wooden floor. He grabs her hair and pulls her head back while kissing her neck. His heart is pumping in his chest just from the smell of her skin.

"You can't," he whispers between breaths. "You can't let him know about us. He'll kill the both of us."

Olivia lets out a gasp as Blake reaches up under her skirt and places a hand in her panties, and then rips them off. He pushes her up against a table, then lifts her up, leans over her naked torso and puts his mouth to her breasts. He closes his eyes and takes in her smell, drinking the juices of her body, then pulls his shorts down and gently slides inside of her with a deep moan. She puts her legs around his neck, partly strangling him when she comes in pulsing movements back and forth, her body arching.

"Oh, Blake...oh, Blake ..."

The sensation is burning inside of him and he is ready to explode. Olivia is moaning and moving rapidly. His movements are urgent now, the intensity building. He is about to burst, when suddenly she screams loudly and pushes him away. Blake falls to the floor with a thud.

"What the...?"

Blake soon realizes why Olivia is screaming and feels the blood rush from his face. A set of eyes is staring down at him.

The eyes of Detective Chris Fisher.

"Blake Mills, you're under arrest," the voice belonging to the eyes says.

3

SEPTEMBER 2015

"I'm sorry, Mary, there's nothing I can do."

I stare at my boss, Chief Editor, Markus Fergusson. He is leaning back in his leather chair in his office on the twenty-eighth floor of the Times-Tower on the west side of mid-town. Behind him, the view is spectacular, but I hardly notice anymore. After five years working there, you simply stop being baffled. However, I am actually baffled at this moment. But not because of the view. Because of what is being said.

"So, you're firing me, is that it?" I ask, while my blood is boiling in my veins. What the hell is this?

"We're letting you go, yes."

"You can't do that, Markus, come on. Just because of this?"

He leans over his desk and gives me that look that I have come to know so well in my five years as a reporter for *The New York Times*.

"Yes."

"I don't get it," I say. "I'm being fired for writing the paper's most read article in the past five years?"

Markus sighs. "Don't put up a fight, will you? Just accept it. You violated the rules, sweetheart."

Don't you sweetheart me, you pig!

"I don't make the rules, Mary. The big guys upstairs make the decisions and it says here that we have to let you go for *violating the normal editing process.*"

I squint my eyes. I can't believe this. "I did what?"

"You printed the story without having a second set of eyes on it first. The article offended some people, and, well..."

He pauses. I scoff. He is such a sell-out. Just because my article didn't sit well with some people, some influential people, he is letting me go? They want to fire me for some rule bullshit?

"Brian saw it," I say. "He read it and approved it."

"The rules say *two* editors," he says. "On a story like this, this controversial, you need two editors to approve it, not just one."

"That's BS and you know it, goddammit, Markus. I never even heard about this rule. What about Brian?"

"We're letting him go as well."

"You can't do that! The man just had another kid."

Markus shrugs. "That's not really my problem, is it? Brian knew better. He's been with us for fifteen years."

"It was late, Markus. We had less than five minutes to deadline. There was no time to get another approval. If we'd waited for another editor, the story wouldn't have run, and you wouldn't have sold a record number of newspapers that day. The article went viral online. All over the world. Everyone was talking about it. And this is how you thank me?"

I rise from the chair and grab my leather jacket. "Well, suit yourself. It's your loss. I don't need you or this paper."

I leave, slamming the door, but it doesn't make me feel as

good as I thought it would. I pack my things in that little brown box that they always do in the movies and grab it under my arm before I leave in the elevator. On the bottom floor, I hand in my ID card to the guard in the lobby and Johnson looks at me with his mouth turned downwards.

"We'll miss you, Miss Mary," he says.

"I'll miss you too, Johnson," I say, and walk out the glass doors, into the streets of New York without a clue as to what I am going to do. Living in Manhattan isn't cheap. Living in Manhattan with a nine-year old son, as a single mom isn't cheap at all. The cost for a private school alone is over the roof.

I whistle for a cab, and before I finally get one, it starts to rain, and I get soaked. I have him drive me back to my apartment and I let myself inside. Snowflake, my white Goldendoodle is waiting on the other side of the door, jumping me when I enter. He licks me in my face and whimpers from having missed me since I left just this morning. I sit down on my knees and pet him till he calms down. I can't help smiling when I am with him. I can't feel sad for long when he's around. It's simply not possible. He looks at me with those deep brown eyes.

"We'll be alright, won't we, Snowflake? I'm sure we will. We don't need them, no we don't."

SEPTEMBER 2015

"Do you come here often?"

Liz Hester stares at the man who has approached her in the bar at Lou's Blues in Indialantic. It is Friday night and she was bored at the base, so she and her friends decided to go out and get a beer.

"You're kidding me, right?"

The guy smiles. He is a surfer-type with long greasy hair under his cap, a nice tan, and not too much between the ears. The kind of guy who opens each sentence with *dude,* even when speaking to a girl.

"It was the best I could come up with."

"You do realize that I am thirty-eight and you're at least fifteen years younger, right?"

Kim comes up behind her. She is wearing her blue ASU —army service uniform—like Liz. They are both decorated with several medals. Liz's includes the Purple Heart, given to her when she was shot during her service in Afghanistan. Took a bullet straight to her shoulder. The best part was, she took it for one of her friends. She took it for Britney, who is also with them this night, hanging out with some guy further down the bar. They are friends through thick and thin. Will lay down their lives for one another.

Liz's eyes meet those of Jamie's across the bar. She smiles and nods in the direction of the guy that Liz is talking to. Liz smiles and nods too. There is no need for them to speak; they know what she is saying.

He's the one.

"So, tell me, what's your name?" Liz asks the guy. She is all of a sudden flirtatious, smiling and touching his arm gently. Kim giggles behind her, but the guy doesn't notice.

"I'm Billy. My friends call me Billy the Kid."

"Well, you are just a kid, aren't you?" she says, purring like a cat, leaning in over the bar.

The guy lifts his cap a little, then puts it back on. "You sure are a lot of woman."

Liz knows his type. He is one of those who gets aroused just by looking at a woman in uniform. She has met her share of those types. They are a lot of fun to play with.

"Well, maybe I can make a man of you," she whispers, leaning very close to his face.

The guy laughs goofily. "You sure can," he says and gives her an elevator look. "I sure wouldn't mind that. I got an anaconda in my pants you can ride if you like."

Liz laughs lightly, and then looks at Jamie again, letting her know he has taken the bait.

"Well, why don't you—Billy the Kid—meet me outside in the parking lot in say—five minutes?"

Billy laughs again. "Dude! Whoa, sure!"

Billy taps the bar counter twice, not knowing exactly what to do with himself, then lifts his cap once again and wipes sweat off his forehead. He has nice eyes, Liz thinks, and he is quite handsome.

As stupid as they get, though.

He leaves her, shooting a finger-gun at her and winking at the same time. The girls approach Liz, moving like cats sliding across the floor. Liz finishes her drink while the four of them stick their heads together.

"Ready for some fun?" she asks.

They don't say anything. They don't have to.

5

SEPTEMBER 2015

She waits for him by the car. Smoking a cigarette, she leans against it, blowing out smoke when she spots him come out of the bar and walk towards her. Seeing the goofy grin on his face makes her smile even wider.

"Hey there, baby," Billy says and walks up to her. "I have to say, I wasn't sure you would even be here. A nice lady like you with a guy like me? You're a wild cat, aren't you?"

Liz chuckles and blows smoke in his face. "I sure am."

Billy the Kid moves his body in anticipation. His crotch can't keep still. He is already hard.

What a sucker.

He looks around with a sniffle. "So, where do you want to go? To the beach? Or do you...wanna do it right here...?" he places a hand next to her on the car. "Up against this baby, huh?"

Liz laughs again, then leans closer to him till her mouth is on his ear. "You're just full of yourself, aren't you?"

"What?" he asks with another goofy grin.

"Did you really think you were going to get lucky with me? With this?" She says and points up and down her body.

The grin is wiped off his face. Finally.

"What is this?" he asks, his face in a frown. "Were you just leading me on? What a cunt!" He spits out the last word. He probably means it as an insult, but Liz just smiles from ear to ear as her friends slowly approach from all sides, surrounding Billy. When he realizes, he tries to back out, but walks into Jamie and steps on her black shoes.

"Hey, those are brand new! Dammit!"

Jamie pushes him in the back forcefully and he is now in the hands of Britney. Britney is smaller than the others, but by far the strongest. She clenches her fist and slams it into his face. The blow breaks his nose on the spot and he falls backwards to the asphalt, blood running from it.

"What the...what...who are you?" Billy asks, disoriented, looking from woman to woman.

"We like to call ourselves the Fast and the Furious," Liz says.

"Yeah, cause I'm fast," Kim says and kicks Billy in the crotch. He lets out a loud moan in pain.

The sound is almost arousing to Liz.

"And I'm furious," she says, grabbing him by the hair and pulling his head back. She looks him in the eyes. She loves watching them squirm, the little suckers. Just like she loved it back in Afghan when she interrogated the *Haji*.

Haji is the name they call anyone of Arab decent, or even of a brownish skin tone. She remembers vividly the first time they brought one in. It was the day after she had lost a good friend to an IED, a roadside bomb that detonated and killed everyone in the truck in front of her. They searched for those suckers all night, and finally, the next morning they brought in three. Boy, she kicked that sucker till he could no longer move. Hell, they all did it. All of them let out their frustrations. Losing three good soldiers like that made them furious.

Liz was still furious. Well, to be frank, she has been furious all of her life.

Everybody around her knows that.

Liz laughs when she hears Billy's whimper, then uses two fingers to poke his eyes forcefully. Billy screams.

"My eyes, my eyes!"

Liz lets go of his hair and looks at her girls. They are all about to burst in anticipation. She opens the door to the car, where Jamie has placed a couple of bottles of vodka to keep them going all night. She lets out a loud howl like a wolf, the girls chiming in, then lifts Billy the Kid up and throws him in the back of the Jeep.

6

FEBRUARY 1977

When Penelope and Peter get married, she is already showing. It is no longer a secret to the people at the wedding, even though her mother does all she can to disguise it by buying a big dress. By the time of the wedding, Penelope has grown into it and her stomach fills it out completely. Peter's mother tells her she looks radiant and gorgeous, but Penelope's own mother hates the fact that people will talk about the marriage as a necessity, or *the right thing to do,* and their daughter as only getting married because she is pregnant. Because she has to.

But that is just the way it is, and no one cares less about what people think than Penelope and Peter. They are happy and looking forward to becoming parents more than anything.

Soon after the wedding, the bank approves a loan for them and they buy their dream house in Cocoa Beach. As a young lawyer who has just been made partner, Peter is doing well, and even though it is one of the most expensive locations in Cocoa Beach, Penelope doesn't have to work anymore. She quits her job as a secretary and wants to focus on her family and later charity work. It is the kind of life they have both dreamed of, and no one is more thrilled to see it come true than Penelope.

"I can't wait to become a family," she says, when Peter is done fixing up the nursery and shows it to her.

Seeing how beautiful he has decorated it makes her cry, and she holds a hand to her ready-to-burst stomach. Only two more weeks till she will hold her baby. Only two more weeks.

She can hardly wait.

Peter is going to be a wonderful father; she just knows he will. He has such a kind and gentle personality. She has done right in choosing him. She knows she has. This is going to be a perfect little family. Penelope already knows she wants lots of children. At least two, maximum four. She herself comes from a family of four children. Four girls, to be exact. There was a brother, but he died at an early age after a long illness. Being the oldest, Penelope took care of him, and it was devastating for her when he passed away. It is a sorrow she can never get rid of, and often she blames herself for not being able to cure him. Later in life, she played with the idea of becoming a doctor, but she never had the grades for it.

Peter, on the other hand, is an only child. His mother has spoiled his socks off all of his life. She still does every now and then. And she still treats him like a child sometimes. It makes Penelope laugh out loud when she spit-washes him or corrects his tie. But she is nice, Peter's mom. She has always loved Penelope, and there is nothing bad to be said about her.

It was always the plan that Peter would follow in his father's footsteps and go to law school, and so he did. He met Penelope right after he passed the bar and started working at the small law firm in Rockledge where she was a secretary.

Soon he moved on to a bigger firm and now he had made partner.

Peter's career exploded within a few years, and now he is talking about going into real estate as well. He has so many plans for their future, and she knows he will always take care of them. She is never going to want for anything.

Two weeks later, her water breaks. Penelope is standing in the kitchen admiring the new tiles they have put in, with a coffee cup in her hand. The water soaks her dress and the floor beneath her. Penelope gasps and reaches for the phone. She calls Peter at the office.

"This is it," she says, with a mixture of excitement and fright in her voice. "Our baby is coming, Peter. Our baby is coming!"

"I...I'll be right there."

Peter stumbles over himself on his way out of the office and the secretary has to yell at him to come back because he has forgotten his car keys.

Peter rushes her to the hospital, where the contractions soon take over and after a tough struggle and fourteen hours of labor, she is finally holding her baby girl in her arms.

"Look at her, Peter," she says through tears. "I...I simply can't stop looking at her. I am so happy, Peter. You made me so happy, thank you. Thank you so much."

7

SEPTEMBER 2015

I spend the evening feeling sorry for myself. I cook chicken in green curry, my favorite dish these days, and sulk in front of the TV watching back-to-back episodes of *Friends* with Snowflake and my son Salter next to me.

"They can't fire you!" Salter exclaimed, when I told him as soon as he got home from school. He knew something was wrong as soon as he saw that I'd made hot cocoa for the both of us and put marshmallows in it.

That is kind of my thing. Whenever I have bad news, I prepare hot cocoa with marshmallows. I have also baked cookies. That is another diversion of mine. Nothing keeps me as distracted as baking or cooking.

"You're the best damn reporter they have!"

"I am, but there's no need to curse," I say.

I enjoy spending the rest of the evening with the loves of my life, both of them, and decide to not wonder about my future until the next day. Salter is so loving and caring towards me and keeps asking me if there is anything he can do for me, to make me feel better.

"Just stay here in my arms," I say and pull him closer.

He has reached the age where he still enjoys my affectionate hugs and holding him close, but lately he has begun to find them annoying from time to time, especially when it is in front of his friends.

I named him Salter because I have been a surfer all of my life, growing up in Cocoa Beach, and so is his dad. Salter means *derived from salt*. We believed he was born of our love for the ocean. How foolish and young we were back then.

It feels like a lifetime ago.

"So, what do we do now?" Salter finally asks when the episode where Phoebe fights with a fire alarm is over.

I take in a deep breath. I know he has to wonder. I do too, but I try not to think about it. Mostly to make sure he isn't affected by it.

"I mean, now that you don't have a job?" he continues. "Can we still live in this apartment?"

"I have to be honest with you, kiddo," I say. "I don't know. I don't know what is going to happen. I am not sure any newspaper will have me after this. I pissed off some pretty influential people."

"That's stupid," he says. "They're all stupid. Your article had more views than anyone's."

"I know, but that isn't always enough, buddy."

I sigh, hoping I don't have to go into details, when suddenly my phone rings. I let go of Salter and lean over to pick it up from the coffee table. My heart drops when I see the name on the display.

It's my dad.

"It's Mary," I say, my heart throbbing in my throat. I haven't spoken to my dad in at least a year. He never calls me.

"Mary." His voice is heavy. Something is definitely going on.

"What's wrong, Dad? Are you sick?"

"No. It's not me. It's your brother."

I swallow hard. My brother is the only family member I still have regular contact with. I love the little bastard, even if he is fifteen years younger than me.

"Blake? What's wrong with him?"

"It's bad, Mary. He's been arrested."

Arrested?!?

"What? Why...for what...what's going on, Dad?"

My father sighs from the other end of the line. "For murder. He's been arrested for murder."

8

SEPTEMBER 2015

They take him for a ride. Billy the Kid is crying in the back when the girls take him first to the Super Wal-Mart in Merritt Island that is open 24/7. Placing a knife to his back, they walk through the store and pull bottles of wine, gin, and tequila from the shelves. They even find a fishing pole that they think could be fun to buy. Along with some chips Jamie wants, and sugarcoated donuts. Kim has a craving for cheesecake while Britney wants chocolate. And loads of it. Liz holds the knife in Billy's back and asks them to throw in some Choco-mint ice cream for her. Then she grabs a bottle of drain cleaner. They tell Billy to take out his wallet and pay for everything.

"If you as much as whimper, I will split you open," Liz whispers, as they come closer to the cashier. "I'll make it look like you attacked me. Who do you think they'll believe, huh? A surfer dude or a decorated war-veteran? A female one on top of it."

After he pays, they open a bottle of gin and take turns drinking from it while they drive, screaming and cheering, back to Cocoa Beach where they park in front of Ron Jon's surf-shop, which is also open 24/7. Yelling and visibly intoxicated, they storm inside with Billy and take the elevator to the second floor. They run through the aisles of bikinis and pull down one after another.

"I always wanted yellow one," Kim yells.

"I'm going red this time," Britney says. "Wouldn't this look cute on me?"

"Grab me one of the striped ones over there," Liz says. "Size medium."

Kim giggles cheerfully then grabs one. They don't bother to try them on. There is no time for that. Kim also grabs a couple of nice shirts from Billabong, and then some shorts from Roxy for Liz.

"Oh," Britney says and points at the surfboards on the other side of the store. She looks to the others. "I always wanted a surfboard!"

"Me too," Jamie exclaims. "Let's find one!"

"I...I can't afford that," Billy whimpers. "Aren't they like four hundred dollars?"

"This one is five hundred dollars," Jamie says, and looks at a seven-foot fun-shape. "Doesn't it look GREAT on me?"

"Adorable," Liz says and laughs.

"I can't afford this," Billy whimpers over and over when they pull the boards out.

"Grab one for me too," Liz says, ignoring his complaints. She presses the knife into his back, puts her arm around his neck, then kisses his cheek, making it look like they are a couple.

"You'll have to," she whispers. "I'll make a scene. Make it look like you tried to rape me."

"Okay, okay," he says with a moan. "Just don't hurt me, okay? Just let me go after this, alright?"

She doesn't make any promises. That's not how Liz rolls.

They charge everything to one of Billy's credit cards, then run out of the store carrying surfboards and plastic bags with bikinis, hollering and laughing. They throw everything in the car and strap the boards onto the roof before driving to the International Palms Resort a few blocks further down A1A, where they book a suite for all of them, charging it on his credit card again.

"Please don't make me pay for any more," he says in the elevator.

They ignore his complaints, and then storm into the room. It is huge and has great views of the ocean. Liz lets go of Billy, then throws him on the white couch. Jamie grabs one of the bottles of Vodka and places it to her lips. She drinks it like it is water. Liz laughs and pulls the bottle from Jamie's hand. She places it to her lips and closes her eyes while it burns its way down her throat.

"Hey, leave some for the rest of us," Kim yells, and grabs the bottle out of Liz's hand.

The vodka spills on Liz's white shirt. Liz looks angrily at Kim. "What the hell...?"

Kim laughs, then drinks from the bottle. Liz clenches her fist before she slams it into Kim's face as soon as she lets go of the bottle again. Kim falls backwards, then stares, confused, at Liz.

"What...what happened?" she asks.

Liz grabs the bottle out of her hand forcefully. Jamie and Britney remain quiet. They dare not make a sound. The feeling of power intoxicates Liz. Liz looks at Billy the Kid, who is squirming on the couch while staring at them with terror in his eyes.

Liz approaches him. He squirms again. Liz leans over and kisses him forcefully. He tries to push her away, but two of

the other girls grab his arms and hold him down while Liz
has her way with him. She pulls off his pants and then she
laughs.

"Is that all? Is that the anaconda you wanted me to ride?"

"Please, just let me go," Billy says, crying in humiliation
"I've done everything you wanted me to. I've paid for everything. Please, just let me go."

"Now he wants to leave. You finally have the chance to get
laid and now you want to leave? No no, Billy, tsk tsk. That's
not what a woman wants to hear, is it, girls?"

The three others shake their heads.

Liz puts her hand on his penis and starts to rub. Soon, his
anaconda grows sizably and he starts moaning.

"Please...please..."

She puts her lips on it and makes him hard, then sits on
top of him and rides him. The other girls are screaming with
joy. Liz rides him forcefully, and soon they both come with
deep moans.

Liz smiles when Billy arches in spasms and she feels his
semen inside of her, then leans over and kisses his forehead.

"If you tell the police what we did tonight, I'll tell them
you raped me," she whispers. "That you were holding a gun
to my head and you raped me. Boy, I do believe I even have
three witnesses. Three VERY reliable witnesses."

Liz finishes with a laugh, then climbs off Billy. "Come on
girls," she says. "Let's get *really* drunk."

She grabs a bottle and drinks from it. It is strange how it
feels like she can't get drunk anymore. Not like *really* drunk.
Not like in the old days. Liz likes being really drunk. It makes
her forget. It is the only thing that can make her forget.

The girls throw themselves at the chips and candy they
bought at Wal-Mart. Liz looks at them with contempt. They
have no self-control, these girls. Kim buries her hands in the

cheesecake and eats it, licking her fingers. Jamie stuffs her face with donuts and has sugar all over her mouth.

Liz sighs.

"You want some ice cream?" Jamie asks.

"I don't want some stupid ice cream," Liz says, mocking Jamie. "I'm bored." She looks at Billy, who doesn't dare to move on the couch. "He bores me."

"What do you want to do?" Kim asks.

"Yeah, do you want to have another go?" Jamie asks.

Liz throws the bottle in her hand against the wall. It breaks and leaves a huge mark that Billy is probably going to pay for. Liz growls and kicks the ice cream bucket.

"I'm sick of the prick. He's no fun to play with."

Liz grabs the drain cleaner and walks towards Billy with firm steps. The girls all look at her. Serious eyes follow her every step. The atmosphere in the room immediately changes. No one is laughing anymore. No one is eating.

"What are you doing with that, babe?" Jamie asks.

"Don't do it," Kim yells.

But Liz doesn't listen. She opens the lid and grabs Billy's jaw. She forces it open. Billy is squirming too much and she can't do it on her own.

"Help me, dammit," she yells.

The girls hesitate, but don't dare not to do as they're told. Who knows what Liz might do next? Who will be next? They have seen too much to be able to say no.

Britney is first to grab Billy's right arm and hold it down. Jamie then grabs the left one. Kim holds his head still, while Liz pours the liquid drain cleaner into his mouth and down his throat. The three girls stare at her while she empties the bottle completely. They dare not even to speak. Billy's screams pierce through their bones. No one dares to move.

Liz throws the empty bottle on the ground, then looks at her friends. "Let's get out of here," she yells.

Her words are almost drowned out by Billy's scream.

9
———

SEPTEMBER 2015

I land at Orlando airport around noon the next day. Salter and Snowflake are both with me. We have packed two big suitcases, not knowing how long we are going to stay. My dad tried to convince me there is no need for me to come down, but I didn't listen. I need to be there. I need to help my brother.

"What about my school?" Salter says, as we walk to the rental car.

"I called them and told them it's a family emergency," I say. "They told me you have to be back in ten days or your spot goes to someone else. They mean business, that school."

It is one of the best schools in New York and one of the most expensive ones too. I haven't decided if I like it or not. The uniforms I can do without, but that kind of comes with the territory. It is mostly the way they shape them into small soldiers there, always running all these tests, making them stand straight, and never having time to play. It is all Salter knows, so to him, it is fine. But there is something about the school that I don't like. I find it hard to enjoy that my child is going to a school like this. Joey and I are both surfers and free spirits. This school is not us at all. Yet, we signed Salter up for it as soon as we moved to New York.

We moved because of my job, but unfortunately it turned out to be the end of our little family. Joey had nothing to do up there, since no one would hire him, and soon we grew apart. Staying at home and not having anything to do wore on him. He never felt like he accomplished anything or that he was supporting his family, and that is important to him. He started to feel lonely and sought comfort in the arms of a young girl who worked at a small coffee house on our street. He would go there every day to drink his coffee and write. He wants to be an author and has written several books, but no publisher will touch them. I think they are beautiful and inspiring, but I guess I am biased. I love Joey. I still do. But when he told me he had slept with the girl at the coffee house several times a week for at least a year, I threw him out. Well, not right away. First, I gave him a second chance and we tried to make it work for a couple of weeks, for Salter's sake, but I couldn't stand thinking about it all day, whether he'd been with her again. It tore me apart. I have never been a jealous person, but this I couldn't handle. I tried hard to, but realized I wasn't as forgiving as I thought I could be. I didn't have it in me and I felt like I could never trust him again. So, I finally asked him to move out.

"Where do you want me to go?" he asked.

I shrugged. "Go live with that coffee house girl. I don't know."

He decided to go back to Cocoa Beach where we grew up together. That was four months ago now. I miss him every day. But I can't forget what he did. What hurts the most is the betrayal, the deceit. I don't know how to move past it. I don't know if I ever can.

He calls as often as he can and talks to Salter. It's been

hard on our son. He loves his dad and needs him in his life, needs a male role model. Salter went to visit him during summer break, and it is the plan that he will be going down for Thanksgiving as well.

"You think I can call Dad now?" Salter asks, as soon as we are in the car and hit the beach line.

I sigh. It is such a big blow to Salter that his dad moved this far away. I know he is excited to see him again. I hate to see that look in his eyes. He doesn't know his dad cheated on me. He only knows that he left, and that is enough. I know he feels guilt and questions if he had something to do with it. I try to tell him it wasn't because of him, that sometimes grown-ups grow apart, that they can't make it work anymore. I am not sure he is convinced.

"Sure," I say.

Salter smiles and grabs my phone and finds his dad's number. While driving towards the beach and listening to him talk to his father, I feel a chill go through my body. I watch the big signs for Ron Jon's surf shop go by and realize my hands are shivering. Everything about this place gives me the creeps. I haven't been back in almost twenty years. Not since I left for college.

Blake was three years old back then. Joey and I have lived all over since. He worked with whatever he could get his hands on, mostly as a carpenter. I spent five years working for CNN in Atlanta, which became my biggest career jump. Before that I held a position with *USA Today* in Virginia. I started my career as a journalist at *Miami Herald* and we lived for a while in Ft. Lauderdale before my job took us out of the state, something I had dreamed of as long as I could remember. To get away.

Salter puts the phone down.

"So, what did he have to say?" I ask, as we approach the

bridges that will take us to the Barrier Islands. In the distance, I can see the cruise ships. A sign tells me I can go on a casino cruise for free. Gosh, how I hate this place...with all its tourists and tiki bars.

"He can't wait to see me," Salter says.

I turn onto A1A, where all the condominiums and hotels are lined up like pearls on a string.

"At least you'll have fun seeing your dad," I say, while wondering what is waiting for me once I arrive at my childhood home. What is it going to be like to see my dad again? What about Blake? I haven't seen him in several years. He visited me in New York five years ago, but other than that, we have mainly spoken over the phone or on Facebook. We aren't very close, but he is still the only one in my family I like. He is all the family I have, and I will do anything to help him out.

Anything.

10

APRIL 1977

Penelope and Peter take the baby home to their new house a few days after the birth. In the months to follow, they try everything they can to become a family. But the sleep deprivation is hard on them. Especially on Penelope. She gets up four or sometimes five times a night to breastfeed, and all day long she feels sick from the lack of sleep.

Only a few weeks after the baby arrived Peter gets a new case. It is a big deal, he explains to Penelope, one of those cases that can make or break a career. And Peter is determined to make it.

But that means long days at the office, and Penelope is soon alone for many hours at the house. Sometimes, he even stays away the entire night just to work, and when he finally comes home, he is too worn out to even speak to his wife.

Penelope, on the other hand, longs to speak with an adult and can hardly stop talking to him and asking him questions.

"How was your day? What's the latest on the case? Do you think you'll be done in time?"

Peter answers with a growl and tries to avoid her. As soon

as he comes home, he storms to the restroom and stays in there for at least an hour, reading a magazine or the newspaper just to get a little peace and quiet.

The first weeks, Penelope waits outside the door and attacks him with more questions or demands as soon as he pokes his head out again.

"The garage door is acting up again. Could you fix it or call someone who could? We need to start thinking about preschool. I've looked over a few of them, but I need your help to choose the right one. What do you think? I was thinking about painting the living room another color. A light blue, maybe?"

One day he comes home at nine in the evening after a very stressful day and all he dreams of is throwing himself on the couch, putting his feet up, and reading the newspaper, enjoying a nice quiet evening. When he enters the house, Penelope comes down from upstairs holding the baby in her arms with a deep sigh. The look in her eyes is of complete desperation.

"Where have you been?"

He sighs and closes the front door behind him. He doesn't have the energy to explain to her what's been going on at the office.

"A long story," he says, and puts his briefcase down.

The baby wails. Penelope looks at her with concern. "No. No. Not again. Please don't start again." She looks at Peter. "She's been like this all day, Peter. I don't know what to do. I don't know anymore. I just really, really need time...just an hour of sleep. I'm so tired."

Peter looks at her. Is she kidding him?

"We're both tired," he says.

"No. No. It's more than that, Peter. She's driving me nuts. It's like torture. I can't eat. I can't think. I can't..."

"Could you shut up for just one second?"

Penelope stares at her husband. "Excuse me?"

"Do you have ANY idea what kind of day I've had? Do you have ANY idea what I am going through these days? I think you can manage a little crying baby, all right? I would give anything to be in your shoes and not have to deal with this case."

Peter snorts, then walks past her into the living room, where he closes the door. Penelope has a lump in her throat. She feels so helpless. So alone and so so incredibly tired. She looks at the baby, who is still crying.

"Why are you crying little baby, huh? Why are you crying so much?"

She puts her lips on the baby's forehead to kiss her, but the kiss makes her realize something. Something she should have noticed a long time ago. The baby isn't just fussing.

She is burning up with a fever.

END OF EXCERPT...

ORDER YOUR
COPY TODAY!

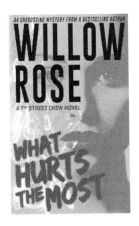

.

Printed in Poland
by Amazon Fulfillment
Poland Sp. z o.o., Wrocław